FRIENDLY FIRE

ALSO BY MARLISS MELTON

The Taskforce Series

The Protector

The Guardian

The Enforcer

The Echo Platoon Series

Off-Duty SEALs (An Echo Platoon Anthology)

Danger Close

Hard Landing

Friendly Fire

Hot Target

Insider Threat

FRIENDLY FIRE

THE ECHO PLATOON SERIES

BOOK THREE

MARLISS MELTON

ePublishingWorks!

Cover by Northern Lake Publishing LLC

Revised: August 2025
ISBN: 978-1-61417-848-4

ePublishing Works!
644 Shrewsbury Commons Ave, Ste 249
Shrewsbury, PA 17361, USA
www.epublishingworks.com
Phone: 866-846-5123

For my daughter Grace, my soulmate.

"...and when one of them meets the other half, the actual half of himself, whether he be a lover of youth or a lover of another sort, the pair are lost in an amazement of love and friendship and intimacy and one will not be out of the other's sight, as I may say, even for a moment..."

— *PLATO ON THE TOPIC OF SOUL MATES, THE SYMPOSIUM*

ACKNOWLEDGMENTS

I've often remarked that writing books is like having babies. It takes about nine months—at least for me. And the questions are all the same. 1) Where did you get your inspiration? (Who's the father?) In this case, former Navy SEAL Michael Jaco, author of The Intuitive Warrior—a book I highly recommend you read—inspired the hero of the story. 2) How hard was the book to write? (Was the pregnancy difficult?) Once, with a previous title, I wrote myself into such a corner that it took me four weeks to resolve the tangled plot. With this book, I only got stuck twice, so I'd say the pregnancy was easy. 3) Did you have any help? (Who attended the birth?) Just as it takes a village to raise a child, it likewise requires many hands and minds to write a single book. Ladies, you know who you are. My baby is beautiful, and I give you full credit. Thank you all so much!

CHAPTER 1

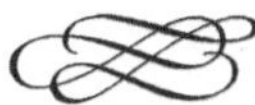

As he stepped aboard the gleaming white cruise ship *Escapade*, Navy SEAL First Class Jeremiah Winters used his six-foot-three height to observe the scene unfolding ahead. Crew members had formed a line on either side of the boarding passengers. Some hurled confetti, while others shook hands and offered words of welcome. On a balcony overhead, musicians played upbeat jazz—a fitting choice for the port city of New Orleans.

Combined with the warmth of an April morning, the festive atmosphere brought a smile to Jeremiah's face. A sidelong glance at his teammate showed Tristan grooving to the music as they made their way through the cheerful reception. This Caribbean cruise was just what Tristan needed to get over his breakup with a longtime girlfriend.

A frisson of alarm skittered up Jeremiah's spine. In the next instant, the sound of automatic weapons erupted in his mind, and civilians crumpled, their blood spattering the cruise ship's pristine fiberglass.

No, no, no! Clapping a hand to his forehead, he tried to banish the image. *It's just my imagination.* It was natural, after all, for a Navy SEAL to picture worst-case scenarios in unfamiliar environments.

The festive energy aboard this boat—so unlike the disciplined world he usually inhabited—was stirring his unease, that was all.

Then again, having spent years learning to harness his sixth sense, he'd be a fool to dismiss a vision out of hand.

"Wait." He tugged on Tristan's T-shirt, sweeping his gaze fore and aft in search of a threat.

"What's wrong?" Tristan's denim-blue gaze flicked to Jeremiah's face, then around, as if catching the same whiff of danger.

Up ahead, crew members were pulling passengers aside to take boarding photos, which would be available for purchase later.

The cameraman called out instructions. "You, pretty lady—turn to the right. Husband, give her a hug. Now, both of you smile!" Holding his camera to his eye, the sandy-haired man snapped a few shots.

Click. Click. Click.

But what Jeremiah saw wasn't a camera—it was a rifle. The sound of bullets punching through flesh sent a wave of nausea through him. The couple's blood sprayed the canvas backdrop.

He blinked, and the vision disappeared. "Damn it."

Tristan elbowed him. "Dude, what's going on?"

Jeremiah pressed his lips together and shook his head. What could he say? *I've got a bad feeling about this?* His teammates respected his gut instincts, but he didn't want to burst Tristan's bubble—not when this was the happiest the guy had seemed since Mariah left him. And Jeremiah certainly didn't want to ruin their vacation before it began.

"Nothing. Forget it."

As the cameraman waved off the couple and called up the next group, Jeremiah's attention snagged on the long auburn tresses of a woman in her early thirties. She approached the photo station with a preteen and a blonde woman.

He stared, his swirling thoughts forgotten. *Wow. She looks just like…*

Heeding the photographer's direction, the trio turned and smiled. The breath tangled in Jeremiah's throat.

Professor Albright? It can't be.

He squinted. It had to be. The college professor who had captivated him, changed his life's direction, and lingered in his dreams for five long years—there she was. Thinner now, almost willowy, with more defined cheekbones, but otherwise unchanged. The rosy lips that curved into a playful smile as she made bunny ears behind her daughter's head—those lips had once brought Wordsworth and Coleridge to life for him.

He and Emma had shared a brief but extraordinary connection. She'd felt it, too—had felt it so strongly that she'd barred him from further visits to her office. Devastated by her rejection, he'd dropped her class, quit school altogether, and devoted himself instead to becoming a modern-day knight errant—a U.S. Navy SEAL.

What were the odds that he'd driven all the way from Virginia Beach to New Orleans, only to run into her here?

Click. Click. Click.

As the shutter snapped again, the same horrific vision returned—flesh punctured, blood spattering, bodies falling. The blood drained from Jeremiah's heart to his feet.

Jesus, no. Not her.

When her gaze flicked toward him, intercepting his horrified stare, his heart stilled. Did she recognize him?

Her long lashes dipped as she looked, just for a moment—but then she turned away, throwing an arm around her daughter's shoulders. The three walked off, chatting as they rejoined the crowd.

A prick of hurt pierced his chest.

Of course she hadn't recognized him. Six years ago, he'd been a lanky twenty-two-year-old with a head full of hair. The Navy hadn't just shaved his head—it had packed fifty pounds of raw muscle onto his frame.

Even if she *had* recognized him, would they even cross paths again? There were 2,400 passengers aboard this ship. They could sail all the way to the Western Caribbean and back and never see each other again.

But that's not what he hoped would happen, was it?

~

"We have our own balcony!"

Twelve-year-old Samantha reached the cabin's glass door in two lanky strides, hauled it open, and stepped outside. The only thing to look at was the Carnival cruise ship moored next to them. Once they cast off, the view would improve substantially.

Emma smiled smugly at her sister. "Told you the upgrade was worth it."

Their room also came with a queen-sized bed—she and Juliet would share it—and a sofa chair that extended into a cot for Samantha, whom they both called Sammy.

Hefting one of the suitcases waiting in the cabin, Juliet carried it toward the wardrobe. "I know you did the upgrade for me. You shouldn't have spent the extra money."

Juliet's claustrophobia had been a factor, but not the only one. "I did it for all of us," Emma said. "Remember, the cruise was free."

She'd won a seven-day cruise for three after entering a fundraiser drawing at church. Not only had she never expected to win—she hadn't even wanted to. Cruise vacations under starry skies were for people who still had husbands… who still believed in romance.

Sitting abruptly on the bed, she sighed. "Maybe this cruise was a mistake."

Knowing Sammy couldn't hear her over the breeze outside, she admitted her misgivings to Juliet, who had begun unpacking.

Juliet brushed a lock of honey-blond hair from her face and gave her a pointed look. "It wasn't. Trust me, you need this cruise—and you'd better try to enjoy yourself."

Emma dredged up a wan smile. "Or else what?"

Juliet sighed. "It's time to move on, Em." Her gray eyes flicked toward Sammy, who was leaning over the railing, peering down the side of the immense ship. "You need to relax and meet people. And this is the place to do it."

By *people*, her sister no doubt meant *men*.

Emma scoffed. "You're one to talk. You haven't taken a vacation from your P.I. firm since you opened it."

More than that, Juliet had never been married—had barely even dated. Her private investigation business consumed all her free time.

"True. But I'm here now, and I plan on cutting loose." Juliet waggled her head playfully. "And you should, too."

"Let me guess." Emma smoothed the comforter under her palms. "What happens on a cruise ship stays on a cruise ship?"

"Exactly. So promise me you'll try to have fun."

Emma blew out a breath. "Fine."

Juliet stepped closer and held out her hand. "Shake on it."

An unexpected tingle of excitement danced up Emma's arm as she and her sister sealed their private pact.

Just then, Sammy stepped back into the room, sliding the door shut behind her. The wind had mussed her shoulder-length dark hair, and her green eyes shone with excitement.

"This is awesome!" She started to explore the room. "We have everything we need—a coffee maker—"

"Oh, you drink coffee now?" Juliet asked, still unpacking.

"No, but you do. A television, even a video game console." Sammy laid a hand on each item as she passed it. "What's in there?" She pointed to the closet Juliet was filling.

"Storage space. How about you unpack with me and stow your suitcase under your bed?"

"Okay." But she kept exploring, opening the door next to the exit. "Tiny bathroom." Her voice came through the door. "Actually, the shower's pretty big."

Emma, deciding to unpack later, lay back on the queen-sized bed to test the mattress. It was firm but surprisingly comfortable. Gazing at the ceiling, she tried to summon that earlier spark of excitement—but it was gone, swallowed by the same somberness that had plagued her since Eddie left her for another woman two years ago.

"Mom, there's no toilet paper."

Juliet called out, "It's in the dispenser."

"Nope. The dispenser's empty."

"Look under the cabinet."

A thumping sound came from the bathroom.

"There's none there, either."

Emma rolled to her feet. "I'll go ask the cabin boy."

Sticking her head into the crowded corridor, she looked for Shiv, their cabin steward—only to be blocked by the tall, broad-shouldered man she'd glimpsed earlier on the deck. Was he a celebrity? A professional athlete?

From ten meters away, his gaze caught hers, and his stride slowed. As he drew nearer, recognition struck like lightning. "Jeremiah?"

His features had matured—his jaw stronger, his neck thicker. The lanky frame she remembered had transformed into muscular perfection. His T-shirt stretched across his broad chest.

Letting the door bump shut behind her, Emma stepped forward to meet him. Their eyes remained locked. "Is that really you?" she asked softly.

The blond Adonis behind him peeked around his shoulder, bumping into him as Jeremiah stopped. Without any visible surprise, Jeremiah shifted the backpack to his left hand and extended his right.

"Professor."

He must've seen her earlier—on the receiving deck, when she'd first spotted him without realizing. An ironic smile carved dimples into his cheeks. Heavens, how she'd missed that smile.

"It's a small world," he added, his voice deeper, more resonant. "How are you?"

Stunned to the point of speechlessness, she accepted his hand, registering the warmth and firmness of his grip.

"You grew up." Stupid thing to say, but she couldn't take him all in fast enough. The intelligence in his gaze was exactly why she'd cherished him as a student. His calm, thoughtful demeanor hadn't changed—nor had his expressive hazel eyes, ringed by long lashes.

"And you look exactly the same," he said, his tone rich with admiration.

Self-consciously, she pulled her hand back. More likely, the demise of her marriage had aged her beyond her thirty-three years, turning the six-year gap between them into a gulf.

His handsome companion split a puzzled gaze between them. "Who's this?"

Jeremiah gestured. "Professor, this is my friend and colleague, Tristan Halliday. Tristan, Emma Albright."

Tristan's megawatt smile hinted at no shortage of adoring fans. "Professor," he repeated, engulfing her hand in his. "Did you teach this guy?"

Heat climbed into Emma's cheeks. "Yes, at George Mason University. Jeremiah took my Romantic Lit class."

"Hah. We call him Bullfrog now. You know, like the song."

Jeremiah was a bullfrog. Emma smiled. "Of course."

"Plus he's wicked fast in the water."

In the water? She looked to Jeremiah for an explanation, but he averted his gaze.

"Excuse us," said a corpulent couple behind them.

Emma backed against the wall, freeing the men to move on. "It's good to see you again, Jeremiah."

"You, too." His gaze lingered until he was forced to focus forward.

Tristan sent her a wink as he followed his friend.

Watching them walk away, Emma asked herself what they did for a living. Tristan's remark about the water hinted at competitive swimming… but they had to be too old for that. Maybe diving instructors?

Now that the large couple had passed her, she spotted Shiv and moved against the flow of traffic to catch him.

A backward glance showed Jeremiah and his friend entering a room just down the hall—directly across from hers. Pleasure surged through her, followed by that earlier tingle of excitement. With Jeremiah on board, she just might enjoy herself after all.

What a marvelous coincidence.

Romantic thoughts bubbled up only to be squashed ruthlessly by experience. She wasn't the wide-eyed idealist she'd been six years ago. If she'd known then what she knew now—that love was a fragile illusion—she wouldn't have been so appalled by her attraction to a younger, *other* man. She wouldn't have worked so hard to save a marriage that was already doomed.

But none of that mattered now.

For the next seven days, Emma was going to let her hair down—just as she'd promised Juliet. The tingle returned, stronger than ever.

Happily-ever-after might be a myth, but *happy-in-the-moment*? That was still a distinct possibility.

~

"Your professor has the hots for you, brother."

Tristan's observation, offered as they took in the layout of their interior cabin, pushed Jeremiah's thoughts deeper into confusion.

He hadn't realized how much seeing Emma up close would rattle him. Damn it, he wasn't a young man anymore. As a Navy SEAL, he'd seen and done things his twenty-two-year-old self couldn't have imagined. But gazing into her soft blue eyes and hearing her melodic voice had stirred the same rush of longing that had led to heartbreak. At twenty-eight, he ought to be old enough to resist her appeal.

"Are you going to make a move on her?"

Tristan's question brought Jeremiah's head around. He'd been inspecting their cabin—no window, two captain's beds, decent amenities—without really seeing it.

"Of course not." He shot Tristan a quelling look and tossed his duffel onto the nearest bed.

"Why the hell not?" Tristan flopped onto the other bed—the one closest to the bathroom.

"Because she's married."

"No, she's not. No ring, and there hasn't been one for a while, from what I could see. You really ought to notice things like that."

Under normal circumstances, Jeremiah would have. But he hadn't been able to tear his gaze from Emma's stunned expression. Turning his back on Tristan, he unzipped his bag, intending to move his clothes into the dresser under the bed.

Emma wasn't married? What had happened to Mr. Albright—

the very reason she'd begged him to stop coming to her office? Curiosity clawed at him.

What did it matter? She'd sent him away—not with his tail between his legs, exactly, but with enough finality to keep him gone. He wasn't about to grovel for her good opinion now—not even if she was the first and only woman he'd ever loved.

Of all the places for their paths to cross—why here? Considering the disturbing images he'd foreseen on the receiving deck, this couldn't be a worse time or place to reconnect.

"Hey." Tristan slapped him on the back, jarring him from his spiraling thoughts. "What's your problem, Bullfrog? We're on vacation. Let your hair down and loosen up a little, would you?"

Jeremiah cracked a smile at Tristan's wordplay. Considering he buzzed his chestnut hair to the scalp for hydrodynamics, there wasn't much hair to let down—unless the bar was already open.

"Let's go grab a drink." He left the duffel to unpack later. Maybe a strong one would drown the haunting visions.

"Now you're talking." Tristan beat him to the door.

Juliet waved an arm to encompass the marshes lining the canal as their cruise ship slowly motored from the port toward the open sea. "I bet all this marsh vanishes whenever there's a hurricane."

Emma smiled at her sister, noting Juliet's straw hat was tied beneath her chin, while Emma's own hat, without ribbons, had to be held down in a breeze. They'd come prepared to shield their pale complexions from the tropical sun ahead. In another twenty minutes, the ship would clear the tidal marsh and steam into the Gulf, where warmer temperatures awaited.

Following her sister's gaze, Emma imagined the area gripped by a hurricane. Thank goodness it was April, and the captain had assured them the weather on their way to Cozumel would be mostly sunny, with just a chance of rain while in Belize.

Sammy tugged on Emma's arm. "Can we go swimming now?"

Emma looked to Juliet, who shrugged. "Sure, why not?"

With a squeal of glee, Sammy hurried toward the pool's exterior steps. The sisters followed. In addition to their hats, they both wore full-length sundresses over their swimsuits—not exactly the look of women ready to cut loose.

Sammy made a beeline for the tube slide, leaving her mother and aunt to scout two empty lounge chairs in the shade. After adjusting the backs to sit upright, they spread their towels, sat down, and extended their legs.

Emma pulled up the hem of her dress, exposing her pale limbs to the sun, then fished sunglasses from her pool bag. Sliding them on, she exhaled, trying to clear her thoughts. *So this is what a vacation feels like.*

Glancing at Juliet, she found her with her hands folded over her stomach, her expression distant. The long sundress covered her runner's legs.

"Having fun yet?" Emma asked.

Juliet's frown deepened. "I'm getting there." The faraway look in her eyes suggested she was thinking of an unfinished case.

Emma hummed softly. "I don't think we have the foggiest idea how to cut loose."

Juliet's lips twitched. "Maybe we should get drunk or something."

"Hey, there."

Both women turned to see a hunky, blond Adonis approaching. They'd missed his advance—surprising, since every female nearby seemed to be ogling him. He wore a sleeveless white T-shirt that highlighted his broad, tanned shoulders and sculpted pecs.

His dark blue focused on Emma, then shifted to Juliet.

Emma snapped her fingers. "Tristan, right?"

He smiled. "Hey, you remembered. And you're Emma. But who is this?"

Juliet's gaze darted in Emma's direction, demanding, *How do you know this guy?*

"This is my sister," Emma said. "Juliet."

"I thought you might be sisters." Tristan held out his hand.

Juliet sat forward offering her own.

"Pleasure to meet you, Juliet."

Silence. With a "You, too," she snatched her hand back.

Tristan jerked a thumb toward the bar. "Care to join us for a drink?"

"Us?" Emma's stomach flipped as she scanned the bar and spotted Jeremiah seated under an awning, his back to the pool. He probably had no idea Tristan was inviting them over.

"Oh, I don't think—"

But Juliet was already pushing out of her chair. "We'd love to."

Emma followed with deep reservations. What more did she have to say to Jeremiah after all these years? Catching Sammy's eye, she pointed toward the bar. People likely thought the sisters easy marks, letting a handsome stranger pick them up so effortlessly.

Jeremiah glanced back as they approached. The flaring of his eyes confirmed Emma's guess and brought her to a standstill. What if he didn't want her interfering with his vacation? After all, she was the one who'd chased him out of her life, likely humiliating and hurting him in the process. Who could blame him for wanting nothing to do with her?

CHAPTER 2

Before Emma could summon an excuse to slip away, Tristan backtracked, catching her arm and tugging her toward the bar.

"Come on, he's dying to talk to you." His low-pitched words suggested he knew more than he let on. Grabbing Juliet's elbow again, he towed them both toward the empty barstools flanking his colleague.

"Hey, I found your professor, Bullfrog. Turns out she has a sister."

Jeremiah swiveled on his stool, eyeing them with cool reserve.

"Bullfrog, this is Juliet." Tristan pushed the introductions forward. "And, of course, you already know your English professor."

Juliet's face whipped in Emma's direction. "He's one of your students?"

"Used to be," Emma said softly. "Years ago."

Having acknowledged them, Jeremiah turned back to his tumbler of—scotch, maybe? Emma's heart sank again. Clearly, he still held a grudge over her desperate rejection.

"Have a seat." Tristan practically pushed them onto the stools, one on either side of Jeremiah while he leaned on the corner of the bar next to Juliet.

Emma, self-conscious and at a loss for words, propped her sandaled feet on the footrail and smoothed her dress over her knees. Being this close to Jeremiah left her tongue-tied.

He'd always been tall, which suited her well, but who'd have guessed that her lanky student would grow into such a formidable man? Concealing her gaze behind her sunglasses, she noted the rippling under his forearms and calves. Even his bare feet in flip-flops looked powerful and manly.

"What can I get you ladies to drink?" Tristan, undeterred by his friend's aloofness, pulled a folded strip of drink tickets from the pocket of his board shorts.

"We have our own tokens." From her own pocket, Juliet produced the tickets they'd purchased on boarding, casting Tristan a sweet but defiant smile.

"Cool." He shrugged carelessly.

Emma caught the bartender's eye. "I'll have a glass of pinot grigio." Maybe gulping it down would give her courage to talk to Jeremiah.

"No, wait." Juliet gave her a pointed look. "I think you'd rather have something fun and frozen, with a little umbrella, wouldn't you?"

Emma nodded in concession. "What do you have that's frozen?"

The bartender pointed to a placard behind him. "I recommend our mojitos—lime, mint, and rum."

Tristan lifted his glass. "That's what I'm drinking."

"I'll put an umbrella in it," the bartender offered.

Juliet chose for Emma. "We'll take two."

Beyond her, Tristan was looking her over, from her long blonde hair down to her hot pink toenail polish. Emma was intrigued to see a blush bloom on her usually impervious sister's cheeks.

Tristan put an elbow on the corner of the bar. "Well, Juliet, I know what Emma does for a living, but what about you?"

Emma willed her sister to flirt.

"I'm a PI," Juliet said, voice firm and businesslike. "I run an investigative firm out of Fairfax, Virginia."

Emma sighed inwardly at Juliet's matter-of-fact reply. At this rate, neither one of them would have fun on this cruise.

A spark of interest lit Tristan's deep-blue eyes, nonetheless. "Is that right? I bet you see all kinds of things people don't."

Juliet shrugged. "I hope so. What do you do?" Her gaze flicked to Jeremiah. "I assume you work together."

"Why don't you guess?" Tristan leaned an elbow on the bar, a small smile on his face.

Juliet hesitated, then, "Okay." She subjected both men to thorough scrutiny. "Well, you're both athletic, but I'd know if you were professional athletes."

Tristan's eyebrows rose. "A woman who follows sports," he noted with approval.

Juliet ignored him. "I'm going to say you're in the military."

"Whoa." Tristan looked amazed. "You nailed it. But can you guess which branch?"

The bartender interrupted, sliding two tempting drinks toward the women while swiping their tokens.

Emma grabbed her drink, relieved to have something to do while Juliet leisurely sipped her mojito and inspected the men a second time.

"I'll need more clues," she admitted. "Show me your tattoos, if you have any."

Tristan glanced around. "Here? You sure?"

A rusty laugh escaped Juliet. "How far do you have to strip?"

Emma smiled. Now *that* sounded flirty.

Tristan waved off the question. "Just teasing. It's on my back."

With scant warning, he lifted his T-shirt, revealing a rock-hard abdomen sculpted like a fitness magazine model. Every woman near the bar gaped.

Turning around with his shirt still raised, he displayed a red, black, and blue eagle spanning his upper back—wings outspread, talons extended, beak wide open as if attacking prey.

Juliet visibly swallowed. "That's—"

"Magnificent," Emma supplied, pulling off her sunglasses for a better look. As she laid them on the counter, Tristan lowered his shirt as he faced them again.

"Does that narrow it down?"

"A little." Juliet's eyes flicked to his glossy golden hair. "How long have you been on leave?"

"Two days."

"Then your branch doesn't care much about hair length." She glanced toward Jeremiah's close-cropped hair. "Though your silent companion keeps his short."

Jeremiah tore his gaze from his tumbler.

"That being the case, I'd say… either Air Force or Navy."

Tristan smacked his forehead in astonishment. "You really are good. What if I said Navy."

She cocked her head, then nodded. "Okay. You're Navy pilots."

"Hah." Tristan laughed, sounding both amused and a little offended. "What if I said we're more like frogs than sea gulls? Think underwater ordnance and that kind of thing."

Juliet's gray eyes widened, darting between the two men. "You're Navy SEALs."

Even as she stated it confidently, Tristan hushed her. "We can't advertise that. But you're right. I have to say, I'm pretty damn impressed."

Aware that she hadn't said so much as "hello" to him, Emma stared in astonishment at Jeremiah's profile. Navy SEAL?

After a swig of his drink, he met her gaze as if curious to see her reaction.

Beyond him, Juliet was looking pleased with herself, and Tristan was explaining that SEALs were high-value targets, so discretion was the better part of valor. Something that had been puzzling Emma for years became suddenly crystal clear.

"That's why I couldn't find you," she blurted.

Silence fell.

Jeremiah's brows knit as he stared back at her. "You looked for me?"

"Of course." How could he sound so surprised? "I wanted to know what you did after college. I never saw you again."

His face hardened subtly. "I thought that was what you wanted."

Pain as fierce as they day she'd begged him to stay away from her gripped her. "No." She shook her head vehemently. "That's not what I wanted. That's what had to happen. There's a difference."

He seemed taken aback. Breaking eye contact, he looked everywhere and nowhere at once. As Tristan chatted with Juliet about finally visiting resort towns instead of drug-infested villages, Jeremiah rubbed a hand over his face.

Regret pushed Emma to add, "Please forgive me, Jeremiah. I should never have encouraged you. You were just a kid. I should have known better."

His large hand covered hers unexpectedly, halting her apology, turning her breath shallow.

"Stop." His rich voice held frustration. "You didn't lead me on. I wasn't that young. Nor do I regret a single minute."

Pleasure warmed her at his confession. But then he pulled his hand away, drained the rest of his drink, and stood. "Excuse me." With those two words, he strode off.

Mortification burned Emma's cheeks. He'd accepted her apology, but hadn't forgiven her. Wiping condensation from her glass, she caught Juliet's questioning gaze.

"Don't mind him." Tristan helped himself to Jeremiah's empty stool. "He's in a weird mood. Plus, he's out of practice with the ladies."

Juliet cocked an ear. "Out of practice?"

"Well…" Tristan hesitated, realizing he'd said too much. "Bullfrog's complicated. Me? I'm simpler to figure out." He put a hand over his heart.

Juliet snorted. "Admitting you're shallow?"

"Nope. Just uncomplicated—and easier to satisfy." He winked.

Juliet stirred her drink while arching an eyebrow at him. "What makes you think I'm here to satisfy you?"

Emma bit her lower lip. Bravo—Juliet was finally flirting. One of them might have fun on this cruise, after all.

Tristan waved a finger at her. "You know, you remind me of something. It's called a rambutan. Ever heard of it?"

Juliet lifted her chin. "You're comparing me to a type of fruit?"

"Not just any fruit," Tristan assured her. "Rambutan's covered in prickly yellow hairs—same color as yours, only yours looks softer. From the outside, it just looks like a tough, prickly ball. But if you peel off the rind, the fruit inside is incredibly sweet and succulent."

Juliet narrowed her eyes even as her cheeks turned pink. "That's a line you use on all blondes, isn't it. But it's telling one. You've traveled exotic places if you've eaten rambutan."

As Tristan rattled off the names of places he'd visited, Emma replayed Jeremiah's parting words in her mind: *You didn't lead me on. I wasn't that young. Nor do I regret a single minute.*

Her heart softened at the suggestion that he cherished their shared memories as much as she did. How could he believe she'd simply dismissed him from her life without a second thought? Nothing could be further from the truth.

Granted, she had tried to forget him, at first, to focus on her marriage, which was already struggling. But two years later, unable to push him from her mind, she had attended the graduation ceremony the year he should have received his diploma—only to never hear his name called. That led her to search for any trace of him online, only the Jeremiah Winters she had cherished as both a student and a friend was nowhere to be found. Now she understood why: he had dropped out of college to become a U.S. Navy SEAL.

She had seen the documentaries—the brutal training program that whittled down candidates until only a few remained. Considering the slender, intellectual young man he had been, it must have been his mental toughness alone that kept him from ringing the quitting bell. Pride in his accomplishment dulled the sting of his silence.

A droplet of water splashed onto her shoulder, pulling her attention to Sammy, standing behind her, drenched. "Mom, I'm thirsty."

Nearby, Juliet and Tristan's conversation had shifted into a heated debate over national security. They clashed over the administration's aggressive stance on drug cartels and terrorists.

Emma shook her head, thinking what a shame it would be if politics clouded Juliet's hopes for a cruise-ship romance.

Leaving her sister and the SEAL to their discussion, Emma slipped her sunglasses back on before leading Sammy to the free lemonade station. Her heart remained heavy. Would Jeremiah forgive her for the past? They could be sharing a delightful conversation if he would only allow it.

Stop it. She pushed her yearning aside with the reminder that the feelings Jeremiah had sparked in her—then and now—were fueled by hormones and illusions.

At the time, it had seemed a lot like love, which was awful considering she was married. But she had learned since then that love wasn't the constant she once believed. She had loved Eddie when she married him, and in just a few short years, those feelings had all but disappeared.

The only reason that hadn't happened with Jeremiah was because their relationship had been cut short. Her feelings for him were suspended in time, like an insect caught for an eternal moment in a drop of amber, forever pure and intact.

It was better this way.

If they allowed their relationship to progress to the next level and the next, their attraction would eventually burst into flame, then burn itself out before turning to ash.

And she couldn't bear to lose him a second time—not like that.

Juliet's first impressions were usually right—but she had to admit, she'd been wrong about Tristan. He wasn't all brawn and no brains. Of course not. All SEALs had high IQs. They endured far more mental and physical hardship than most and thrived in hostile environments.

Plus Tristan had traveled to places she'd never even heard of, let alone wanted to visit, and he argued his views on national security with such clear reasoning, citing historical examples to back himself up, that Juliet found herself respecting his point of view—even if she didn't quite agree.

"Hey, listen." He leaned an elbow on the bar and lowered his voice to a conspiratorial murmur, his eyes on her sister at the snack bar. "I could use your help."

"Oh?" Juliet's cautious nature asserted itself. "With what?"

His dark blue eyes locking into hers made her insides flutter—an unfamiliar sensation. Where men were concerned, Juliet called the shots. Besides, the men she usually dealt with were either colleagues or criminals, and she kept her distance from both.

"I happen to know my teammate's in love with your sister."

She laughed out loud. "What?"

"Seriously. It all clicked when they ran into each other this morning in the hallway. He's always talked about this one perfect woman he loved and lost. It's her. She's the one."

The assertion intrigued her. "But he was her student," she replied. "And Emma was married back then. She would never have acted inappropriately."

"Maybe not. But something happened between them. I overheard her apologize just a moment ago."

"Yeah, me too." Looking back at Emma, she watched her hand Sammy a paper cup at the lemonade fountain. Her pained expression said it all.

"Okay, I agree they might have had a spark." Juliet looked back Tristan. "But I *know* Emma. She would have sent Jeremiah packing before she cheated on her husband."

"Maybe that's exactly what happened."

"Huh." Juliet glanced at Emma again. "So what do you need my help for?"

He leaned in, voice dropping even lower, though no one was close enough to hear. "I want to keep throwing them together, see what happens."

Juliet wondered if Emma's heart was ready for romance. "Why not? My sister's been single for over two years."

"And Bullfrog is the purest person I know. He deserves to be happy."

"Purest? That's an interesting word for a man."

"If you get to know him, you'll see what I mean. He's like a monk. He reads instead of going out, meditates so he never loses his cool. He came on this cruise just to make me happy—not for himself. A man like that deserves a good woman, and I think your sister's the one for him."

Juliet pursed her lips together. He'd given her a lot to think about. One of Tristan's sentences finally registered. "What were you unhappy about?"

Tristan grimaced and looked away. "You don't miss much, do you?"

"Not usually." She crossed her arms, signaling she expected an answer.

"All right." He had the grace to look chagrined. "I had *planned* to bring my girlfriend on this cruise and propose, but she broke up with me two weeks ago. Bullfrog offered to take her ticket."

An unpleasant feeling flickered in Juliet. "You had no idea she was going to bail?"

He exhaled sharply. "Maybe I did. I thought the cruise might spark something new. Things had definitely flatlined."

"How long were you together?" The nosy question slipped out.

He smiled firmly. "That's not the topic of our conversation. Are you in or not?"

Juliet couldn't see why not. Even if only for the cruise, having Jeremiah around for Emma to flirt with couldn't hurt. Emma had played the dour divorcée far too long.

"Sure. What do we do?"

"Should be easy."

He leaned in, the scent of soap—or maybe shaving cream—causing her to inhale.

"You tell me what excursions y'all are taking, when you plan to eat or go out, and I'll do the same. That way we hit the same spots, and they get thrown together. If it's meant to be, Mother Nature will handle the rest."

His plan sounded simple enough. To keep him from stepping back—because his closeness was unexpectedly thrilling—Juliet whispered, "Just so you know, Emma's cynical about romance. Eddie's abandonment shattered her."

"Her ex?"

"That's the one."

Tristan settled back onto his stool, fingers threaded in his lap, a thoughtful look in his eyes. "Let me guess—you don't believe in romance either."

She parodied his earlier line. "That's not the topic of our conversation."

Her sass made him laugh. "Fine. We'll stick to the topic. So, you're in?"

Juliet searched for Emma, who'd returned to the poolside recliners. Since Eddie ran off with another woman, Emma had lived like a spinster—hiding in her condo with her daughter and two cats, avoiding chick flicks and romance novels. At this rate, she'd be single for the rest of her life.

Facing Tristan again, Juliet stuck out her hand. "Let's do this."

For the second time that afternoon, his hand engulfed hers. The strength and warmth sent her pulse racing. She panicked and yanked her hand free.

He didn't comment on her awkwardness. "Let me get your next drink."

"Nope. I'll get my own."

Jeremiah's uneasiness mushroomed as he and Tristan shuffled along in the mandatory safety drill.

"This is nuts," Tristan muttered, voicing Jeremiah's own agitation as they moved like mindless sheep down the narrow hallway.

Passengers had been sent to their cabins an hour earlier, to prepare. At exactly 8 p.m., a grating alarm had blared over the intercom, summoning everyone to the stairwells. Half the people staggered like drunks, unsure where to go. The corridor clogged, the line crawling to a near halt. If a fire had broken out, they'd have been roasted alive.

Finally, the captain's Dutch-accented voice sounded over the clamor, reminding passengers to report to their assigned muster stations.

"Where's our muster station?" came cries from all along the passageway.

Had so few people read the directions left in their cabins? Jeremiah searched the hall for Emma, certain she knew what to do.

Tristan herded the mindless masses in the right direction. "Up the stairs to the promenade deck, people. Let's go!"

They were halfway up the stairs when flashes of gunfire and splattered blood flooded Jeremiah's mind without warning. He clenched the handrail to stay grounded as the visions surged, accompanied by the barrage of gunfire and the metallic scent of blood. *Oh, God.* Sweat trickled down his back, unrelated to the stuffy hallway.

It's just my imagination, he tried telling himself, but, of course, it wasn't. He knew a psychic hit when he suffered through one. Licking salt from his upper lip, he accepted the truth: something terrible was coming—but when? Sometimes days passed after a psychic hit before his visions became reality; other times, only hours. *Please give me time to fix this.*

Fresh air rushed over him as he ducked through a hatch onto the promenade deck. A mellow sky and calm Gulf waters offered a brief balm. The sun had set, heralding an evening that promised to be lovely. For now, everyone was safe. There was still time to act.

One of the stewards doling out life vests was a young Malaysian steward.

"Thank you." When Jeremiah's fingers brushed the man's in the hand off, shock stopped him in his tracks.

The steward's hand felt as lifeless as a corpse's.

Dismay slammed into Jeremiah. His sixth sense had never lied. This man was a dead man walking. But who would kill him? How could terrorists have boarded this ship when every passenger and their luggage had passed through metal detectors? No one could've brought assault rifles onboard—not like the ones in his visions. He himself didn't even have a weapon.

Vulnerability gnawed at him. His mind raced. Maybe weapons had been smuggled in through the service entrance, hidden under a food pallet or in a band member's instrument case. If he could find the guns before the attack, he might prevent the horror. His visions had saved lives before.

His gaze swept over the lifeboats, lashed tight like chicks tucked under a mother swan's wings. They hadn't been lowered—not even for the drill.

"Put your backs against the ship, keeping away from the railings." A safety officer was barking orders through a megaphone.

Just beyond him, a flash of long auburn hair caught Jeremiah's eye. Emma stood with her daughter and sister with the ship against their backs. When Tristan spotted them too and headed in their direction, Jeremiah braced himself for the pull Emma still had on him as he followed his friend.

Emma's cautious smile as she acknowledged their approach softened the resentment still lingering in his chest. Her confession earlier that she had looked for him had already eased the ache he'd carried for years. She must have loved him in return to have searched for him.

That being the case, was there anything to stop them from picking up where they'd left off? Oh, yeah. Just the bloody act of terror about to be unleashed on all of these unsuspecting vacationers—Emma included.

CHAPTER 3

Following Tristan to the opening next to Juliet, Jeremiah realized his best friend was dead set on pursuing Emma's sister. Those two stood between him and Emma, both wearing expressions that looked suspiciously smug.

Sensing Emma wished to say something to him, Jeremiah leaned forward to look at her.

This drill is a joke, said her gentle blue eyes.

He nodded grimly. *Tell me about it.*

But the humor died in his throat. The threat was real, and no one here had a clue. The crew of the *Escapade* probably had no idea how to evacuate passengers quickly, let alone handle a massacre in progress. The more he thought about it, the more a ringing filled his ears.

As the safety officer marched past, bellowing into his megaphone, Jeremiah tipped his head back against the hull of the ship, closed his eyes, and willed his anxiety to ease.

At last, the officer called, "Enjoy your evening!"

Passengers cheered, eager to resume their entertainment. Jeremiah kept Emma in sight as she flowed into traffic with a hand on her daughter's arm. Torn between wanting to talk to her and wanting just to keep her safe, he slipped past the passenger between them and drew up right behind her. "At least it's not raining," he said in her ear.

Tipping her head back, she sent him a wry smile. "Thank goodness."

As they lined up to return their life vests, his gaze fell to Emma's pink shoulders. She'd stayed in the sun longer than she should have. Her daughter, all arms and legs with shiny dark hair, stood beside her, wrestling with a vest that swallowed her petite frame. Premonition strummed his consciousness.

"Um, your daughter needs a smaller vest than that one."

Emma gave it a cursory glance as she handed it to the attendant. "Good thing it was only a drill."

They filed back into the stairwell where more visions panned through Jeremiah's mind. *Oh, Jesus. Not again.* The same horrors panned through his mind. *Okay, I get it. It's not my imagination!*

So much for striking up a conversation with Emma. Automatic gunfire blended with the tramping of feet, keeping him from speaking. Blood sprayed the walls, spiking his adrenaline as he scanned for the source of the violence. The face of the attacker eluded him, and time was running out to communicate his willingness to start over.

"Listen." His mouth felt dry, his words stilted. Instead of saying something clever or flirtatious, he heard himself advise, "If the emergency is ever real…Come find me."

Her brows pulled together. "Okay."

"Tristan and I can keep you safer than anyone else on this ship." Maybe that was why they'd crossed paths again. Maybe his purpose was to protect her—nothing more.

After descending to the level of their cabins, they ran into Tristan and Juliet waiting in the crowded hallway.

"Hey, Bullfrog. Let's take these pretty ladies to the Lizard Lounge. I hear they like karaoke."

"And Emma has a beautiful voice," Juliet tacked on. "Just wait till you hear it."

Still grappling with dark thoughts, Jeremiah didn't answer. Maybe this wasn't the time for rekindling his friendship with Emma. He didn't need a distraction; he needed to stay alert.

"I can't go to a bar," he heard Emma protest. "What would I do with Sammy?"

Passengers pressed in around them, annoyed with them for standing in their way.

Sammy bounced on her toes. "Oh, you could take me to Kids' Zone! That's where my friend Sophia's going."

"Well, that's an option," Emma agreed. "But I need to sign you in first."

"Look, there's Sophia!" Sammy pointed to a girl entering the elevator with her parents. "Can we go?" She tugged on her mother's hand drawing her away.

A stream of people promptly came between them. Looking back, Emma caught Jeremiah's eye. "Maybe I'll meet you there."

He doubted he would go.

"I'm sure she'll join us," Juliet said at his elbow.

"Come on, brother." Tristan gestured up the hallway toward the interior staircase. "Let's go hang out."

Hang out? Jeremiah couldn't afford that luxury. He had to stop the violence before it started.

Lifting a hand in farewell, he backed toward the stairwell he'd just exited. After climbing back to the promenade deck, he pushed out into the cool evening air. Taking advantage of the promenade deck, which wrapped around the entire circumference of the ship, he began to walk, willing more visions to come to him regardless of how they sickened him.

With enough clues, he could piece together the plot and stop the attack.

Come on, Universe. Talk to me.

To increase their odds of beating the enemy—whoever that might be—he would have to tell Tristan soon what he'd foreseen. But for now, he was the only soul aboard who knew what was coming.

Maybe *this* was the reason he and Emma had crossed paths

again. Maybe he was meant to protect her, not build his life around her as he wanted to. Starting over again—that would take energy and focus that he didn't have right now. Then again, if she wanted him back in her life—if she came after him with an open heart, he knew he'd cave in an instant.

Emma was the one and only woman he had ever loved, and falling in love with her again would be as easy as breathing. But a dark force stirred by the evil in men's hearts threatened to keep them apart.

Will we never get a chance to love each other as we could?

"I can't believe neither one of them showed up."

Tristan's annoyance slipped out as he leaned back against the plush seat across from Juliet. He left his half-empty Foster's bottle on the glass coffee table and locked eyes with her across the space between them.

"I can." Juliet nibbled thoughtfully on a peppermint leaf from her mojito.

Watching her lips and teeth move delicately over the leaf heated Tristan's blood. Unlike his insecure, raven-haired ex-girlfriend, Juliet radiated quiet confidence. She didn't fill the air with endless chatter like Mariah. When Juliet spoke, it was sharp and insightful. Her honey-blond hair, steely-gray eyes, and athletic frame made her beautiful—tough, not fragile. She looked like she could take you down in a wrestling match.

The mental image of their bodies tangled, sweat slicked and mouths fusing, ignited a fire in him. Ordering himself to slow down, he steered to safer ground.

"You seem like the older sister, but you're younger, right?"

She pointed a finger at him with mock severity. "First of all, I'm going to forgive you for suggesting I look old."

"That's not what I meant."

"I know. That's why I'm forgiving you." She set her glass down and leaned back. "Emma's older by four years. I'm the practical one. She was the romantic dreamer."

"Was?" He cocked his head at the tense past-tense.

"Yep. Now she's just disillusioned. Probably holed up in our cabin, nose in a book."

"No!" He gaped. "How could she do that when there's so much to do here?"

"Spoken like a true non-reader."

"I read." Her judgment made him sit straighter.

"Read what?"

"Thrillers. Mostly." He rattled off a couple of favorite authors.

She waved a hand. "Okay, fine. I stand corrected. You can't know everything about someone in just a few hours."

He smiled slow and easy. "What about a few days?"

She shrugged. "We'll see."

He narrowed his gaze. "Bet I can tell you something about me that you would never guess."

Her gaze sharpened, weighing the wager. "Go ahead."

"I used to be a NASCAR driver."

"Hah!" Her eyes flew wide. "You're kidding."

"See? Surprised you." He grinned. "Four years on the circuit before the SEALs."

"That adrenaline rush wasn't enough?"

"Hey, I like pushing limits—finding out what I can do."

"You must be crazy to race cars, let alone join Spec Ops."

"Call me crazy to my face. I'm used to it."

Ignoring his sarcasm, she studied him through her eyelashes. "What makes you so…?"

"Reckless?"

"I was going to say devil-may-care."

Having asked himself that question more times than he could count, he grimaced. "I don't know." The beer he'd consumed on an empty stomach loosened his tongue, causing him to add, "I'm not like the rest of my family."

She leaned in. "In what way?"

"Let's see." He glanced at the ceiling. "My parents are doctors. My brother's a lawyer. My sister's a financial advisor."

Her gaze cut through him. "So, you're the black sheep. But to be a SEAL, you have to be smart."

Her faith warmed him. "Thanks, darlin'. Actually, I was adopted. Maybe that's why the white-collar career path never called to me."

"Adopted." She cocked her head. "Is there a story there?"

"Oh yeah. My birth mom left me in the hospital ER lobby. My parents, who worked there, called social services, got permission to take me home. Six months later, my adoption became legal."

She blinked as if deciding if he was serious. "So, you push yourself to the limit because…?" She motioned for him to finish.

He held back the full truth—that he felt like a mistake, an unwanted child left behind like a bag of trash. That feeling drove him to reckless extremes—not to die, but to find meaning.

"Want to hear me sing?"

Her eyebrows rose at the sudden shift. The karaoke singers had been abysmal all night, and it was driving him crazy.

"Are you any good?" she asked doubtfully.

He flashed a grin. "You be the judge."

Leaving her at the table, he approached the DJ. Out of the corner of his eye, he caught a middle-aged man swagger over to Juliet, trying his luck and taking the seat Tristan had just left.

Possessiveness flared. He was about to intervene when the man hung his head and slinked off.

Admiration surged. Juliet could definitely hold her own.

Tristan chose a country song about love growing cold on a stormy night and stepped onstage, grabbing the mic.

The room fell silent—a reaction he had come to expect. Men scowled with envy; women stared like he was a prize.

Once, he'd soaked in the attention. Now, it felt hollow. What he craved was depth.

The music started. Focusing on the screen, he gave the song everything he had. Midway through, he glanced up—Juliet's mouth was hanging slightly open.

He smiled. Nobody expected this from the SEAL. The boy could sing.

The song ended with thunderous applause.

"Thank you, thank you very much," he said with a mock Elvis drawl, then hopped offstage back to Juliet.

Still no sign of Bullfrog or Emma.

"So?" he asked, plopping back down.

"Not bad." She smiled, eyes glinting with interest. The look on her face made him feel ten feet tall.

"Your turn." He gestured to the stage.

"No way." She shook her head. "Emma's the singer."

"Maybe we should find her."

"What time is it?" She stood and leaned over to check his watch.

"Quarter after eleven."

She sighed, collapsing back in the chair. "Nah, she won't come out now. Plus, I've got to pick up my niece from Kids' Zone. Long day—we left Dulles at dawn."

Disappointment hit him, but he understood, so he stood, offering his hand.

She ignored it, standing on her own, before slipping her hands into the pockets of her sundress in what looked like a clear message to keep this distance. Huh. He could've sworn she was warming up to him.

They headed for the exit, stepping out into the common area with its grand, sweeping staircase. Tristan came to a stop. "Wait, we haven't compared itineraries yet. How are we getting Bullfrog and your sister together?"

She paused and exhaled, thinking. "Meet me in the Fiesta Galley at nine? Breakfast and coffee help me think."

The thought of seeing her again so soon made him want to skip sleep.

"Cool." He smiled. "Want me to walk you to Kids' Zone?"

She gave him a deer-in-the-headlights look. "No."

With that, she turned on her sandals' heels and strode toward the elevator, shoulders back, head high.

Okay, so clearly she wasn't as into him as he was into her. Maybe he was the only one who'd had fun.

Puzzled, he scanned the bar for other women. They were pretty enough, but none held a candle to Juliet—who'd quietly captured his attention without him realizing it until now.

He smiled wryly, heading for the grand staircase. Maybe he'd find Bullfrog and figure out why he was dodging Emma when it was obvious he was obviously still crazy about her.

Emma laid her book on the bedside table and glanced at her cell phone—then remembered she'd turned it off to avoid roaming charges. Rolling out of bed, she hunted for the watch she'd tucked into her luggage.

It was thirty minutes to midnight. Sammy must be exhausted by now, while Juliet was out with the hunky Tristan. Normally, Emma could count on her sister to bring Sammy back to their cabin as promised earlier. But these weren't normal circumstances. Peeking into the Lizard Lounge earlier, she'd caught Juliet looking completely smitten, and that was a first. Her sister worked side-by-side with hard-nosed cops and smart-ass lawyers. Not one of them had ever put a captivated expression on Juliet's face.

If Jeremiah had been there, Emma would have joined them. His absence could only mean one thing: no interest in rekindling their connection. The conclusion panged her way more than it ought to. It made her want to break her promise to Juliet. Forget about having fun on this cruise. Juliet could have fun for the both of them.

Instead, Emma had headed back to their cabin, picking up a book from the ship's library en route, which she'd been reading since. The non-fiction account of Mayan culture was fascinating—especially since they would soon be visiting the ruins of Tulum.

But with the hour so late and Juliet still out, Emma supposed she ought to fetch Sammy from Kids' Zone herself, just in case Juliet found herself… indisposed.

"After all, what happens on a cruise ship stays on a cruise ship," she quipped as she slipped back into the sundress she'd worn earlier.

The subtle movement of the ship rocking beneath her feet drove home the fact that the *Escapade* was surging across the Gulf waters. How astonishing. Even more astonishing was that Jeremiah Winters was aboard this same floating cosmos, bound for the same sandy shores.

Her thoughts drifted back to their very first meeting. She'd been grading essays in her office when a knock drew her attention to one of her new Romantic Lit students, standing at the open door with a backpack slung over one shoulder and a tentative smile.

The only reason she'd remembered his surname was because he'd distinguished himself from day one. "Oh, hello, Mr. Winters."

"Jeremiah." He looked deep into her eyes, reminding her of his first name.

Something inside her seemed to swivel. "How can I help you?"

"Um." He glanced at the note outside her door. "It says here you have office hours now?"

"Yes. Come in. Have a seat."

Her office seemed to shrink as he entered. Dropping into the chair next to her desk, he reached between his long legs, unzipped his backpack, and pulled out their textbook.

"I've been reading some poems we skipped." He cast her a sheepish smile, flipping to William Wordsworth's section. "I really wanted to talk about these two."

With long, sensitive fingers, he pointed to *Ode on Intimations of Immortality from Recollections of Early Childhood.*

"I don't know why, but these reminded me of William Blake's *Songs of Innocence.* Especially this one."

He read it in a low, resonant voice that sent goosebumps to her skin. *Here's someone like me. He gets it.*

"Or am I way off?"

His insight was brilliant. "Not at all. You've brought up something recognized by literary experts." She flipped to Blake's text and read a line, striving to match his tone.

Looking up, she caught him watching her intently.

"Do you believe in soulmates?" he asked her.

The question hung between them, alive. Her heart yearned to say yes.

"You said in class this morning that Wordsworth and his sister are considered soulmates. That made me wonder if you believe in them."

Her thoughts went to her husband, Eddie, whom she'd met as a junior undergrad. Having lost both parents two years before, she'd latched onto him with relief. Eddie was steady and reliable—but not a soulmate as much as a pillar of strength.

"I guess so. After all, I teach Romantic Lit."

"Except you taught us on day one that 'romantic' has nothing to do with romance."

"Sad but true." The awareness arcing between them made her search for lighter ground, and, just then, the length of his thumbnail caught her eye. "Oh, do you play guitar?"

He glanced at his thumb, smiled wryly. "Classical guitar. I try, but I'll never be as good as Baden Powell—he's a Brazilian guitarist."

Surprise flared. "Yeah, I know exactly who he is—or was," she amended. "I have all his CDs." She'd never met anyone else who knew Baden Powell.

"That's funny. I have all his music on Spotify."

His reply underscored their age difference, easing some of her incredulity. "Small world."

"You're not much older than me."

His unexpected words made her laugh self-consciously. Had he read her mind? "Oh, no? How old are you?"

"Twenty-two."

"Oh." At least he wasn't a teen, still. "So you didn't go to college straight out of high school?"

"No, I backpacked through Europe, doing odd jobs."

Envy flickered, tempered by happiness for him. "Lucky you." She'd only been to Europe on her honeymoon and ached to return.

He closed the textbook reverently. "I *am* lucky. My parents insisted. Traveling puts everything I'm studying into perspective."

She admired his enthusiasm. "Please tell me you're an English major."

"No, Philosophy with a minor in French. But I really like your class."

His tone said *I really like you.* And, God help her, she liked him just as much.

"Well—" she took the higher ground, reminding herself she was his professor and married—"if anything else grabs your imagination, come by and discuss it. I'm always available during office hours."

"I will." He started to put the book away, then stopped and looked back at her. "You didn't say how old you are."

She summoned a prim smile. "Twenty-seven." Yet in that instant, she'd have given anything to be younger—and not married.

"Six years is nothing." Standing, he slung his backpack over one shoulder. His slow smile revealed dimples. "I'll see you in class, Professor."

"Bye." Feeling her world tip on its axis, she watched him walk away.

Rousing from her daydream, Emma shook off the feelings and slipped on her sandals. Grabbing her room key, she left the cabin to fetch her daughter.

She hadn't taken five steps when the object of her daydream rounded the corner. Their gazes locked and both slowed to a stop. Jeremiah's hazel eyes seemed to see straight into her soul.

"Hi." She recovered first and moved toward him.

He did the same until they met in the middle. "You never made it to the Lizard Lounge." His tall frame blocked the lighting, casting his face in shadow. The hurt in his voice was unmistakable.

How could he know that—unless…? "Well, I saw you weren't there, and Juliet was having such a good time with Tristan that I didn't want to interrupt."

His mobile mouth twisted sardonically. "That's pretty much what I did, too."

So he *had* shown up. But what had he been doing since then? Talking to another woman?

He stepped closer, and the air reversed in her windpipe. A whiff of balsam filled her nose. Her eyes stung at the realization he still smelled the same.

When he raised a hand and stroked her cheek, the six years apart melted away. His touch flustered her just as it had the day he stroked her knuckles and said goodbye.

Whether she backed against the paneled wall or he pressed her there, she couldn't recall. But there she was, aware of his tall, muscled body pressed against her softer one. She fought to keep her eyes open, to witness what she'd always hoped for.

"I've missed you, Professor."

Both the title and his words brought tears surging to her eyes. Then he lowered his head and covered her mouth with his.

His kiss was electric—frustrated and anguished. Imprisoned in its colliding emotions, she spun in helpless enthrallment.

Then a child's voice floated toward them, and he released her suddenly. Emma gasped and straightened, distancing herself just as Juliet rounded the corner with Sammy.

Her heart pounded erratically.

Glancing back, she found Jeremiah striding toward his cabin, footsteps silent on the carpet.

Emma gathered composure as she greeted her daughter and sister. "You remembered to collect her?"

"Of course." Juliet's discerning gaze flicked between Emma's flushed face and Jeremiah's retreating back. No doubt she sensed the lingering electricity.

"Thank you. Did you have a good time, honey?" Emma put an arm around Sammy, drawing her toward their door.

"Yes, it was awesome. I want to go back tomorrow."

"I think we can arrange that." Using her key card, Emma let them in.

Why the turbulent kiss? If she had to guess, something was troubling Jeremiah—beyond the shock of running into her again.

As Sammy darted into the bathroom, Juliet brushed past murmuring, "Sorry about my timing."

Emma waved off the apology. Words eluded her as she imagined what might have happened if the kiss hadn't been interrupted. They might have ended up in his cabin making love like she'd only ever imagined.

Should she be grateful or resentful for Juliet's timing?

I'm grateful. Given what she'd learned about love's transience, she'd be a fool to get swept up again. Love was an illusion—and his pull could vanish in a blink, leaving her more devastated than when Eddie pulled the plug on their marriage.

No. She was better off keeping her distance.

CHAPTER 4

Popping the last bite of toast into his mouth, Jeremiah looked up to see Emma's sister, Juliet, approaching Tristan's and his table in the Fiesta Galley. The galley offered an all-you-can-eat buffet free to passengers, though some preferred the half-dozen upscale restaurants that were anything but free.

Upon arriving ten minutes earlier, Jeremiah had spotted Emma and Sammy seated by the window among the hundred or more guests. In her white sundress, backlit by the sweeping sea and sky, Emma resembled a Titian angel—slimmer than the voluptuous figures in the painter's works but every bit as radiant. Juliet, however, had been nowhere in sight.

Embarrassed for having kissed Emma so intensely, he'd steered Tristan away from the pair. His only excuse was that the ominous feeling he'd been carrying around had overwhelmed him in the moment, clouding his judgment. Worse, he'd broken his own rule to wait for her to make the first move.

But now he was sticking to that plan. With Tristan none the wiser, he'd selected a table near the ship's prow and out of Emma's line of sight before they went off one at a time to fill their plates with breakfast.

Now Jeremiah's plate was empty. Juliet stood before him, balancing a tray piled with pastries and two cups of coffee.

"Hi."

Her terse greeting came with a pointed smile as she set the tray down across from him.

Oh. Okay.

He slowly pushed back his chair.

"You don't have to leave."

Her protest was clearly insincere.

Tristan offered him a bland smile. "Bye."

Jeremiah picked up his coffee cup, now nearly empty, and went to refill it. Seeing Emma and Sammy still seated by the window, his resolve to make her come to him faltered. Perhaps he should apologize for his behavior and offer up an explanation. As a mother, didn't she deserve to know about the threat hurtling toward them?

Yes, she did.

With his will weakened, he topped off his coffee and headed in her direction.

"With all the options on the buffet line, I can't believe you're only eating Raisin Bran," Emma chided her daughter. Spotting Jeremiah headed in their direction, her pulse doubled its beat. *Where did he come from?*

"I'm not. I'm having ice cream next."

With a stifled laugh, Emma shook her head and gave up.

"Mind if I join you?" Jeremiah loomed over them, carrying a cup of coffee and wearing an apologetic expression that melted Emma's defenses.

Sammy glanced up in surprise.

"Not at all." Picking up the tray across the table, Emma made room for him to sit there. As he pulled his chair in, their knees bumped, and her nerves jangled.

"Hi," he said to her daughter.

"Sammy, this is Jeremiah," Emma introduced formally, though they'd met at the safety drill. "He used to be a student of mine."

Jeremiah held out his hand, but Sammy was busy stifling a burp.

"Excuse me." She sounded so genteel in contrast to the hearty burp that his laugh spilled out. Emma's face warmed with chagrin.

"Can I go to the pool now?" Sammy's green eyes begged to escape.

"I thought you were going to have ice cream next."

"I am. I'm taking it to the pool to eat there." Without waiting for her mother's permission, she slipped out of her seat and pushed her chair in.

"Don't forget your pool bag." Emma snatched it off the floor and thrust it at her. "And put on sunscreen before you swim, especially on your nose and shoulders."

Grabbing the bag without a word, Sammy headed for the soft-serve dispenser.

Emma hid her humility behind a sip of orange juice.

"How long have you been divorced?"

The unexpected question caught her off guard. She choked on the swallow, citrus burning her throat. Setting her glass down, she coughed into her napkin. "Almost three years."

Jeremiah looked away toward Sammy's retreating form. "Is she still close to her father?"

"Not really. He moved out of state. She sees him two weeks a year."

His gaze softened with compassion. "I'm so sorry."

He must be wondering how the man she'd trusted could have abandoned them both.

"Listen." He dropped his gaze to the tabletop. "I'm sorry about last night."

A prick of hurt touched her. Did he regret kissing her?

"Well, not that sorry," he quickly added with a devilish smile that chased away her pain. "My mind was in the wrong place. I need to tell you why. Would you walk with me when you're done with breakfast?"

So much for keeping her distance. Faced with his request, Emma chose to share his company. "Sure."

They pushed back their chairs simultaneously and rose. Though ship staff would clean after them, it still felt wrong to leave their dishes behind as she followed Jeremiah toward the exit.

"Thanks." She brushed past him as he held the door ajar. A cool breeze wafted through the weave of her white cotton dress.

"This way." Jeremiah led her up a set of exterior steps headed for the prow. As they climbed, he slipped on sunglasses, making her wish she'd brought her own.

As the sun warmed her shoulders, it occurred to Emma that, apart from the safety drill, she and Jeremiah had never *done* anything together. Their encounters had been confined to her office walls; their adventures vicarious and cerebral. They'd traveled through space and time in stories, but never taken a simple walk—until now.

Invigorated by the sun and fresh breeze as much as by his presence, she looked around as they reached the large deck at the boat's front. A netted enclosure stood before them.

"What's that?"

"The sports court. We're standing on the track that runs around it."

The stripes beneath her feet confirmed his words. Following the track, they circled the sports court. Peering inside, she saw a blacktop basketball court and a pickleball area. A netted ceiling prevented stray balls from sailing into the sea—or worse, the open-air dining balcony above.

Jeremiah pointed to the court floor. "See the big X? With the nets down, it doubles as a helicopter landing pad."

The random fact seemed important to him.

"Where'd you find out that?"

His mouth firmed. "From the security officer."

She cocked her head. "You've talked to the security officer? What for?"

"Well, you know, we SEALs are big on safety. He only gave me a minute."

"I see."

They had the track to themselves; the courts stood empty. Feeling the wind whip her hair into tangles, she reached up to restrain it. Jeremiah slowed his step, watching. Through his dark sunglasses, she caught his eyes lingering on her upturned face. His gaze made her self-conscious as she twisted her hair into a knot.

"There. That's better." Dropping her hands, she moved forward again.

Hadn't he wanted to discuss something? The silence was killing her. "Do you like your job?" she asked to break it.

A small smile touched his lips. "For the most part. I tell myself I'm a modern-day Don Quixote—except the giants I fight are real."

She could only imagine how terrifyingly real they were. "Well, I'm proud of you, Jeremiah." Her throat tightened with awe and respect. "You've done something so few men can."

He inhaled as if savoring the compliment. "Thanks. That means a lot."

Curiosity got the better of her. "So, have you found your Dulcinea yet?" With Jeremiah, she never worried whether he understood literary references—in this case, to the woman Don Quixote loved from afar while charging into battle in her name.

He slowed and met her gaze, holding it. "You know it's you, Emma. There's never been another."

The frankness swept her off her feet until reality brought her sharply back. She gripped the railing to steady herself.

He joined her, facing the open sea. "The water is lighter today than yesterday."

Jeremiah's observation drew her gaze to the tiny whitecaps foaming and fading on the swells. The breeze kissed her bare skin; sea birds wheeled overhead calling to each other. The romantic setting made her think of the famous scene in *Titanic*, in which Jack held Rose secure on the prow of the unsinkable ship while she pretended to fly. *Dreamy nonsense*, Emma reminded herself.

"We've entered the Caribbean Sea."

Clearly, he knew more about bodies of water than she did.

"You know that by the color?"

"Yes. It's changed from cobalt blue to teal. See the difference?"

Men were supposed to have only a basic palette—dark blue, light blue, navy. But Jeremiah wasn't most men; he'd read *Pride and Prejudice* and loved it.

"This view reminds me of a poem by Wordsworth."

His comment confirmed her insight. She held her breath, confident he'd recall a few lines. His gift for memorizing verse had amazed her the first time she heard it—and every time since.

A rapt audience, she rested her hip against the railing and admired his arresting profile. With his head cocked as if listening for the words, he spoke to them in a serene voice.

"'And I have felt a presence that disturbs me with the joy of elevated thoughts; a sublime sense of something far deeper, whose dwelling is the light of setting suns, and the round ocean and the living air, and the blue sky, and in the mind of man.'"

The words hung between them—too perfect to be sullied by anything ordinary. Despite herself, Emma's heart lifted like a kite caught in a steady breeze. *They're just words,* she told herself. Still, they captured something true and eternal—something worthy of her gratitude.

"I wish I could do that." She nodded toward Jeremiah's effortless recall of the poem. "My memory's terrible."

He shrugged, glancing her way. "Can't take credit. That's just how my brain works."

His brain—that had drawn her to him first. But as he turned to face her, her heart skipped with the thought of another kiss. She wished she could see his eyes through the dark lenses of his sunglasses.

"Reciting poetry hasn't helped much in the military."

She chuckled softly. "I can imagine."

"But I've developed another skill."

"Oh?" Her mind leapt straight to the bedroom.

He finally removed his sunglasses, dropping them in his breast pocket while revealing his deep-set hazel eyes, a kaleidoscope of browns and greens. The dead-serious look on his face chased away her wandering thoughts. What he had to tell her wasn't good.

"You know when you sense something right before it happens? I've developed that ability."

She blinked, trying to process what he meant. "Like when I know my sister is about to call?"

"Exactly. That's prescience—our sixth sense. If you exercise it like a muscle, you can enhance intuition. After a while, you get good at picking up on energy and intent—warnings of danger."

A sliver of alarm cut through her. "Sounds useful in your line of work."

Jeremiah smiled, a brief crack in his serious mask. "Very. In Native American culture, warriors learned to see far ahead—remote viewing. I'm still learning that skill."

She frowned. "What if there's a bend in the road?"

"I take the bend in my mind's eye to see what lies beyond—a puddle or a wall concealing the enemy."

The word *enemy* tolled in her head until a sudden thought struck her. "Did you know we'd cross paths again?"

"No."

His simple answer put the thought to rest.

"But I had a vision yesterday right before I saw you." His jaw clenched as he looked toward the pilot house.

She swallowed hard. "You've seen something bad, haven't you?"

He grimaced. "Yes."

That explained his odd behavior. Her stomach tightened. "What kind of bad?"

A heavy silence fell before he said, "I'd rather not say. I just want you to remain alert, and if you see anything suspicious—tell me."

Goosebumps rose on her skin. Her thoughts darted to Sammy, alone at the pool. "What should I watch for?"

He lifted a hand and stroked her bare arm in a soothing gesture. "Anything that strikes you as hostile—a look, a shout. . . someone with a weapon."

At a loss for words, Emma kept quiet. His warning was the last thing she expected to hear while on vacation. It jarred her sense of reality.

"Maybe that's why we crossed paths again," he added, dropping his hand. "Maybe I'm here to keep you safe."

Without his comforting touch, vulnerability surged. She wet her lips. "Now I'm nervous."

His lips firmed. "I'm sorry. I want you thinking happy thoughts. They're safer—and lead to better outcomes."

When his gaze rested on her lips, and Emma's breath caught. As he leaned in, her heart pounded—equal parts hope and caution. In ten minutes, Jeremiah had captivated her again. The warrior he'd become could ambush her heart before she even sensed the danger.

His lips brushed hers, quieting her fears. This wasn't an assault—it was tenderness inviting her to accept what she might otherwise resist. Now that she wasn't married, nothing stood in the way but fear.

But if Eddie's abandonment had hollowed her, what would losing Jeremiah feel like? The need to protect herself had her pulling free. She faced the sea again.

From the corner of her eye, she saw him bow his head and sigh. His hands gripped the railing, mirroring her stance.

"I shouldn't have told you." His voice held regret. "You think I'm crazy now."

"No." She shook her head. "I sensed something was troubling you. Now I know why."

Against her better judgment, she covered his hand with hers—planning to pull away immediately—but the smooth swell of his knuckles enticed her to caress them.

"Do you still play guitar?"

He let her touch him, making no move to stop her. "Rarely. Not much time. Always fighting windmills, taking online classes."

"To get your Master's? Your Doctorate?"

"Still finishing my bachelor's."

She pulled her hand back to face him. "You didn't graduate?" No wonder she hadn't seen his name in commencement.

"No. I left that semester. Never went back."

"Oh, Jeremiah." Dismay clenched her chest. "I'm sorry."

"You apologized already." He smiled firmly. "You were the best thing that ever happened to me."

The words jolted her again. "Please don't say that." Her body stiffened. "What we feel—then and now—it isn't real."

His brows rose. He gave a humorless laugh. "It isn't *real*?"

"No." She grasped the rail as the ship shifted once beneath her feet. "It's biochemistry. Hormones, endorphins that make you blind to faults, unable to think straight. Psychologists call it limerence."

"Limerence." He sounded skeptical.

"Yes. Lasts six months to two years, maybe longer if it's forbidden. But it fades, and reality returns."

He loosed a humorless laugh. "So you're saying love isn't real."

Her traitorous heart gave a skip at the word love. "*Falling* in love isn't real," she corrected. "It's a temporary madness."

His thick eyebrows knit. "If that's true, then why did Tennyson write, ''Tis better to have loved and lost than never to have loved at all'?"

She cast about for an answer. "I don't know. But good for you—most people think Shakespeare said that."

Still frowning, he folded his arms across his chest while planting his feet to counter the ship's subtle movements. "Some risks are worth taking, Emma. If no one had ever fallen in love, think of all the art lost. Every masterpiece ever created was likely born out of limerence, as you call it. And for the record—I've always seen you clearly." A hint of anger sparked in his hazel eyes.

His logic cracked her defenses. If she wasn't careful, limerence might convince her what they felt was real.

"I'm sorry." She searched for distance. "This isn't a good idea."

"This?" Dropping his arms, he gestured at the ship, the ocean spread out before them. "Or this?" Catching her chin, he brushed his thumb over her lower lip.

She stepped away from his electrifying touch. "I need to think." Her voice wavered. "I'll see you."

Turning, she hurried down the stairs, aching for him to chase her, to promise it was safe to feel this way.

How pathetic.

Love wasn't safe. Love wasn't even real. And he was a Navy SEAL—didn't ninety percent of SEAL marriages end in divorce? Why was she even thinking about love when she only wanted a little fun?

At the bottom, she glanced back. Jeremiah stood at the top, arms once more folded, his expression thoughtful but not discouraged.

Her heart leapt. *Come after me.*

She crushed the weak thought and made a beeline for the pool.

Jeremiah spun around to face the wind. Well, that hadn't gone the way he hoped.

Blowing out a slow breath, he pressed onward up the track toward the prow, turning over Emma's words in his mind. Where on earth had she picked up all that nonsense about limerence? It had to be the fallout from her failed marriage—some desperate search for meaning as to why love had failed to keep her and her husband together. Probably the result a self-help book, full of airy theories.

But the real reason for her broken marriage—he hoped—was that the spark between him and Emma had outshone anything she'd ever known with her husband.

She couldn't be more wrong about love. Of all the forces in the universe, love was the most real, the most powerful, the most enduring. It could stretch across time, shield the weakest soul, and stare down evil without flinching. Imagine the gift he could give her when he showed her what love truly was.

But first, he had to keep her alive—and every one of the other 2,398 souls aboard this ship.

At the prow, he faced forward, letting the wind whip over him, sharpening his senses. Centering himself, he gripped the rail and closed his eyes, seeking to remote-see, a skill he was just beginning to hone.

He pictured their route, envisioning Roatan Island rising from the sea—mountainous, cloaked in dense, tropical rainforest. Was that where the hostile forces would board, or were they already lurking aboard, waiting for the perfect moment?

He pushed beyond Roatan, but Emma's strange ideas about love echoed stubbornly in his mind, sabotaging his focus.

With a frustrated sigh, he opened his eyes and released the rail. What now?

After his frustrating run-in with the tight-lipped security officer last night, he'd combed the ship from stem to stern, poking into hidden corners known only to the crew—hunting the source of his unease.

He'd gathered what he could about the crew's backgrounds. Some were Palestinian refugees from Gaza—but none carried the dark zeal of jihad. Many were Africans and Ukrainians fleeing war in their homelands. Were any of them the threat he'd sensed on board?

A flicker in the water directly below him caught his eye. A family of dolphins was escorting the *Escapade*, diving and leaping with joyful abandon alongside the ship.

The sight eased his tension and brought a smile to his face.

Leaning over the rail, he watched the sleek mammals in quiet awe. They swam faster than he ever could—making him feel feeble by comparison. But the Universe had made its point. He wasn't alone. The forces for good were with him, still.

CHAPTER 5

"I can't believe I let you talk me into this."

Emma gasped for breath, pausing behind her sister on the forested path winding toward the hill where their zip line adventure would begin. Gazing upward, she spotted the gleaming metal wire stretching high above the branches that bowed overhead. She slowed to a stop. *Am I really going to do this?*

"You'll be fine." Juliet, fit and unruffled by their steady uphill climb, glanced back and slowed to for her.

"Hurry up!" Sammy called from the staging platform. She'd left them in the dust, bounding up the hill like a young goat. Her impatient shout jarred the rainforest's peaceful hush.

Emma reached for Juliet's arm as she started forward again. "Wait—you know I'm still not great with heights." She searched for a way out.

Juliet tugged free of her hold and turned her back. "No quitting now. You need to do this, Em. First, conquer the fear. Then you'll enjoy it."

Emma dragged her feet. "Enjoy dangling a hundred feet in the air with only a harness strapped to my thighs?" A cold sweat prickled her skin. "I wanted to relax on this cruise, not jumpstart my adrenal system."

Juliet kept moving. "You need to jumpstart *something*."

Emma easily overheard the muttered words. Juliet was talking about her love life, wasn't she? Her thoughts flicked to Jeremiah. If only she weren't tangled in the illusions of limerence, she'd welcome that jumpstart. But one never came without the other.

With a groan, she chased after her sister. If only she'd chosen a different excursion like scuba diving in Mahogany Bay, as Tristan and Jeremiah were doing. Why hadn't she chosen that excursion? Oh, yeah. Sharks.

By the time Emma reached the wooden shelter perched atop the hill—the launch platform—her thighs burned from the climb.

"Look at this view, Mom!" Sammy leaned far over the platform's edge, peering into the lush forest below.

"Honey, be careful!"

But then she looked, and her breath caught at the panorama awaiting her. Here above the treetops, a sea of green leaves rolled away in every direction, bordered in the distance by a turquoise ocean. Stunning. The view was worth every bit of the climb, especially when two yellow parrots burst from a *gumbalimba* tree, fluttered briefly, then disappeared. Jeremiah would probably recite a poem right now if he were here.

Remembering what she was about to do, Emma wished he was.

One of their dark-skinned guides began explaining the zip line's mechanics. As he demonstrated how to wear the harness properly, Emma's stomach churned. Her mouth dried.

Then she glanced at Sammy's bright eyes, and a spark of her daughter's excitement leaped into her.

Maybe this could be a thrilling adventure, not a terror.

"Who wants to go first?" the guide asked, shaking off his halter.

Sammy shot her hand up. "Me!"

Emma's heart pounded as she watched her daughter climb into the oversized harness. With a grin of anticipation, Sammy stepped to the platform's edge.

"Careful, baby."

Without a backward glance, Sammy stepped into thin air. The harness caught her, and she zipped down the wire, her exhilarated cry echoing through the forest.

It couldn't be as bad as Emma imagined.

Snippets of a William Wordsworth poem floated through her mind as she steeled herself to follow. *"When the green woods laugh with the voice of joy, And the dimpling stream runs laughing by…"*

Juliet turned toward her. "You're next."

"No, no. I'll go after you. That way you can catch me at the bottom."

Emma's words earned a stern look. "Don't you dare chicken out."

"I won't. I need to do this." Emma nodded, determined.

"Okay." Juliet turned away. "Watch me. Do exactly what I do."

Juliet whooped as she sailed into the forest. Emma summoned every ounce of courage and stepped into the guide's offered harness.

"Relax, ma'am. Go with it. You'll be fine."

Her heart hammered as she gripped the vertical cable hooked to the horizontal one. The guide gave her a gentle shove off the platform.

She swallowed a scream as she dropped.

Air rushed up—cool, sweet, scented with frangipani. *"Come live, and be merry, and join with me, To sing the sweet chorus of 'Ha ha he!"*

The line went taut, and instead of falling, Emma began a smooth, swift glide over the leafy treetops. Cool wind kissed her face. Leaves brushed the tips of her sandals. A fragile sense of safety stirred within her.

Through the branches ahead, she spotted Sammy on the distant landing pad, clapping wildly for her mother's feat.

Emma loosened her grip just a little. With a long, steady breath, she let go of her fears and opened herself to the vivid greens rushing past and the thrilling freedom of flight. Beneath the canopy, dappled sunlight flickered through the leaves. *So this is what it feels like to fly.*

Juliet was right. She needed this.

Some risks are worth taking.

Jeremiah's words echoed in her mind. He risked everything day after day for their country, living fully and fiercely. So what if her heart teetered on the edge of love's illusions? Without taking that leap, she'd never create memories like this.

It was time to embrace life—danger and all.

"Dude, the reef was incredible. You feeling any better?"

Tristan's sudden entrance caught Jeremiah off guard. He shoved the ship's blueprints under his pillow—but not fast enough.

Tristan's gaze tracked toward the papers peeking out. His diving mask had left a pale oval around his eyes and nose, while the rest of his face was bronzed by the sun.

"What are you doing? Thought you were sick. Don't tell me you're cramming for some class!"

Jeremiah chuckled. "Studying sounds like the worst punishment ever. These aren't class notes." He pulled the blueprints free. "Research."

Silence.

"Research on what?" Tristan's tone tightened.

Jeremiah met his teammate's wary gaze. "I've been getting some hits." He couldn't keep it bottled up any longer. He needed Tristan's help figuring out where the threat might be.

Tristan groaned. "Seriously? Here? On this ship?"

"Yes. The day we boarded, I saw something."

"I thought you were acting weird. What'd you see?"

"Men with assault rifles gunning people down." Jeremiah's voice dropped. "Haven't seen anything today, though."

Tristan brightened. "That's good, right?" He started putting away his underwater camera. "You said those visions aren't set in stone. Maybe the threat's gone."

Jeremiah shook his head. "No. I still feel it coming." His eyes darted to the blueprints. "And when the shit hits the fan, I want to know the safest places to send people."

Tristan's face tightened with reluctance. "Please don't say that, brother. No way semi-automatics made it onboard. Everything passed through X-rays and metal detectors."

"That's true—even crew stuff." Jeremiah nodded. "Found that out from a mechanic in the engine room. He's the one who lent me these blueprints. But I think there's a way in."

"How?"

"In instrument cases. Too big for the X-rays. Plus, no point running them through metal detectors—the instruments trip those anyway."

"So *this* is what you did all day? You said you were feeling queasy."

Jeremiah shrugged, avoiding Tristan's gaze.

"You lied to me!" Tristan's eyes widened with mild offense, then softened as he looked at the blueprints. "You wanted me to enjoy myself. Damn it, Jeremiah—you're too good for this world." He clapped him on the shoulder. "Forget it. We're safe, brother. Besides, we've got a date with two hot women tonight. We'll be late if we don't move."

Jeremiah stiffened, scanning Tristan's face. "Women? They better not be strangers."

"Juliet and Emma, dude. Who else?"

"Oh." Relief and excitement washed over him. "Well, why didn't you say so?" He dropped the blueprints on his bunk and sprinted for the bathroom, beating Tristan there.

"You schmuck!"

Half an hour later, the two SEALs stepped into the disco-themed bar and hesitated. The place was packed with baby boomers—not a millennial or Gen Zer in sight. A mirrored ball spun overhead, flinging glittering shards of light across the parquet dance floor, while a live band played the theme from *Grease*. The lead singer sported a foot-tall Afro, and the rest of the band wore sequined hippie attire.

"There they are."

Tristan spotted their targets and started toward them.

A surge of exultation hit Jeremiah's bloodstream when he saw Emma sitting in a booth beside her sister. She'd come. And her welcoming smile hinted at a change of heart.

"Ladies." Tristan greeted Juliet and Emma with a cheek kiss each, making Juliet stiffen while Emma's eyes brightened in surprise.

If only Jeremiah had Tristan's confidence. Instead, his gaze drifted admiringly over Emma's dress—a skimpy coral number that matched the flush riding her cheekbones. In the glittering light, her skin shimmered like mother-of-pearl. Suddenly, a vivid image flashed in his mind—him peeling back her dress to bare her breasts.

Well, hot damn.

Welcoming the intuitive hit, he slid into the seat across from her.

"How was the scuba diving?" Emma asked the moment they sat.

"Good." Tristan answered before Jeremiah could. "Not the Great Barrier Reef, but the coral was still impressive."

Jeremiah shot Tristan a grateful glance for not revealing he'd snorkeled alone.

Juliet lowered her drink. "You've been to Australia?"

Tristan wagged a finger. "Good on you, mate." Then, leaning toward Jeremiah, he added loudly, "Nothing gets past her. I love it."

Jeremiah's attention flickered to the band. The frenetic electronic synthesizer notes distracted him briefly. His gaze locked on the lanky keyboard player with shifty eyes. The synthesizer's large vinyl-and-steel frame looked capable of housing several assault rifles.

Was that an intuitive hit—or a wild guess? Either way, the band deserved closer scrutiny. But not now.

Facing Emma, Jeremiah marveled at the thought that he might actually be undressing her later. The devil-may-care lift at her mouth's corners told him something inside had surrendered to the inevitability of their coming together. Why question it when the reward promised an unforgettable night?

A waiter appeared. "What can I get you gentlemen to drink?"

Tristan pointed at Juliet's glass while pulling a token from his shirt pocket. "I'll have what she's having."

"And you, sir?"

"Macallan Scotch." Jeremiah's affection for the whiskey dated back to a summer in Scotland when he was twenty.

As they waited, Juliet recounted their zipline adventure. "I thought Emma was going to back out on me, but she didn't."

Jeremiah caught the flush on Emma's face—reliving the thrill.

"No, it was great. Life-affirming." She met his eyes, and his libido jumped awake.

At that moment, a sultry Lionel Richie song replaced the disco beat.

Jeremiah nodded toward the dance floor. "Care to dance?"

"Oh." Emma's pulse jumped at the invitation. She glanced at the couples already dancing. No one was getting too intimate, and dancing certainly qualified as living more fully.

"Sure. Why not?"

Besides, leaving the table would give Juliet and Tristan a moment alone—one step closer to Juliet's goal of making the most of this cruise. No doubt, her sister would beat her to their mutual aim of cutting loose.

As she and Jeremiah rose and wove through the tables toward the dance floor, his warm hand settled at the small of her back, sending a quiet thrill through her. Heads turned as they passed, letting her know they made a striking couple. He guided her to a corner near the band, then slipped his arm around her waist and gently drew her in.

When their bodies met, her breath caught. She tried to appear casual, draping an arm around his neck, but her nerves were jangling. As he caught her free hand, she realized—they'd never held hands before.

And it felt… stunningly perfect. Her palm nestled into his, their fingers twined. Swallowing hard, she looked up at him—only to find him studying the band.

"Where's Sammy?" he asked on a serious note.

She drew back slightly to search his face. "At Kid's Zone. Why?"

He met her eyes briefly before returning his attention to the stage. "Just curious."

It was more than that, she was sure. But before she could press, another thought surfaced.

"I thought of you today," she said, steering the conversation.

That got his attention. "Oh?"

"I wondered what poem you might've recited if you'd been with me—gazing down at the rainforest canopy, watching it ripple in the breeze."

A smile flickered across his lips. "You're the only person who actually enjoys my recitations. My teammates usually groan—'Seriously, brother? We're about to take out insurgents, and you're quoting Shakespeare?'"

She laughed. "Why not? No one says it better than Shakespeare."

"True. One night we were huddled in position, about to ambush the enemy. Guess what popped into my head?"

"'Something wicked this way comes'?"

"Bingo." He chuckled. "Another time we were working with the DEA, helping capture a drug lord. The DEA agent started listing off our target's crimes, and I couldn't resist—'There is something rotten in the state of Chiapas.'"

She laughed, delighted by his dry delivery. "So I take it this won't be your first trip to Mexico."

"I've seen the interior. Never the beaches."

"Chiapas… that's where you caught the drug lord?"

His expression darkened. "Yeah, we caught him. But he escaped from prison six months later."

"El Cuchillo, right? I think I saw that on the news. Doesn't his name mean *The Knife*?"

"Sí. And yeah… you can imagine how he earned it."

A shiver passed through her—not entirely due to the air conditioning. "Was he caught again?"

"Not yet." The weight in his voice made her ache for him.

"That must be discouraging. But you still like your work, don't you?"

He paused, considering. "I like it because of my brothers. My teammates are my family. They make me feel indispensable. And most of the time, what we do really matters."

She pictured them—warriors bonded by hardship and triumph. Her lips curved as another Shakespearian quote surfaced. "'We few, we happy few, we band of brothers.'"

He smiled. "Couldn't have said it better. And thanks to the Navy, I've had access to some great education." A quick glance at the band. "I'm actually a medic now."

"Really?" But he still seemed distracted. Maybe he was just nervous.

"Yeah. I get to sew guys up, push morphine, tie tourniquets…"

"I guess you don't faint at the sight of blood."

"Only my own."

Before she could respond, the song faded out. The keyboard player held the last note, then leaned toward the mic.

"That's it for the band tonight," he announced, in a thick Irish accent. "But don't leave just yet—Jason's here to spin your favorite soundtracks from the '60s and '70s. Thanks for listening. We're the Sequels, and we'll be here all week."

A smattering of applause. The band began to pack up.

Jeremiah didn't move.

The DJ queued up a Bee Gees track, but it was obvious Jeremiah's mind was elsewhere.

"Care to take a walk?" he asked, confirming her suspicion.

A quick glance at their table showed Juliet and Tristan deep in conversation. "Sure."

Jeremiah led her out of the club at a brisk pace, into the carpeted corridor. Without pausing, he turned toward an exit, holding the door for her.

They stepped onto a moonlit deck. The sea stretched dark and endless beneath a waning moon. But it wasn't the view Jeremiah was watching.

Emma followed his gaze to the smoking area, where the keyboard player had lit a cigarette. Intrigued—and slightly put out—she let him steer her to the railing, where he pretended to admire the ocean.

She waited, then leaned in. "Why are we following the guy from the band?"

He cast her a guilty glance. "Sorry. I didn't think you'd notice."

"A woman always knows when she's not the center of attention."

That earned a laugh. He propped an elbow on the railing and turned toward her.

"Don't sell yourself short, Professor. Trust me, I'd rather be taking you on a romantic stroll right now. But I need to know more about that man's intentions."

She studied his face in the shadows. "You think he's planning… something violent?"

It was hard to imagine the rather tired-looking man becoming dangerous.

He followed her gaze, then sighed. "I'll talk to him another time. Right now, I want to show you something. Do you trust me?"

The suggestion of a secret adventure made her heart flutter. It wasn't him she didn't trust—it was herself. "Fully."

"Good. Come with me."

He caught her hand and led her back inside, down the corridor, and into an elevator. He pressed the button for the fourteenth floor—the highest level on the ship, aside from the pilot house.

Definitely not headed to his cabin.

The elevator chimed, and the doors opened onto a short hallway with violet carpeting.

Excitement fluttered in her stomach. Sneaking around with a SEAL was kind of… fun. How much trouble could they get into?

Jeremiah put a finger to his lips and beckoned her toward a door labeled CONFERENCE ROOM.

He tried the handle—locked. Then pulled a credit card from his wallet.

"Oh my God," she whispered. "What are you doing?"

His hazel eyes sparkled with mischief. He worked the card into the doorframe, popped the lock, and opened the door with a soft snick. Gently, he propelled her inside and shut the door behind them.

"We're going to get into trouble," she warned.

"Not if we don't get caught."

The room smelled of lemon polish and leather seats. In the dark, she made out a long conference table.

"This way."

He led her to a window, swept aside a floor-length curtain, and exposed a sliding glass door. After flicking the lock, he cracked it open and drew her onto the balcony.

Warm, briny air met them. Unlike the balcony off her cabin, this one was expansive, situated at the ship's stern between two large lights—one red, one green. Crossing to the railing, Emma stared at the ship's frothy wake, a pale ribbon unraveling on the black sea.

Jeremiah joined her, his gaze fixed on her profile.

"If something goes wrong on this ship," he said quietly, "I want you to come here. If the door's locked, use your cabin key and break in—just like I did."

She turned to him, unease skittering down her spine.

"There aren't any exterior cameras," he added. "No one would know you were back here. A helo could hover overhead and drop a line to pick you up."

The scenario made her zipline adventure seem like a kiddie ride. But surely he was exaggerating. Cruise ships were safe… weren't they?

"You can't stop worrying, can you?"

His tormented gaze skimmed her face, lingered on her mouth, then dropped to her chest. "I was hoping you could help me with that."

Blood surged through her veins. Just like the day she'd banished him from her office—terrified she'd fall for him—she now stood at the edge of that same precipice. Only this time, she had no marriage to protect. Just her heart.

And maybe the fall would be worth it.

Emma opened her arms in silent invitation.

He kissed her immediately, surrounding her with heat and hunger, flooding her with a desire that scared her for how right it felt. This time, there was no reason—not really—to stop. Only fear. And she was tired of letting fear dictate her life.

"I've missed you," she admitted between kisses.

He groaned and pulled her closer.

Feeling his tumescence against her pelvis, anticipation shimmered low in her belly, sweet and terrifying. She clung to him like a drowning woman clutching a life raft, wanting more.

Then he tore his mouth from hers with a ragged breath. "Okay. Let's slow this down." He glanced around, nodding toward two padded lounge chairs—the only ones on the balcony. Releasing her, he pushed them together.

"Lie down with me?"

She kicked off her sandals and slid onto the far chair. Jeremiah stretched out beside her. Without hesitation, their fingers found each other, twining tight.

Lying back, Emma looked up—and gasped. "Oh, wow."

The stars stretched endlessly overhead. The sky was velvet-black, the cosmos glittering like diamonds just out of reach.

"We have the universe to ourselves," Jeremiah murmured, smiling. He pointed upward. "There's the Little Dipper. And Orion."

"That must be Venus," she said, nodding toward a brilliant point of light. "Planets don't twinkle like stars."

He rolled onto his side, prompting her to do the same. His free hand trailed slowly down her bare arm, then up again, stirring goosebumps in its wake. Their faces were inches apart, close enough for her to see the starlight reflected in his eyes.

"There are over eight billion people on Earth," he said softly. "What are the odds we both ended up on this ship?"

The question settled between them. Maybe he was right. Maybe it wasn't chance.

"It's not a coincidence," he said, reading her silence.

She dropped her gaze. "Did you bring me out here to gaze at stars and talk about fate?"

He didn't answer. Instead, he tilted her chin and met her eyes—gently, deliberately—then kissed her again.

This kiss, like the one outside her cabin, wasn't smooth or easy. It was stormy. Uncertain. Like a bolt of lightning, it lit her up from the inside, flooding her with a craving to be known, to be touched, to be filled.

Above the thrum of engines and the whisper of waves, she gave in—to desire, to fate, to him.

CHAPTER 6

The kiss deepened. Passion beat Emma's heart like a native on a drum, accelerating the tempo of their merging. Curling her fingers into his shirt, she drew Jeremiah closer, craving his essence, his heat. He reached behind her, releasing the bar that propped up her seat, and lowered the back steadily. When she was lying flat, he rolled up and over her, causing the chair to groan in protest.

He nibbled the length of her neck, summoning a shiver of desire that tightened her nipples against the fabric restraining them. His clever fingers found the zipper at the side of her tight dress and tugged it open. Then, kissing her again, he slid the spaghetti straps from her shoulders.

Emma's toes curled at the sensual undressing. Before long, he'd peeled her dress down, exposing her modest breasts like a priceless gift unwrapped with reverence.

Glancing down self-consciously, she was pleased by how beautiful she looked—her nipples erect, bathed in moonlight. Never in her life had she felt more alluring.

"I've been waiting six years to do that."

Her heart gave a pang, but she thrust the memories away. "Naughty boy."

He chuckled, clearly taking no offense.

Lowering his head, he worshiped each breast with swirling licks of his tongue, making her cradle his closely shaved head. His hair, though shorn, was soft to the touch. Her yearning spiraled to dizzying heights. Cool air touched her heated center as he rucked up the hem of her dress. She lifted her hips, easing his seduction.

With one foot on the deck and a knee braced beside her, he paused to gaze at her. She'd never felt more desirable, lying half-naked and wanton, her dress bunched around her hips, her lace panties a feeble barrier.

"I am dying to quote Byron right now," he growled, "but I don't want to sound corny."

The confession pulled a laugh from her. *She walks in beauty, like the night…* Of course that was the poem he meant. Her heart swelled with feelings she dared not name. How she longed for him to see her as the best of dark and light. Yet even if he did, those feelings would be fleeting. Passion always faded. Romance was a tragedy by nature.

The thought sobered her as she watched Jeremiah tackle the buttons on his shirt. When he shrugged out of it, revealing lean muscle and dusky chest hair, desire roared back—heightened by the sight of scars marring his perfect torso.

"Oh, Jeremiah." She reached for him, brushing her fingers over the thick, shiny seam just above his right hip. "What happened here?"

"I'll tell you later."

He reached for the front of his trousers, unbuttoning and unzipping them. All thoughts of battle scars vanished as he exposed himself, fully aroused, to her hungry gaze. How many times had she imagined this moment—only to discover that reality eclipsed her every fantasy? He was magnificent. The prospect of his possession nearly sent her over the edge.

Then the buzz of a phone shattered the moment.

Jeremiah glared at the Android he'd left on the table. "Damn it."

"Your phone works out here?" Frustration sharpened her tone.

"Yeah. Sorry. I can't ignore it." He picked it up, let it scan his face, then read the message aloud. "Oh, wow."

She almost didn't want to ask. "Wow, what?"

"Tristan just won five grand at the slots."

"Good for him." *Too bad he couldn't have waited another thirty minutes.*

"And your sister says she can't pick up Sammy. She needs you to do it."

Emma shot to her elbows. "Oh my God. What time is it?" She'd completely lost track.

"It's only eleven-thirty." Jeremiah killed the screen and set the phone down.

Emma sank back with relief. "Then I have twenty minutes. As long as I'm there by ten to twelve, I'm okay."

He climbed onto the lounge chair beside her—not on top of her, as she would've preferred. With a sigh, he tucked a strand of hair behind her ear and grimaced. "I'm sorry, but that's not enough time."

Disappointment steamrolled her. "It's not?" She would unravel in seconds if he simply claimed her.

"I don't want twenty minutes, Professor. I want forever."

His words struck her mute. She stared at him, stunned.

"No answer?" He pulled back slightly.

"Why would you even bring that up?" Her voice came out stricken. "Didn't you hear anything I said yesterday? What we feel for each other isn't real. It never was. Love is a lie, Jeremiah."

Eddie would've exploded if she talked to him that way. Jeremiah simply stared—long and thoughtfully. "Are you sure you're not trying to convince yourself?"

"Yes, I'm sure." She sat up, forcing space between them, threading her arms back into her spaghetti straps. "I'm telling you what I *know* to be true."

A frown finally creased his brow. "So what are we doing here, then? All you want is a fling?"

Shame burned her cheeks. But who was he to judge her? She hadn't had sex in nearly three years. "Well, why not? Men do it all the time. Doesn't mean a thing to them."

"I'm not like that, Emma." He rolled onto his back and fastened his pants. With his gaze on the stars, he added, "And I don't do temporary."

She climbed off the chair, yanked her skirt down over her hips, and searched for her sandals. Behind her, Jeremiah rose and stalked to the railing, tugging his shirt on—his back rigid, his face turned from her.

Awash in chagrin, Emma struggled with the zipper he had lowered so effortlessly minutes earlier. Finding her sandals, she wriggled her feet into them, trying to ward off the regret and remorse pressing on her chest. An apology stuck in her throat. She had chased him away—again—repeating history without meaning to. Couldn't he just accept that they had no future, but could still share an affair neither of them would ever forget?

Or maybe *she* was the one who needed to accept Jeremiah's romanticism—and relent to the possibility of forever?

The mere thought of a relationship terrified her. *Never again.* The bond Jeremiah believed would endure would only wither, as all passionate love did. She couldn't bear to watch that loss unfold. Better to walk away from the illusion of happiness. One of them had to be the realist.

"I think I should go." Her body still pulsed with longing. *If only Jeremiah were an opportunist, like most men.*

"I'll walk you out." He turned and led the way off the deck.

Emma followed on shaky knees, her stomach churning with the fear that Jeremiah must think even worse of her now.

They crossed the dark conference room in silence. At the corridor, he peeked out, then motioned for her to slip through ahead of him before closing the door softly behind them.

They rode the elevator in silence as thick and heavy as cement. Back on the tenth floor, they passed through the bustling corridor and entered the casino, where Tristan and Juliet were exchanging their buckets of coins for dollar bills. As they approached, Juliet glanced over—and did a double take.

Her gray eyes locked onto Emma's no-doubt tense expression. Handing her bucket to Tristan, she hurried over and caught

Emma's arm, pulling her deeper into the casino while Jeremiah remained by his teammate.

"Are you all right?"

Emma swallowed the knot rising in her throat. "I'm fine. Congrats on winning all that money. Is he giving you some?"

"Half." Juliet studied her, frowning. "We interrupted something with our call, didn't we? I'm so sorry."

Emma couldn't reply. "I'm going to go get Sammy now." She turned away, forced to pass Jeremiah on her way out.

The look on his face—disillusioned, hurt—was the same one he'd worn the day she told him not to visit her office anymore.

Averting her gaze, she walked stoically into the hallway and struck out toward the Kids' Zone.

I did the right thing. I did the right thing.

If she said it enough, maybe she wouldn't feel so awful.

Juliet heaved a sigh in the wake of Emma's exit. Not five seconds later, Bullfrog clapped Tristan on the back and stalked off in a different direction.

As she watched him go, Tristan joined her with a fat wad of bills in his hands.

"I wish we hadn't texted them," she admitted. "They needed more time to work things out."

He slapped the bills against his palm, thinking. "Well, tomorrow, we wake up in Belize. Maybe we can get them together again."

"Except that you and Bullfrog are riding ATVs while the three of us are tubing through the Mayan caves."

"Right. And tubing lasts all day. Hmm."

Juliet met his deep blue eyes. "We need to change things up."

"Right. And I think I know how. I'll tell Bullfrog I'm dying to impress you with my driving skills. Then *you* ask him to trade his excursion ticket for yours."

"Oh, so I have to ask him?" The crinkling at the corners of his eyes made her wonder at his thoughts. Did he really want to show off—or was he mocking himself again, as she'd noticed he tended to do? It was one of the things she liked about him. He didn't have the ego that usually went with his looks.

"Naw, I'm just messing with you. I'll ask him."

She propped her hands on her hips, thinking. "There's only one flaw with your plan."

"Oh, yeah? What's that?"

"You're assuming I'd willingly give up my tubing ticket just to be with you." She raised a brow. "You might be exaggerating your charm just a little."

He belted out a laugh that made her lips twitch.

"I was hoping you wouldn't notice that part. But seriously, Bullfrog would much rather go tubing through Mayan caves than get his thrills and chills watching me drive. He gets enough of that whenever we train in the desert."

Picturing Tristan behind the wheel of a desert patrol vehicle made him hotter than ever. The crazy nut had to love every minute of being a SEAL.

"What about me?" she demanded. "Am I going to enjoy myself four-wheeling?"

He flashed her a grin. "I'll make sure of it. Plus, I'll take you shopping in Belize City afterward and spend my half of the winnings on you." He waggled his eyebrows and started counting out the money.

She grunted. "Too bad I hate shopping."

He glanced up, astonished. "A woman who hates shopping?"

"There are a few of us."

"Damn." He shook his head and looked back down at the bills. "Where have you been all my life?"

Her pulse skipped at the words, muttered just under his breath. Was he serious? Apparently not, since he kept counting. "Two thousand five hundred. Here's your half." He held it out to her. "Don't spend it all at once—unless you want to buy me a new motorcycle."

"Right." She grabbed the money.

But Tristan didn't let go. "Can I get a thank-you kiss for sharing my money with you?" The question was asked artlessly, accompanied by a hopeful look.

Juliet squashed the kindling of desire that sparked to life inside her. "Technically, I won it all because I pulled the handle." She shrugged. Too bad.

His smile deepened, but he still didn't release her half of the bills.

Heaving a sigh of mock disgust, Juliet slid her free hand into his wavy hair and tugged his head down, glimpsing surprise in his eyes as she turned the tables on him. Trying not to smile, she molded her lips against his sensual mouth and kissed him soundly.

Mmm. Nice. Lingering just long enough to hint at what he'd be missing, she pulled away, tugging the money from his slack fingers.

"I'll see you in the Fiesta Galley at eight-thirty. Bring Bullfrog's excursion ticket, and I'll bring mine."

With a smile that felt far more flirtatious than she intended, she brushed past him, sliding the money into her shorts pocket as she walked away fast.

Don't follow me. Don't follow me. Heart pounding, she hustled toward the elevator. Keeping Tristan on his toes appealed to the feminist in her, but she probably came off looking experienced in seduction—which she most definitely was not.

Oh, God. Her stride faltered. What if Tristan's appeal caused her to fall for him? Where would she be then? Just another one of his conquests, memorable only for helping him get over Mariah, whom she'd heard enough about in the past seventy-two hours to consider the most manipulative woman on planet Earth. Juliet had zero intention of following in her footsteps.

"Juliet."

Oh, crap. He was coming after her. Resisting the urge to glance back, she darted around a corner and quickened her pace. He could move a lot faster in loafers than she could in three-inch heels.

"Wait."

She pretended not to hear him. If she waited for the elevator, he'd catch up. And then she knew what would happen—he'd back her into a corner and finish the kiss she'd just started. Only he'd give it to her long and deep. Her knees weakened at the thought.

If she took the stairs, she might get away yet.

Too bad that option didn't sound nearly as exciting.

But Emma would be looking for her. Since Juliet had always been the down-to-earth sister, she couldn't let her down now.

Kicking off one heel and then the other, Juliet held both shoes in one hand and bounded down the stairs, taking two at a time. By the time Tristan reached the elevator, she'd be long gone.

"Wait. Where are you going?" Emma stared in disbelief as her sister crossed the boardwalk, veering away from them. "We're over here!"

When Juliet glanced over her shoulder, Emma pointed dramatically at the excursion sign labeled *Bottoms Up Cave Tubing*. "It's right here," she repeated.

With a grimace, Juliet turned back toward Emma and Sammy, tugging the brim of her pink golf cap lower to shade her eyes. "I forgot to tell you." She gestured toward another group, where Tristan stood out—conspicuously fit and tan among paunch-bellied men and scrawny teenagers. "I'm switching excursions with Bullfrog so I can hang out with Tristan. I hope that's okay with you."

Emma snapped her mouth shut and divided a glare between her sister and Tristan, who stood scratching his neck, trying to look like he hadn't orchestrated the whole switcheroo.

"You're setting me up," she accused, although a quick glance around revealed no sign of Jeremiah.

Juliet hitched her backpack higher. "Look, caves really don't do anything for me. Claustrophobic, remember? Plus, I'd really like to spend the day with Tristan." She lifted her chin, as if that settled everything.

Torn, Emma looked back at the golden-haired SEAL. He and Juliet *did* make an attractive couple. Good for her—living up to their pact and having some fun.

"Fine." She pressed her lips together. "Just… watch yourself."

Juliet's eyes narrowed under the brim of her cap. She stepped closer. "What's that supposed to mean?"

Emma shot a quick glance at Sammy, who was talking to her friend Sophia, then lowered her voice. "I've heard Tristan's never really been alone. And I know how much you value your freedom. That's all."

Juliet stared at her for a long moment. "Thanks."

Turning away, she strode toward Tristan's group without another word.

Emma searched the pier for Jeremiah. After last night's emotional derailment, she wouldn't blame him for skipping the excursion altogether.

One by one, groups boarded their buses and departed—including Juliet and Tristan's. But the Bottoms Up Cave Tubing group lingered, still waiting on a missing passenger. Emma eyed the thunderclouds looming inland, surging toward Belize City. Maybe today wasn't the best day for tubing anyway.

"Well, I guess our last passenger's not showing. Time to go." Their guide waved them onto the bus.

Emma's steps dragged with disappointment. Jeremiah wasn't coming. And why should she feel let down? *She* had been the one to insist they had no future.

As the bus idled and the guide launched into a brief history of Belize, Emma barely listened. The vehicle suddenly shuddered, and she looked up just in time to see Jeremiah making his way down the aisle.

Her spirits lifted instantly.

He shot her a grin that made his dimples flash, then dropped into an empty bench across from her and Sammy's.

To her surprise, there was no trace of resentment in his expression—just that same intellectual curiosity she'd noticed from their first meeting.

"Why is *he* coming?" Sammy muttered, glum.

"The bus is moving," the guide called.

Emma frowned and leaned toward her daughter. "Aunt Juliet gave him her ticket."

Sammy's sullen expression didn't change.

"Don't you like him?" Emma asked under her breath.

Sammy shrugged and turned to gaze out the window.

Emma sighed inwardly. Well, if that wasn't a sign. Sammy clearly didn't want another father figure in her life—and who could blame her, after what Eddie had done?

Still, the instinct to defend Jeremiah—to list his endless virtues—caught her off guard. Why should Sammy's opinion even matter?

Jeremiah wasn't going to be part of their lives.

The thought weighed on her chest, heavy as the rainclouds rolling in over the flat, green terrain.

Sammy Albright trailed her mother down the narrow jungle path. With every step, the tube slung over her back bounced against her calves. The hot bus ride into the remote countryside had been followed by a lunch of yellow rice and chicken. When she heard a rumor the meat was actually iguana, she lunged for the last hamburger—only to have some man swipe it from under her hand. Turned out, iguana *did* taste like chicken.

After lunch, they were handed life jackets and headlamps and told to pick an inner tube. Hers was almost as tall as she was, so she had to carry it balanced on her head while holding the straps on either side. Through the thin soles of her water shoes, every rock on the trail gouged at her feet. They'd already crossed the stream twice, the water warm as bath water.

"Can I carry that for you?"

"No thanks." Sammy sneaked a glance at Jeremiah Winters.

He nodded and stepped around her, leaving her to wrestle the oversized float.

She studied him. He looked too old to have been one of her mom's students. Plus, he had a nice face. Hard to hate a guy with a nice face. But she didn't have to *like* him either.

Her mother did, though. That was obvious. Even now, Mom's eyes tracked him as he loped to the head of the line. He didn't shuffle like everyone else—he practically bounced, like this hike was nothing. At the front, he struck up a conversation with their new guide, a short, nut-brown man who proudly announced he was one hundred percent Mayan.

Sammy's conscience nipped at her heels. If Mom *really* liked Jeremiah, maybe she should be nicer to him. But she'd seen what her dad had done to them. Men didn't stick around.

Once the cruise was over and they went home to Fairfax, Mom would forget about him. She'd go right back to spending weekends indoors, reading and watching thrillers on TV. Maybe she deserved more than that.

"You won't see any toucans unless you look up."

At her mom's reminder, Sammy tilted her head to the canopy overhead. No toucans, but a little monkey leapt from branch to branch. It slipped, tumbled, and caught itself. Sammy let out a relieved breath.

Finally, they reached what had to be the start of the ride. Tubes floated on a wide, tea-colored swath of water ahead. As Sammy emerged from the tree line, fat droplets of rain began to fall, dimpling the stream's surface.

A low rumble of thunder had the group glancing up.

"Don't worry," the guide called out. "You're going to get wet anyway!"

Following instructions, they waded into the shallows and flopped onto their tubes, bottoms dunked in the water. The guide lashed the floats together, and Sammy found herself beside her mom—with Jeremiah's knees bracketing her head from behind. Mom pretended not to notice how close he was, but her eyes were shining.

The guide began pulling them toward the center of the stream.

"Bottoms up!" he shouted, dragging them over smooth pebbles.

So that's where the name comes from.

The rain came faster now, pelting Sammy's arms and legs. It was warm—like the stream—and oddly soothing. The guide swam ahead, the rope clamped between his teeth to free his arms. Soon the current picked up, and he no longer needed to tow them, just held tight to the lead tube.

Sammy glanced around, enchanted. The jungle hemmed them in as they drifted, water turning from clear to cloudy as runoff bled in from shore.

Her mom cast a worried glance back at Jeremiah, but he said nothing.

The rain didn't bother Sammy. If anything, it felt like a warm massage. She'd stayed up too late two nights in a row, and her eyelids were getting heavy. Letting her head fall back against her life vest, she turned her cheek to the sky and closed her eyes. The adult-sized vest rode up her torso, and her chin tucked into it, like a turtle's head into its shell.

"Honey, don't fall asleep," Mom warned. "You'll miss the *cenotes*."

"Wake me up when we get there." Sammy unfastened the top buckle on her vest so it wouldn't scrape her chin. The current rocked her gently. Once or twice, the bump of a neighbor's tube stirred her, but she drifted back to sleep immediately.

A warm hand shook her shoulder. "Honey, wake up. We're going into the caves."

She forced her eyes open just as the sky gave way to a rocky ceiling. Darkness swallowed them.

"Turn on your lamps," their guide's voice echoed.

Too groggy to move, Sammy didn't bother. She let the sound of rushing water and the guide's melodic voice wash over her—something about bats nesting in sandstone crevices and ancient Mayan rituals evidenced by pottery shards far below.

"Sammy, look up," her mom urged. "You're missing the waterfall."

Lifting her chin from her vest, Sammy glimpsed a shaft of sunlight piercing the cave roof. Rainwater poured through the opening, crashing into a natural basin and splashing the nearby tubes as their guide led them around it.

It's like that scene in the movie Coco, she thought.

The cool air, the roar of water, and the darkness pressed in. She let her eyes drift closed again.

"This sinkhole is rumored to be bottomless," the guide said.

His voice mingled with a dream about an underwater treasure.

"Can't you slow us down?" a man snapped, jarring Sammy from her doze. "We're going too fast."

The tubes bumped and jammed together. The guide must've braced his body to slow them. Jeremiah's tube bumped hard into Sammy's, causing her head and shoulders to slip down into the hollow of her life vest. She came abruptly awake as her head kept sliding, down the inside of her tube and out the bottom.

I'm under water!

Sammy flailed, groping the slick rubber above her. Nothing to hold on to. She clamped her knees around the tube, but the current tore her loose and sucked her under.

Water surged into her nose and ears. *Help!* She tried to rise the way she'd gone down—only to smack her head on the flotilla above.

Panic spiked. *I'm drowning!*

CHAPTER 7

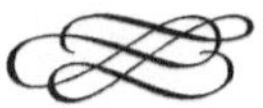

Sensing movement beside her, Emma swung her head toward Sammy. Her headlamp spotlighted flailing feet just as they vanished beneath the surface, leaving behind nothing but an empty life vest.

A scream tore from Emma's throat. "Stop! My daughter just went under!"

Her horrified cry echoed off the sandstone walls as she yanked away the empty vest and plunged a hand through the hole, but Sammy was gone. Jeremiah pulled his leg out from beneath her. The flotilla wobbled.

Emma lifted her headlamp in time to see Jeremiah toss his life jacket back onto the flotilla as he dove cleanly into the water. The guide vanished a second later, headlamp and all. Alarm rippled through the group as the flotilla kept drifting forward.

Terror seized Emma's throat. The current carried them with a velocity no doubt worsened by the rain. Her heartbeat thundered in her ears as she tracked the beams of light darting below the surface. *Please, oh, please, oh, please!* Each second dragged like an eternity.

At last, Jeremiah surfaced, cradling Sammy in his arms. The

guide popped up beside them, sweeping their faces with his light. Sammy's ashen face froze Emma in place as Jeremiah kicked toward the flotilla while keeping her head above water.

"She's okay." His voice, calm and steady, washed over the group like balm. Cries of relief broke out.

Emma burst into tears. *Thank You, God!*

The roar of the falls faded behind them, and a hint of daylight told Emma they were nearing the exit. She reached for Jeremiah, catching his hand and guiding it to the handle on Sammy's raft. With a strength that stunned her, he lifted her eighty-pound daughter back onto her tube before Emma could even assist.

"Mommy."

"Oh, my baby." Emma wrapped her arms around her, burying her face in Sammy's wet hair. Swallowing her sobs, she focused on calming her daughter's trembling body. Gratitude, pure and profound, swelled in her chest. *I owe Jeremiah a debt I can never repay.*

Into that illuminating moment came an irritating voice. "I want a full refund. The tour was interrupted!"

Jeremiah, who'd risen from the water like Poseidon himself and landed atop his tube in one smooth move, cut the man a sharp look. "You will not."

Emma, impressed by the cool command in his tone, pictured the man pouting in silence.

Pulling back, she brushed a lock of wet hair from Sammy's face. "Are you okay, sweetheart?"

"I think so. I almost drowned."

"I know." Emma grabbed the life vest lying across her legs. "Here. Put this back on." As she helped Sammy into it, she noticed the upper buckle was still unlatched. "Keep it buckled this time."

"I will."

The cave brightened gradually as they drifted toward its mouth. Emma closed her eyes, offering a silent prayer of thanks. If Jeremiah hadn't been there…

She shoved aside the awful thought and turned back to him. Sunlight filtering through the cave's opening lit his hazel eyes, making them look like bodies of water. Emotion surged in her chest as she reached out and gave his damp thigh a squeeze.

He caught her hand and held it firmly. The feelings she'd been holding back rose like a tide. Maybe he was right—maybe they *were* meant to be on the same cruise.

"Thank you," she mouthed.

He winked—mischievous, familiar—and with that gesture, a memory of his body atop hers came rushing back. The breadth of his shoulders, the line of hair down his taut stomach. Regret stirred. Last night had been their chance. How good it would have felt to join with him, finally, after all these years.

His gaze held hers, steady and open, and her pulse jumped at the message in it. Jeremiah still wanted all of her.

Slowly, reluctantly, she slipped her hands from his. A part of her rejoiced. Maybe they should finish what they started—if only to appease this hunger before it burned out.

But could she survive the fire without being reduced to ash?

That was the question. And deep down, she already knew the answer.

Tristan taunted Juliet from atop his four-wheeler. "Just remember, second place is the first loser."

Straddling an identical ATV, Juliet wondered how often he'd used that line—and how many times he'd won.

Not even the steady drizzle could dim the competitive gleam in his blue eyes. He couldn't wait to show off his driving skills, could he? But winning wasn't all about speed. Cunning counted just as much, and she'd noticed a shortcut on the trail map tacked to the cabin wall where they'd signed in.

In response, she revved her engine while holding the brake firm.

He threw his head back and laughed.

Their guide, a young woman with ebony skin, zipped up alongside them and eyed them sternly. "Are you all ready?" she shouted over the idling engines.

"Yeah!" chorused the dozen or so riders.

"Okay then. On my count to three and you're off. One, two..."

On three, Juliet released the brake and shot toward the muddy track disappearing into the tree line. Tristan's engine whined behind her as he swiftly pursued, and she promptly increased her speed, startled when flecks of mud flew up off her churning tires to spatter her bare arms and legs.

Within seconds, she was speckled with reddish-brown mud. Thank goodness her hair was tucked inside her helmet.

Ignoring the mess, she pushed her speed higher, streaking past greenery and wildlife at a pace that turned the jungle into a blur and kept adrenaline cycling through her system like engine oil.

No wonder Tristan loved racing. She had to admit—this was thrilling. Focusing solely on the unraveling trail, she kept her eyes peeled for the landmarks she'd memorized.

Tristan's engine sawed in her ear. Glancing back, she found him practically on her bumper. He grinned, a flash of white in a face shadowed by his helmet. Facing forward again, she set her jaw. No way she'd let him pass—not yet.

As they hit a straightaway and the trail widened, Juliet swerved to block him. Her tire bumped his, giving rise to a high-pitched squeal.

"You're crazy!" he shouted, backing off.

A pile of gray rock on a promontory above the tree line—landmark number one—caught her eye. Pretending to be chastised, she veered left and slowed down, letting him pass. He roared by with the smirk of the triumphant.

Just you wait, cowboy.

As he sped ahead, flinging mud in his wake, she slowed to a moderate speed and scanned for the fork that would shorten the course by several hundred meters before rejoining the main trail near the finish line.

Distracted by Tristan's backward glances, she nearly missed it. A rope had been strung across the opening—surely just to keep riders from mistaking the shortcut for the main trail.

As Tristan dipped out of sight over a small hill, Juliet cranked the handlebars and veered hard right, steering around the rope and through two trees before bouncing onto the shortcut. A glance back revealed at least one group member had seen her quick exit.

Within seconds, she hit thick overgrowth. Wet fronds brushed her knees and slapped her face and shoulders. A flash of being trapped in a car with no escape flickered through her mind, and her unease spiked. She tilted her head skyward, using the open view to steady her nerves.

The foliage thinned suddenly—but relief gave way to doubt when she spotted a fast-running creek cutting across her path. On the map, it had looked like a mere trickle. Now it was wide and frothy, the muddy water a café-au-lait swirl. Ten feet across at least, it was impossible to tell how deep it ran.

Should I cross it or not?

Common sense warred with the vision of Tristan's shocked face when she beat him to the finish.

She bit her lip, hesitating. Then, "In for a penny, in for a pound," she muttered. Releasing the brake, she eased into the stream.

The water rose halfway up her tires. *I'm good,* she thought, exhaling.

Then her front tires dipped suddenly. She hit the brake—wrong move. She flew over the handlebars and landed hard on her butt in three feet of water. Her ATV gurgled beside her, wheels spinning uselessly.

"Juliet!"

Tristan's shout and the roar of his engine doubled her humiliation. He must've doubled back.

Tailbone aching, she turned as he abandoned his ATV on the shore and charged into the stream. After cutting her engine, he crouched beside her, getting as wet as she was.

He gripped her shoulders. "Are you hurt?"

Only my pride. "I'm fine," she said, ignoring her throbbing tailbone.

The good news: the cool, mineral-sweet water had mostly washed her clean. The bad news: Tristan looked pissed.

"What the hell were you thinking?" His dark blue eyes blazed.

Apparently, the good-time SEAL had a serious side.

"I was taking a shortcut so I could beat you," she said cautiously, studying him. A man's temper said a lot about him.

"Yeah, I saw that shortcut on the map too."

She blinked. "You did?"

"Didn't you notice the skull and crossbones stamped on it?"

"Um, no." He had to be kidding. Had she really missed that?

Breathing heavily, he surveyed their surroundings. "You violated the most basic safety rule."

She softened. "The buddy system?"

"Damn straight. Where you go, I go. And vice versa."

A flutter of something warm moved through her. "But that would put us on the same team."

His eyes narrowed. "You don't want to be on my team?"

She shrugged. "I can't beat you if we're on the same team."

"True. But we can still beat everyone else."

She blinked. "Oh, yeah."

They both turned their heads to regard the trail on the far side of the creek.

"Don't move. Let me see how deep this is. " He rose and sloshed through the water.

"Careful," she called, then sighed when the water barely reached his knees, even at its deepest.

"I say we stay on this trail," he said, coming back and holding out a hand. "If we're lucky, we'll still come out ahead."

"And it pays to be a winner." She grasped his hand, letting him pull her up.

Tristan's gaze dropped to her sodden T-shirt. The warm water left nothing to the imagination.

"Damn," he muttered, then met her eyes. "Second place isn't looking so bad, you know. We could pretend we got lost."

A vivid image of them tangled together, skin to skin, flickered through her mind, heating her from the inside out. She cleared her throat. "As tempting as that sounds, hotshot, I'd rather be your teammate than your rebound lover."

He flinched and grimaced. “Ouch. A woman who tells it like it is.” Turning away, he grabbed her ATV and started pushing it toward the other side.

Uncertain what to do with herself, Juliet followed him—only to draw up short when he suddenly swung around.

Her breath caught as he stepped closer, released her ATV, and gently nudged her chin upward. Then, without warning, he dropped a surprisingly sweet kiss on her astonished lips.

Before she could react, he drew back. “You’re honest,” he said, voice low and gruff. The sound of it made her insides flutter. “I like that.”

“Thanks?” she managed.

But was she being honest with herself? That was the real question. Denying her attraction to Tristan might cause it to spiral out of control. And she’d *never* not been in control—especially when it came to choosing her sexual partners. She never got involved with anyone who could truly hurt her. That meant avoiding men she liked too much—like him.

Too sticky, this situation. Too soon to untangle it.

She masked her thoughts behind a carefully neutral expression and watched as he turned away again to haul her ATV the rest of the way onto shore.

He gestured for her to mount. “Start her up.”

Juliet saw his gaze drop as she swung a toned leg over the seat and straddled it. She twisted the key, half-expecting silence. But the engine sputtered, then roared to life.

Relief bloomed.

Tristan grinned and clapped a firm hand on her shoulder. “I’ll be right behind you.”

Admiration welled as she watched him cross the creek with purposeful strides. That broad back. That can-do attitude. No wonder she was tempted.

He mounted his ATV and sent her a confident thumbs-up before powering through the shallows to join her. By the gleam in his eye, she could guess what he was thinking: *Let’s go win this thing.*

Juliet accelerated, driving more cautiously now, each bump and curve of the wild path sharpening her awareness.

He stayed right on her tail.

And though she savored the victory she knew was coming, one thought chased her harder than he did:

How far can I afford to go with Tristan?

"Hey, I got your message, brother."

Jeremiah dragged his attention from the musician fingering the keyboard in the corner of the bar and nodded at Tristan. "Hey." He'd left his teammate a note saying he'd be waiting at the Lizard Lounge.

Tristan dropped into the stool beside him. "What's up?"

"I want to show you something." Jeremiah cracked open the lightweight laptop he'd brought along and angled the screen toward him.

"More research?" Tristan leaned in and scanned the document. "This is a rap sheet. Who's Aiden Lawlor?"

"Shh," Jeremiah hushed him, then tipped his head subtly in the musician's direction. "That's him. On the keyboard."

Tristan cast a casual glance at the Irishman, then looked back at the screen. "Where'd you get this?"

"Hack," Jeremiah said, referring to the IT genius in their platoon.

Tristan studied the rap sheet more closely, then looked up sharply. "Wait—you think he's behind the hits you've been getting?"

Jeremiah studied the man's profile. "I don't know. Just because he's got IRA connections doesn't mean he's up to something. Maybe he couldn't get a job back home, so he took to the sea."

Noting the bartender's approach, he smartly closed the laptop.

The bartender nodded at Tristan. "What can I get you?"

As the man stepped away to grab his order, Jeremiah caught a glimpse of movement in the bar's mirror—a small, pale face peeking out from behind a potted plant. Sammy Albright. She was spying on him.

The soft, rippling notes of a jazz riff drew his attention back to the keyboard.

"Well, he sure can play," Tristan remarked.

"And he's versatile," Jeremiah added. Earlier, the guy had nailed a disco piece. Now he was riffing on Miles Davis. Versatility implied intelligence. And smart people weren't always content to entertain others. Sometimes, they had agendas.

Tristan gave him a look. "Had any more hits lately?"

Jeremiah shook his head. "Nope."

"That's good news, right?"

"I guess."

Tristan brightened. "Hey, I heard you saved Emma's kid from drowning today."

Jeremiah glanced at the mirror again. Sammy was still watching him. He shrugged. Maybe his being on the tubing trip instead of the ATV excursion hadn't been a coincidence. Maybe that's why he and Emma had crossed paths again—so he could save her daughter. Not to win her back.

If that was his purpose, then it was fulfilled. But it sure didn't feel like it.

He focused on Tristan. "How about you? Have fun riding ATVs?"

"Hell yeah. We beat everyone else by taking a shortcut through the jungle. Broke the course record, actually. Won a free beer. But then someone reported us for cheating, and we had to buy everyone's drinks instead."

Jeremiah chuckled. "Good thing you're independently wealthy."

The bartender returned, placing a bottle of Foster's in front of Tristan.

He took a long swig, then set it down with a belch. "So, what's the plan with the musician?" He glanced over his shoulder.

"We need to befriend him."

"Oh?" Tristan didn't sound thrilled.

"He gets off at twenty hundred hours. I was thinking we could—"

He stopped mid-sentence as Sammy emerged from her hiding spot and made a beeline for him.

When she tapped his shoulder, he swiveled around, feigning surprise. "Hey there."

"Hi." She nervously bit her bottom lip.

"How're you feeling?"

"Good. I wanted to say thank you." Her words came out in a rush.

"No problem." He thought of mentioning the life vest but figured her mother had already said enough—and Sammy had likely learned her lesson.

Sammy spoke first. "I was wondering if you wanted to watch the *Cirque du Soleil* show with us in the Stardust Theater. It starts in five minutes."

Warmth bloomed through him. "Does your mother want me to come?"

Her wide eyes were unreadable. "Yeah."

"You sure?"

"Mm-hmm. Come on. The theater's filling up."

She gestured for him to follow and strode out of the bar.

Jeremiah looked at Tristan, who shoved him playfully off the stool. "What are you waiting for? Go."

"Put this in our room for me?" Jeremiah slid his mini laptop at his friend.

"Sure."

"Thanks. See you here at nineteen forty-five to talk with Lawlor." Then he followed Sammy out.

Halfway down the corridor, she ducked through a set of double doors. Jeremiah entered the cool, dimly lit theater and spotted Sammy slipping into a row. The unmistakable copper-red of Emma's hair revealed her location.

Sammy squeezed past her and sat down—leaving the end seat empty. Right next to Emma.

When he slid into it, Emma's widened eyes said it all. Sammy had duped him. Emma hadn't been expecting him. The twelve-year-old avoided his gaze, leaving the grown-ups to sort things out.

"Hi," Emma said civilly, then shot a look at her daughter.

"Hello."

They sat in silence for a beat, both taking in the red velvet curtain and spotlight glowing like a sun at center stage.

Then Emma leaned closer and spoke quietly in his ear. "You said you could see things that are going to happen?"

He turned toward her, catching a trace of honeysuckle—her scent. The one that had haunted him for years. "Sometimes."

"When you mentioned Sammy's life vest was too big for her during the drill… was that prescience?"

He'd asked himself the same question. "Probably." He sighed. "But I didn't recognize it for what it was at the time. I'm sorry. I don't always cue in on it."

"Don't apologize." Her soft blue eyes shimmered in the dim light. "You saved her life, Jeremiah. I can never repay you for that."

He gave a half smile. If she told him she still loved him, that would repay the debt a thousand times over. But for now, he'd settle for gratitude. "That's sort of what I do." He shrugged.

"Well, I think it's very admirable."

"Thank you."

She hesitated. "Would you consider going to Tulum with us tomorrow?"

The question caught him off guard. His heart lifted. "Don't you think your sister will want to go?"

"I think she'd rather swim with Tristan—I mean, with the dolphins," she amended, rolling her eyes.

"You did tell her that he's only been single for about a week?"

"Yes, I warned her. But don't worry—my sister doesn't do relationships. She's never been close to anyone outside of the family. So… are you coming?"

He searched her hopeful expression, trying to read her intent. Did she want his company? Or his protection?

"If it's okay with Juliet—and with Sammy…" He glanced at the girl. She was definitely listening in. "I'd love to."

"It's fine with me," Sammy piped up.

"And I'm sure Juliet won't mind. History's never really been her thing."

How much do you want me? The question sat heavily in his chest. But he didn't dare ask it.

What mattered most now was Emma and Sammy's safety. And given the sense of foreboding building inside him, he needed to be wherever they were.

A dark cloud drifted through his mind—too obscure to identify.

What was that?

The lights dimmed. The feeling intensified. Something awful was coming.

From above, a striking brunette unfurled herself from a cross-beam, spinning and gliding down a ribbon of silk.

Jeremiah's thoughts scattered. The woman's descent was mesmerizing, breathtaking in its precision.

And yet, deep inside, one truth pulsed louder than ever: He was almost out of time to convince Emma that love wasn't just real—

It was everything.

CHAPTER 8

As he reached for his tumbler of whiskey, Jeremiah checked his watch before fixing his attention back on Aiden Lawlor. He'd hurried from the theater an hour earlier and intercepted the musician just as he walked off stage. It had taken every ounce of his jazz knowledge—and an offer to buy the man a drink at the poolside bar—to get Lawlor alone and talking. As it turned out, Aiden Lawlor was both a talker and a drinker.

Within minutes, he'd brought up his checkered past and expressed strong political views. But by the time they'd ordered their third round, Jeremiah was convinced that—however rebellious in his youth—Lawlor lacked the radical streak necessary to orchestrate the kind of slaughter Jeremiah had envisioned.

So, who was the party responsible?

"Let me ask you a question," he said, taking advantage of a rare pause.

"Sure, sure, ask away." A decade of banishment from Ireland had done nothing to diminish the man's brogue.

Jeremiah lowered his voice, though the area remained deserted. "Is it possible for someone to bring a cache of assault rifles aboard this ship?"

Lawlor sat back, his expression one of astonishment. "Now, what kind of question is that?"

"A hypothetical one," Jeremiah replied. "I work in security."

"Ah. That makes sense." Lawlor considered for a moment. "Sure, there are ways."

The answer made the top of Jeremiah's head go cold. "Tell me."

"Through the maintenance people," Lawlor said with a shrug, as if the notion had crossed his mind before. "Now and again, the ship gets dry-docked, and workers go in to remodel or fix the engines. There's no security then, so, theoretically, they could stash weapons all over the ship for later."

"Huh." Maybe that was how the attack he'd sensed would happen. But with no further hits since the first day, he had to consider the possibility that he'd imagined everything.

At this point, the only thing he knew for certain was that Lawlor wasn't the source of his unease. And now he needed to extricate himself from the loquacious musician or risk missing his chance to stop by Emma's room and pick up the book on Mayan civilization she'd offered to lend him.

As late as it was, she might've already given up on him showing.

At 10 p.m., Emma laid her book aside, shook off a yawn, and rose from her bed to slip into a pair of workout shorts and a sports bra. With Sammy at Kids' Zone and Juliet out enjoying the evening with Tristan, nothing was stopping her from making good use of the time.

Since Jeremiah had mentioned needing to work out before swinging by to borrow the book on Tulum, she felt inspired to do the same. Besides, she couldn't shake the urge to spend more time with him. Watching *Cirque du Soleil* together had set a precedent—and left her hungry for more of his company.

After lacing up her tennis shoes, she grabbed a water bottle and headed to the gym. Anticipation kept her pulse elevated until she pushed open the clouded glass door—only to find the place empty. Her spirits took a nosedive.

With a silent pep talk, she moved past the elliptical and treadmill machines, which faced a wall of windows overlooking the black expanse of ocean. Crossing to the mat area, she set down her water bottle, tossed her towel across a mat, and began to stretch.

For the next half hour, she moved through a series of yoga postures, chasing the meditative state she sometimes found through exertion. But peace eluded her. Her body thrummed with unsatisfied need.

What if Jeremiah—despite the look he'd given her on the Bottoms Up tour—was still sticking to his guns? What if he *meant* to keep his distance until she made the foolish promises he seemed to want from her? Or worse—what if he'd already given up?

Everything inside her rebelled at the thought. Deep down, she didn't want him to *ever* give up on her. She might not believe in happily-ever-after, but she needed *him* to believe in it.

What's wrong with me? She shook her head, baffled by the illogic of her own desires.

With a heavy heart and a surge of annoyance—at both herself and Jeremiah—Emma snatched up her water bottle, tossed her towel into the laundry bin, and marched out of the gym.

Jeremiah lurched into the elevator, striking his shoulder on the door when it didn't open fast enough. The impact jarred him to his senses. He was in no condition to drop by Emma's room for a book—or anything else.

My mistake. He shouldn't have tried to keep up with Lawlor's drinking. Between the scotch's influence and his body's unrelenting desire for Emma, he might say or do something he'd regret.

As he staggered past her door a moment later, a faint trace of her perfume hit him. Instantly, an image of her in the shower—sleek, wet, gloriously naked—flooded his mind.

If only he hadn't spent the last two hours chasing a threat that might not even exist. He could have been with *her*, discussing the book like they used to in her office at GMU. He could've stolen a kiss, maybe two. Laid her back against the bed and persuaded her she was wrong about the nature of love.

"Idiot." He slammed his cabin door behind him—then nearly plowed into Juliet, who stood with her back to the door, arms crossed.

"'Scuze me."

She whirled to face him, frowning, then turned back toward Tristan, who was rifling through Jeremiah's backpack.

Jeremiah blinked. "Hey, that's mine."

"I need your excursion ticket for the dolphin swim," Tristan said, guilt flickering across his face.

Snatching the pack from his hands, Jeremiah dug through the pockets. "Where've you been all night? You were supposed to meet me in the bar to talk to Lawlor."

"Oh." Tristan looked sheepish. "Sorry, brother. We got picked to be contestants in a game show." He grinned over at Juliet. "Won a free dinner at one of the ship's five-star restaurants."

Jeremiah rolled his eyes. Finding the excursion ticket, he handed it to Juliet. "If you haven't figured it out yet, Tristan's as lucky as a leprechaun. We don't call him the Golden Boy for nothing."

"Really?" She eyed Tristan from head to toe. "Well, he's not lucky on *all* fronts."

Did that mean she hadn't fallen for his charm yet? "Well, good for you." Jeremiah set her a nod of approval.

"Hey!" Tristan raised his arms in protest. "Stop talking about me like I'm not here."

"Wait." Juliet turned to Jeremiah, frowning. "Where's Emma? I thought she was with you."

He winced. "Uh, no. Not for the last two hours. I think she's in her cabin."

Her look of disbelief made him feel even more like a jackass. "I'd better check on her," she muttered. With a huff, she strode out and closed the door quietly behind her.

The moment she was gone, Tristan sat up on his captain's bed and shook his head. "That woman scares me."

Jeremiah stashed his backpack. "Oh yeah? Why's that?"

"She's not like any woman I've ever known. She's fun. She's cool. She's like one of us—only female and smoking hot."

Jeremiah headed for the bathroom, but Tristan wasn't done.

"I'm dying to make a move on her, but I feel like it'd mess things up. I *like* her."

The surprise in his voice made Jeremiah pause at the bathroom door. "More than you liked Mariah?"

Tristan tilted his head, frowning. "You know, I don't think I ever *liked* Mariah."

Jeremiah stared at him, baffled. "Then why'd you stay with her so long?"

He shrugged. "I don't know."

"Security?" Jeremiah offered. "Looking for a mother figure?" He was just drunk enough to share a few of his theories.

Tristan glared at him. "What are you, my therapist?" He grabbed a pillow and lobbed it at Jeremiah's head. "Worry about *your* love life. You're the one scoping out terrorists when you could've been getting laid."

Jeremiah caught the pillow and hurled it back—missed by a mile.

He shook his head, disgusted with himself. "You're right. I'm also drunk. I'm going to bed."

"Loser."

"Yep."

Inside the bathroom, Jeremiah glowered at his reflection. He was batting zero tonight.

And he had no one to blame but himself.

~

Emma glanced back at the empty corridor as the announcement for their excursion played again over the loudspeaker. They couldn't wait any longer for Jeremiah. Maybe he'd changed his mind.

"Passengers taking the excursion to the Mayan Ruins of Tulum, please exit the ship at level five to catch the ferry to the mainland."

Swallowing her disappointment, Emma guided Sammy into the stairwell. "Are you sure we have everything? Did you pack a water bottle and sunscreen?"

"Yes, Mom." Sammy's tone hovered just below snotty.

Emma frowned at her. "I should've made you go to bed earlier."

"I'm fine." Sammy stomped down the stairs headed for the exit. "I just wish I were swimming with the dolphins instead of going to see some stupid old ruins."

"They're not stupid." Emma peeked into her own bag, making sure she'd brought along the library book for Jeremiah, just in case he showed up at the last minute.

When she looked up again, there he was—leaning against the wall at the top of the stairs on deck five, waiting for them. Her heart leapt before she could stop it. Remembering how he'd stood her up the night before, she forced herself to nod at him coolly.

He grimaced and pushed off the wall. "Hey. Sorry about last night—I got pulled into some work stuff."

Searching his gaze, she could tell he wasn't lying—but still. Why not let her know beforehand so she wouldn't have spent the night wondering?

"Well… here's your ticket." She handed it over like a peace offering.

His somber expression melted into a grin as he took it. "Thanks. I have to admit—I'm excited about this." His hazel eyes kindled with anticipation, just like they used to when she'd show him a new essay or poem.

Holding a grudge against him was impossible. Besides, they were about to share another unforgettable adventure—and hopefully, nothing bad would happen to Sammy this time.

"Ready?"

"*Absolument.*" Pairing a grin with his French reply, he gestured for her to precede him out onto the side deck.

A warm breeze threatened to lift the skirt of Emma's lightweight yellow sundress as they crossed the gangplank onto the pier in sunny

Cozumel. Pressing her hand to her hem to avoid doing a Marilyn Monroe impression, she scanned the area for the ferry to the mainland.

Jeremiah pointed. "I think that's ours over there."

Another day of living a little bolder than she had in years. *I can do this.* The feeling was liberating, like soaring over the treetops on the zipline. And sharing this adventure with the two people who meant the most to her made the occasion feel… unforgettable. Like one of the highlights of her life. *This is all I need to be happy. Well… this, and one of Jeremiah's heart-stopping kisses—and maybe his arms holding me close.*

Limerence, she reminded herself firmly. *Don't let yourself be blinded by the illusion of love.*

Jeremiah's optimism soared as they approached the ferry. The choppy sea promised an exciting ride across to the mainland. Emma, who seemed to have forgiven him for standing her up last night, might even get nervous enough to reach for his hand. He had an entire day to convince her that love could last forever—and that anything was possible. Even a relationship with a Navy SEAL. If she just believed in it.

As they followed the pier toward the boat, Jeremiah's steps slowed. *Oh no.*

The crewmember handing out life vests was the same Malaysian who'd passed them out during the drill—the same man Jeremiah had envisioned as a corpse. His stomach clenched as he took in the vest around the man's own neck.

"You're going with us?" he guessed, a cold trickle sliding down his spine like melting ice.

"Yes! My first time to Tulum." The young man's eyes sparkled, tripling Jeremiah's dismay. So much life in him, and yet—death would take him anyway.

Swallowing the lump of dread in his throat, Jeremiah briefly considered warning him off—but that would sound insane. Useless.

The best he could do was stay alert.

He followed as the employee helped Sammy and Emma step off the pier and onto the ferry. Jeremiah boarded last, steering them toward three seats near the front of the craft—the rows behind were nearly full as they were the last to board.

The pilot barked out brief safety instructions over the gurgling engine, while the Malaysian took a seat further back. Crew scurried along the deck, unmooring the vessel. As they drifted into deeper waters, the pilot revved the twin engines. The bow rose, lifting those in the front rows high above the sea. No turning back now.

"You okay?"

The question, soft in his ear, drew his gaze to Emma's blue eyes, shaded beneath the brim of her straw hat as she held it down with one hand, searching his face.

"Perfect." He managed a smile for her, then for Sammy, just as the bow dropped and they hit a patch of waves. "Do either of you get seasick?"

"We haven't before."

A cool spray misted over them. Sammy blinked in surprise, then laughed.

Emma surprised him next by threading her arm through his—and then, even better—twining her fingers between his. "But I guess we'll find out."

Her touch thrilled him, scattering his thoughts. *I guess I'll find out, too—how accurate my hits are.*

What if the blood and bullets he'd envisioned weren't about the boat itself—but the people involved?

The thought had him twisting in his seat to scan their fellow passengers. His gut sank. Right behind them sat the couple he'd seen flattened by gunfire in his vision—the first bodies he'd imagined when they'd boarded the cruise ship.

Overhearing their animated conversation in French, Jeremiah pegged them as Canadian. It made no difference. He could still see their lifeless forms, drenched in gore, burned into his mind's eye. Swallowing hard, he fought the nausea curling upward in his throat.

Think positive. He dragged in a breath, but a cold sweat broke across his upper lip anyway. Sliding his free hand into the backpack wedged between his knees, he retrieved his sunglasses and slipped them on, hiding his restless gaze from Emma.

Her fingers still clung to his, grounding him.

Closing his eyes, Jeremiah focused on the ferry's steady rhythm—rising, falling, slicing through the whitecaps. The hot Caribbean sun baked his shoulders, warmth seeping into him, relaxing some of the tension in his spine. The Yucatán Peninsula drew closer with every beat of the engine.

Mexico. The last time he'd been here, his platoon had worked a joint DEA op to capture El Cuchillo. What a time to think about that. The drug lord had spent a measly six months in prison before escaping with the help of corrupt guards. By now, he was likely back to ruling the streets, controlling every narco and pimp in the region—if not the entire country.

That has nothing to do with today. Cancún was still relatively untouched by the cartel violence plaguing Guerrero, Chiapas, and other Mexican states. They were heading to a tourist site, not a battlefield. He, Emma, and Sammy would spend a beautiful day exploring mystical ruins.

There was nothing to worry about.

"You're the one who gets seasick."

Emma's voice pulled him back. He cracked his eyes open to find her wearing a wry smile. He seized the excuse gratefully. "Don't tell anyone."

She squeezed his hand, though she gave him a lingering, worried look.

Please let me be wrong, he prayed.

CHAPTER 9

"How did they get up there?" Sammy asked, staring up at the red handprints beside the door leading to the Upper Temple.

"What does the book say?" Jeremiah added.

Thumbing through the library book, Emma searched for the answer. Out of the corner of her eye, she watched Jeremiah turn in a slow three-sixty, scanning the archaeological ruins. He'd done that at least a dozen times already, his ultra-vigilance bordering on obsessive. On their tubing expedition, he hadn't been nearly this tense—though obviously observant, or he wouldn't have seen Sammy slip through her tube.

"Here it is." Finding a photo of the famous red handprints, she scanned the paragraph below it. "It says, *'The left hand appears to have seven digits. It is claimed to be a characteristic of the grandfather god, Itzamna—along with the supernatural height that would have been required to place the prints where they are.'*"

"Well, there you have it," Jeremiah said to Sammy. "He was obviously a tall god. Or an alien," he added, "if you believe in the Ancient Astronaut Hypothesis."

His neutral tone didn't reveal whether he actually believed that alien beings were responsible for the Mayans' advanced architecture and astronomy.

"That's silly." Making her opinion clear, Sammy lost interest in the handprints and turned her attention to the six-foot iguana sunning himself on the parapet beside them.

Emma snapped the book shut. "I'm more inclined to think all those fingers were an unfortunate side effect of inbreeding. Cousins married cousins to keep power in the family." Hearing the cynicism in her voice, she shrugged and tucked the book into her bag.

"Can we go swimming now?" Sammy asked, hope filling her expression.

Glancing at the bright azure waters lapping at the cliffs nearby, Emma had to admit—a swim sounded heavenly. But when she checked her watch, her heart lurched.

"Oh my gosh, it's ten minutes to three! We have to be back on the bus in ten minutes!"

Put out by her mother's refusal, Sammy threw herself onto the ledge in a dramatic pout, startling the iguana into a quick retreat.

Emma offered a hand to help her up. "I'm sorry, honey. But beaches are a dime a dozen. There's only one Tulum."

"Thank God." Ignoring her hand, Sammy rose with exaggerated reluctance.

"Oh, come on. You thought it was interesting. I know you did."

"We should go."

Jeremiah's taut tone stole her attention. His expression was tighter than ever. She wished she could read his eyes through those dark triathlon sunglasses, but the grim set of his mouth said enough. Something was eating at him. It wasn't Sammy's sulking—he didn't seem like a man who'd let a kid's mood rattle him.

Maybe it was something else. The cruise was winding down. Soon, they'd go their separate ways. He'd go back to guarding the free world while she...she would go back to her quiet, predictable seclusion. Safe. And dull. And lonely.

"Yeah. Let's go." With that, they followed Jeremiah's long shadow down the steep temple stairs and along the raised walkway, making their way out of the ancient walled city. Nacho, their guide, had warned them—the bus would leave without them if they were late.

To Emma's relief, she spotted other members of their group heading in the same direction. The gray-and-white passenger bus idled where they'd left it, its open door releasing all the air-conditioned air. As the couple ahead of them boarded, Jeremiah caught Emma's arm, stopping her.

"Wait a second." Stepping past her, he addressed the driver. "Where's Nacho?"

The man regarded him blankly. Jeremiah repeated the question in Spanish, but the reply came back garbled and unintelligible.

Emma rolled her eyes. His ultra-vigilance was over the top.

Gesturing toward the open-air bar that Nacho had pointed out earlier, she offered, "He's probably getting a beer."

She scanned the shadowed interior beneath its palm-covered roof but saw no sign of him.

Jeremiah scraped a hand down his jaw, following her gaze, his mouth tightening even more.

"Señor," the driver said, suddenly proving capable of English. "You're letting all the cold air out."

"I'll go find Nacho," Jeremiah offered.

"No." The driver shook his head firmly. "He knows what time we go. *Salimos a las tres en punto.*" *We leave at exactly three.*

"Jeremiah..." Emma touched his arm. Three more tourists from their group had caught up and were trying to board behind them.

He stepped aside to let them through—but still held Emma and Sammy back.

"We can't miss the ferry," she reminded him. It would take at least half an hour to reach Playa del Carmen, and then another forty-five minutes to return to Cozumel by ferry. "The ship leaves at six sharp, and the captain said he won't wait."

"I know." His voice was clipped. "Do you see any taxis?"

What? Why would they need a taxi with a perfectly good bus in front of them? Still, she joined him in scanning the parking area. "No."

He exhaled slowly, the worry in his stance palpable. Finally, he released her arm. "Fine. Let's go."

By the time they climbed aboard, most of the seats were already taken. They had to walk more than halfway down the aisle before finding two empty seats—across from one another.

Sammy slid into the window seat, leaving Emma on the aisle with Jeremiah across from her. As he dropped his backpack onto his knees and began pawing through it, she studied him, wondering what had him so rattled.

Not a minute later, without Nacho or even a headcount, the driver shut the door with finality, threw the bus into gear, and pulled away from the ruins.

Emma glanced around at the sun-kissed faces of their fellow tourists, a faint worry stirring inside her.

Had they left someone behind?

Sitting back in his seat, Jeremiah studied the bus driver's every move as they left the archaeological site and turned onto a highway exit. He braced a hand on the seat in front of him, jaw tight.

Around them, fellow passengers chattered about the haunting ruins, giant iguanas, and sandy cliffs. Emma listened with one ear, noticing the bus approaching an intersection she didn't recognize. Instead of heading north along the coast, the driver turned left—away from the sea—and accelerated down a road that even she could see was taking them inland.

Jeremiah shot upright and powered to the front to confront the driver. Emma stared after him, straining to catch his words.

"Why are we going this way?" he demanded.

The driver murmured something unintelligible.

"We're headed west, not north. Turn this bus around."

The driver shook his head emphatically. "We go this way to avoid the stoplights."

"Hey, sit down," snarled a bald, tattooed man sitting nearby. "He knows where he's going."

Jeremiah ignored him, gripping the bar behind the driver's seat and referencing his tactical watch—likely checking a compass. The road narrowed, flanked by scrub and brush.

When the driver finally slowed and veered onto a smaller road, Jeremiah returned to his seat, casting the bald man an inscrutable glance. Through his dark sunglasses, Emma could see his worry—could feel it bleeding into her.

Dust swirled as leaves brushed the bus's sides. Jeremiah pulled out his cell phone and accessed his contacts.

"What are you doing?" Emma whispered.

He leaned toward her. "Do you trust me?"

"Of course."

He thumbed a series of buttons, handed her the phone, and spoke into her ear: "Take this. I'm going to stop this bus. The driver's not taking us to Playa del Carmen. He's handing us over to very bad people."

"What?" She sounded breathless. "Seriously?"

"When things go south, hit the call button. Just hit it. Don't say anything. Promise?"

She nodded, heart pounding.

Jeremiah rose again. The driver barked at him to sit. The Malaysian crew member spoke up hesitantly. Then the bald guy swung up out of his seat to stop him.

"Joe, leave him alone," protested the woman with him, but Joe ignored her.

Emma heard his warning clearly "Stop bothering the driver. He knows what he's doing."

In a low voice, Jeremiah reasoned with him, but Joe's expression only darkened. In the next instant, he grabbed at Jeremiah, intending to push him back up the aisle—but with a response too fast to see, Jeremiah freed himself, clamped a hand on the man's trapezius and pressed him back into his seat. Whatever he growled in Joe's ear kept him seated as Jeremiah headed for the driver.

That man saw him coming and braked sharply. As Jeremiah flew forward, crashing face-first against the windshield, Emma yelped. He fell into the stairwell by the door, his glasses flying off his face.

"Mom?" Sammy pushed to her feet with concern.

Emma held her thumb over the call button, frozen between fear and action.

When Jeremiah's head emerged from the stairwell, she relaxed slightly. He shook off dizziness and brushed off dust off his shirt, all while staring hard at the driver. The deadly determination on his face made her heart skip a beat.

Suddenly, the bus braked again, but this time for a reason. A slew of uniformed men clutching rifles had materialized on the road just up ahead. Jermiah braced himself, managing not to fall this time. Catching sight of the men responsible for the roadblock, he looked back at Emma. "Now," he mouthed to her.

With her heart jumping in her chest, she pressed the button. It was happening just as he'd predicted.

As the bus came to a jarring stop, Jeremiah hastened to the back to rejoin them. The driver threw the door open, and three dark-haired men charged aboard, pointing their rifles at the passengers while the bus driver fled into the foliage.

"*Manos arriba*!" they yelled. "Hands up, *todos*!"

With his eyes, Jeremiah gestured for Emma to shove the phone into her bag, but she stuffed it under her thigh instead as they all raised their hands.

Emma had never stared into the barrel of a rifle before. She fought to keep control of her bladder. One realization penetrated her shock: *Jeremiah knew this would happen. That's why he was so on edge—all day.*

~

Jeremiah had trained day in and day out for worst-case scenarios like this, but his teammates had always been with him—not a busload of civilians. Jesus. This was worse than anything he'd ever experienced.

Three armed men had boarded the bus, while another five, all wearing military-style clothing, surrounded it. He and Bad-Ass Joe were probably the only passengers on board who could be counted on to fight back—except they didn't stand a chance without a weapon between them.

All Jeremiah possessed of any use was his watch and his cellphone. He could hear the latter buzzing beneath Emma's leg. Master Chief wasn't answering Emma's call. Good. Then his voicemail would pick up and record whatever insanity happened next. A recording could be played again and again. And with any luck, it would be full of clues about what was happening to them.

"¡Quédense con las manos arriba!" bellowed one guerrilla while the other two moved down the aisle, swinging their assault rifle this way and that.

Several people screamed—mostly women. Bad-Ass Joe sent Jeremiah an incredulous look—*How'd you know?*

Jeremiah forced himself to lower his gaze, staring submissively at the seat in front of him as the head guerrilla followed his comrade down the bus. The stench of sweat and cigarettes trailed after them. Jeremiah could feel their bloodlust from where he sat. Showing any kind of resistance right now would get him shot, and then where would Sammy and Emma be?

Master Chief Kuzinsky's tinny voice came from a great distance. "Bullfrog. What's your status?"

Damn it. The call hadn't gone to voicemail.

Fortunately, the pock-faced leader didn't overhear. *"¡Saquen sus tarjetas de identificación!"* he barked, having reached the back of the bus. "Identification." Speaking English with a thick accent, he thrust a hand at the French-Canadian couple.

As the young husband scrambled to find their IDs, Emma, clutching Sammy's arm, searched Jeremiah's expression—maybe for reassurance. He wished to God he could give it to her.

What did they want with their ID cards? The French-Canadian handed over the laminated ship-issued passes required for re-boarding. The guerrilla inspected the man's name and nationality, both printed on the cards. *"¿Es su esposa?"* He gestured to the pretty woman next to him, asking if she was his wife.

"Sí," the young man affirmed.

"Ju estay on the bus." The guerrilla gestured at them to stay put.

Keeping their ship cards, he turned toward an older couple to take theirs.

A relative calm fell over the passengers. Jeremiah could tell they'd convinced themselves this was a government-sanctioned search, and the IDs would be returned. But it wasn't. It was true the guerrillas wore military-style clothing, but it was ragged and mismatched, with no names sewn above their breast pockets, no insignia of any kind. The Mexican National Guard had much higher standards.

The guerrilla took one look at the older couple's ID and ordered them off the bus.

"Bájense." Get off. He yanked the old man up by his collar. His elderly wife jumped to her feet and started forward, the man at the front of the bus protesting that they were too old.

"Son ricos," the leader tossed back. *They're rich.*

Jeremiah's heart sank at the telling words. This was an abduction. They were being taken for ransom. He glanced at the phone still hidden in Emma's lap. *Are you hearing this, Master Chief?*

Three more women and a teenage boy were ordered off the bus—all U.S. citizens. Being told to stay put almost seemed like the better deal, except Jeremiah had already envisioned the French-Canadian couple gunned down the day he'd boarded the cruise ship. The Malaysian crewmember was going to end up dead, too. An awful taste filled his mouth. Sometimes his visions were more than he could stomach.

The leader and his assistant finally reached the row where Emma, Sammy, and Jeremiah sat. The leader thrust out his hand. *"Identificación."*

The laminated cards shook like leaves in a stiff breeze as Emma handed over hers and Sammy's.

One glance, and the leader pointed with his rifle toward the front of the bus before pocketing the cards. *"Bájense." Get off.*

She froze, casting an uncertain glance at Jeremiah.

"I go with them." Simplifying his English and projecting his voice for his master chief to overhear, Jeremiah handed over his own ship card.

As all three guerrillas sized him up, Emma finally slipped his phone into her pool bag without them noticing. *Good job, Professor.*

"Come on, honey." Pulling a wide-eyed Sammy behind her, she squeezed past the guerrillas into the aisle but didn't take a step toward the door until Jeremiah, having surrendered his ID, joined them.

Shadowing them off the bus, he slouched to downplay his warrior's physique. How had he not foreseen the way this evil would play out? They'd been beset by a band of ruffians intent on ransom—and that was the best-case scenario. Clearly, it was easier to transfer money from the U.S. to Mexico than from any other country. That's why non-U.S. citizens were being left behind.

With adrenaline ricocheting through his veins, it was all Jeremiah could do to tamp down his fighting instincts. After stepping off the bus, he led Emma and Sammy as far away from it as the five guerrillas permitted. Making a run for it would get them all shot. He put an arm around their shoulders, holding them close.

I'm responsible for their survival. The realization both humbled and terrified him. *What if I fail?* He squashed the negative thought the instant it surfaced. *Think positive.*

Within minutes, all the U.S. citizens on the bus—thirteen of them, by his count—stood in an uncertain knot on the narrow road, squinting against the bright sun. The pock-faced leader and one other soldier came off the bus carrying women's purses and a bag full of wallets and jewelry. They'd robbed everyone on board.

Jeremiah focused on the last guerrilla still on the bus. Terror sank talons into his shoulders as the man raised his rifle and backed toward the door.

No. Don't. He almost cried the plea aloud. Clapping a hand over Emma and Sammy's ears, he pulled their heads to his chest just as the gunfire erupted.

He forced himself to watch it—punishment for not managing to stop it. Just as he'd foreseen, bullets riddled the French-Canadian couple first, then everyone else, including the Malaysian crewmember, two Japanese couples, three Scots, and four Australians, if Jeremiah had guessed right. Blood and brain matter splattered the bus's windows. Some of the glass shattered, belching gore onto the road, until everyone left on the bus was either dead or dying.

The U.S. citizens screamed in abject terror. The old woman staggered against her husband, who caught and held her. A teenage boy sprinted for the woods, only to be tackled by one of the guerrillas and shoved face-first into a prickly bush.

"Jeremiah!"

Emma's strangled cry urged him to do something. He could seize the weapon of the guerrilla closest to him and kill a few bad guys before they all turned their weapons on him and his companions—but that wouldn't help anyone.

"I can't," he ground out in her ear. "Not yet."

The murdering guerrilla staggered off the bus, limping, blood leaking through a hole in his boot. He'd been struck by a ricocheting bullet.

That's called karma, asshole. Jeremiah resisted the urge to glare at him.

He spoke to Emma and Sammy while keeping them from seeing the carnage. His instincts were screaming that someone on the bus was still alive—injured but savable.

Just not by him.

"Stay calm. We have the phone. We'll be found."

But the guerrillas, forgetting those inside the bus, were now turning their attention to their captives. Pointing rifles in their faces, they ordered them to surrender their possessions.

"Dámelo." Give it to me. A chubby guerrilla, possibly still in his teens, wrenched the pool bag out of Emma's rigid hand. He pointed at Emma's wrists, demanding her watch also.

"*Tu mochila, gringo.*" He demanded Jeremiah's backpack, not seeing his watch as Jeremiah hid his left arm behind Emma's waist.

Hoping to hold onto it and still pained by the individual he sensed fighting for life in the bus, Jeremiah surrendered the backpack without protest.

Sammy, in her distress, had left her own bag on the bus. She tried to get a look at the bloodied windows, but Emma stepped between her and the view.

"Baby, don't look. You'll wish you never had."

The guerrillas began dumping the contents of their bags onto the road. Jeremiah glimpsed Emma's towel and library book tumble out, along with his cellphone. When his wallet fell from the backpack, the guerrillas pounced on it, pilfering the fifty bucks he'd brought ashore. Thank God he'd left his military ID on the ship. That would have gotten him executed on the spot.

His cellphone lay faceup on the road, as yet unnoticed. He hoped like hell Master Chief was still listening. Surreptitiously, he unbuckled his watch, wishing he had thought to hide it earlier. But in that same instant, the chubby guerrilla glanced back at him, catching Jeremiah about to stuff his watch into his pocket.

Aw, hell. Kicking himself for his carelessness, Jeremiah guessed what was coming next as the youth swaggered over.

"Dámelo." Give it to me.

He resisted wanting to fight as the youth's sweaty hand wrestled the watch from his possession. The U.S. Navy had invested thousands in the device. It was waterproof up to two hundred meters and equipped with GPS. Next to the cellphone, it was their best hope for rescue. He didn't want to give it up. But he also didn't want to die—not yet.

Distracted by the suffering of the injured soul on the bus, Jeremiah surrendered his watch with a shudder. The teen quickly stuffed it into his own pocket, clearly intending to keep it for himself. His comrades, too busy scavenging for valuables, didn't notice. In fact, the time was ripe to make a run for it, Jeremiah realized. He could dive for the tree line in a zigzag and maybe, just maybe, their bullets would miss.

Do it! ordered the voice in his head that sounded a lot like Master Chief's. His thighs flexed, ready. But just then, Emma tightened her hold on his arm. A glance at her chalk-white face made his decision for him. He couldn't leave her and Sammy.

It was his fault they were living this nightmare. He'd seen it coming—just hadn't interpreted it right. A dozen cruise ship passengers were dead because he hadn't acted in time. And the one survivor on the bus was slipping away. He could feel it.

Dismay ravaged his heart, and tears blurred his vision. *Please forgive me.*

Then, to his horror, one of the guerrillas finally noticed his cellphone. *"¡Mira, jefe!"*

His boss sauntered over. In his late twenties with acne scars on both cheeks, he resembled Panama's former dictator, Manuel Noriega. *"¿De quién es?" Whose is it?*

"No sé." I don't know. The others shrugged.

Jeremiah squeezed Emma's and Sammy's shoulders in silent warning: *Keep quiet.* Craterface darted him a suspicious look.

"Tíralo en el colectivo." Throw it into the bus.

With dread, Jeremiah watched his cellphone get lobbed through the bus's open door, followed by an iPod, three more phones, and a Kindle. Why leave them? The answer became apparent when another guerrilla hopped aboard with a can of gasoline.

My God. They were going to set fire to everything—including anyone still alive inside. His sixth sense sought out the last survivor, but he or she had succumbed to their wounds, thank God, and wouldn't feel the flames.

Their own situation preoccupied him now. They had one hope left. His gaze slid to Chubby Guerrilla. As long as that youth held onto his watch, Uncle Sam would find them. Because one thing was certain—they weren't all going to stay here.

The stench of gasoline filled the air. A match ignited behind the guerrilla, and the interior of the bus caught ablaze. Almost immediately, the smell of burning flesh and hair overpowered the gasoline. Emma clamped a hand over her mouth and nose, staring at him with disbelief, all while shielding Sammy.

Nausea roiled in Jeremiah's gut. All of this was his fault.

"¡Ándenle!" Move it! the leader barked.

All at once, the guerrillas were ushering them up the road at gunpoint.

But the elderly man holding his wife didn't budge.

Craterface glanced back. *"Mátenlos." Kill them.*

Jeremiah halted. He would draw attention to himself—but he couldn't let the old couple be slaughtered. Releasing Emma and

Sammy, he stepped between the gun-toting guerrilla and the elderly couple, curling his hand around the woman's frail arm.

"Let's go, sir. I'll help you." He pulled them forward, drawing the woman—and thus her husband—along with him.

The old man's eyes met his. "She's diabetic, son. She won't last two days without insulin."

"Just keep walking. Anything can happen in two days. Give it a chance."

With grim acceptance, the old man nodded and kept moving. Tossing them a sneer, Craterface waved them on and barked at them to walk faster.

Emma made her way closer. "I'll help her," she offered. "You protect Sammy, please."

One glance at Sammy assured him she wanted his protection. Plus, the old woman might prefer Emma's gentle hand. But several of the guerrillas were now noticing Emma's striking beauty for the first time. Jeremiah could practically read their minds: She'd fetch a pretty penny on the black market. So would Sammy, on the verge of womanhood. His blood went cold at the thought of either of them disappearing into Mexico's sex trade.

Not on my watch. He hadn't prevented this nightmare, but by God, he'd move heaven and earth before harm came to either of them.

As he trudged along with a protective arm around Sammy, guilt clawed at him. How would Emma ever forgive him? He'd warned her that something violent was going to happen and yet still hadn't stopped it.

Even if she could forgive him, how could she ever love him again?

He shoved the thought aside with sheer force of will. *All will be well. My teammates will come for us.*

They had to.

CHAPTER 10

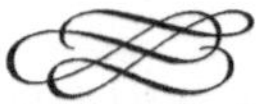

"Well, have you at least alerted the police on the mainland?" Juliet leaned on the security officer's desk aboard the *Escapade*, determined to badger him until he finally *did* something. How could he just ignore the disappearance of an entire excursion group?

The swarthy, mustached officer leaned back in his chair, acting as if nothing was amiss, even though it was nine o'clock at night and the cruise ship had delayed its departure because the ferry had never returned from Tulum. Twenty-six passengers and one crewmember were still missing!

If that weren't alarming enough, Tristan had received a call from his master chief hours earlier. Bullfrog had somehow managed to dial Master Chief's number, and while he hadn't spoken a word, Master Chief had heard gunfire—and screaming. Something awful had happened to Emma and Sammy, and no one seemed to be doing a damn thing about it.

"We alerted the police right away," the officer said at last.

His patronizing stare was one Juliet encountered often in her line of work. "The passengers were seen at Tulum boarding the bus to return to the ferry. The police are searching for the bus now. It must have gone the wrong way."

"How?" Juliet kept her hands planted firmly on the desk. "Isn't there just one main road going up and down the coastline?"

The officer's mustache twitched. "Quintana Roo is a state encompassing over forty thousand square kilometers and many roads."

"There's only one road going up and down the coast," Juliet snapped. "If they're not on that road, then someone must have abducted them."

The man didn't respond. He glanced away, flicking an invisible piece of lint off his uniform sleeve.

His silence drenched her in horror. "Are you saying that's what happened to them?"

He stood abruptly, forcing her to straighten away from the desk. "Of course not. I'm sorry, miss, but I have nothing more to tell you. I need you to leave my office." He gestured toward the door. "I have important work to do."

Tristan, standing behind her, spoke up for the first time. "If you could keep us updated, we'd appreciate it. Room 508." Calmly, he picked up a pen and memo pad from the desk, scribbled Juliet's cabin number, and laid them down where the officer could see them.

"Of course," the man said, already crossing the office to hold the door open.

Juliet planted herself in front of him on the way out. "Promise me this ship won't leave Cozumel until they're found."

He refused to meet her gaze. "That's up to the ship's captain, miss. We have other passengers aboard who would be inconvenienced. We cannot stay here indefinitely."

She briefly weighed the benefits of breaking his nose to get her point across.

"Come on, honey." As if sensing her volatility, Tristan guided Juliet out into the corridor, where laughter floated from the casino, mocking her distress.

Between the security officer's casual dismissal and Master

Chief's grim report, a terrible certainty had taken root in Juliet's mind. She jerked to a halt in the passageway. "We can't just wait here doing nothing." Already a plan was forming.

"I agree." Tristan's dark blue gaze didn't waver. "Want to go to the mainland and look for them?"

She almost hugged him for his action-oriented response. "Yes, but..." She weighed the risk of leaving a ship that might depart at any minute, and the slim possibility that Emma, Sammy, and Jeremiah were already on their way back. "What if we pass them on the open water and never know it?"

He offered an immediate solution. "We'll leave a note in their cabin telling them to call my sat phone."

"Perfect." She couldn't have asked for a simpler solution. "Let's grab some clothes."

As she headed for the stairs, he fell in beside her, taking her hand in his firm grip. This was a novelty—having a partner to help her solve a crisis. Apart from her secretary, Juliet worked alone. The unexpected pleasure of partnership faltered with a sudden thought. "What if they don't let us off the ship?"

Tristan squeezed her hand. "No worries, honey. Bullfrog left blueprints of the ship in our cabin. I'll find us a way off."

"I've told you not to call me that." She knew she ought to wrest her hand from his, but right now she didn't want to. And with her world turning upside down, she could do worse than finding herself in league with a Navy SEAL. "Thank you." The humble postscript slipped out before she could stop it.

Tristan smiled reassuringly. "We'll find them, honey."

The man clearly had short-term memory issues. But she was too grateful for his company to take him to task again.

~

"Emma, wake up."

Emma roused from a light slumber, struggling to orient herself as ugly reality returned, causing her heart to lurch and her stomach to churn. *Not a nightmare, then.*

With Sammy's skinny frame slumped against her side, the memories of the past six hours washed over her, spiking her pulse and drying out her mouth. They'd walked only ten minutes or so before being ushered onto a smaller bus—a *combi*. As it had driven them deeper into wilderness, she'd given up trying to memorize the route. The sky had darkened. Somewhere along the way, she must've drifted off.

A glance across the aisle revealed Jeremiah's silhouette, framed by distant lights. He'd apparently sat vigilant and silent the entire ride, while the other passengers sniffled, moaned, and complained about needing a bathroom.

Now, they were all quiet—perhaps too dismayed to speak.

"What time is it?" she whispered, belatedly recalling that both their watches had been taken.

"Around midnight." His wide-awake tone made her suspect he'd been guarding them, noting every detail of their abduction, no matter how monotonous.

Emma turned to the window. Hours earlier, the *combi* had bounced down rutted roads that wound through endless palm trees and scrubby brush. Watching the sun sink behind that wild, foreign vista had felt like a kind of death. She'd clutched Sammy close, murmuring reassurances she hadn't felt, until her daughter finally slumped into a fitful sleep.

Coming to terms with the fact that they'd been kidnapped had taken much longer. With Jeremiah's cell phone reduced to ashes inside the burned-out bus, there wasn't much hope of rescue.

"Where do you think we are?" she asked softly, careful not to wake Sammy.

Jeremiah shifted, leaning across the narrow aisle to murmur in her ear. "We've been heading northwest, sticking to back roads. I'm guessing that's Mérida coming up on our right."

"Why would they take us to Mérida?" Beyond his shoulder, she glimpsed the faint skyline of a city emerging from the darkness.

When he didn't answer, she gripped the canvas of his cargo shorts. "Answer me."

His hand closed over hers, squeezing tightly. The words

sounded dragged out of him. "Best-case scenario—they put us in a secure building, contact our families, and release us once a ransom's paid."

"Oh God." She choked on the exclamation. *If that's the best-case scenario*… "Okay. Don't tell me the worst."

Her heart threatened to implode from the terrifying images flooding her mind.

The stagnant air shifted as Jeremiah moved close enough to press his forehead to her temple. "I'm so sorry," he whispered. Regret threaded through his voice, thick and raw, as if he believed this was his fault—even after all he'd done to protect them.

Emma caught the side of his face in her palm, holding his gaze through the shadows. "This is not your fault, Jeremiah. You did everything you could."

His jaw flexed beneath her fingers. "I thought something was going to happen *on* the ship. I was wrong."

"I remember. You told me to go to that balcony at the back of the yacht." The bittersweet memory edged aside her terror for a moment. If she could go back to that moment—rescind her decision to visit Tulum—how differently this night might have gone.

"I never would've let you on that ferry if I'd known," he said, his voice thick with guilt.

The torment in his tone twisted her insides. He clearly blamed himself for this nightmare.

Stroking his cheek, she savored the bristly texture of his growing stubble. "We'll be okay," she whispered. "Didn't you tell me recently that happy thoughts lead to better outcomes?"

A faint smile curved his lips. "That's true. And as long as Chubby holds onto my watch and stays close, we'll be found." He nodded toward the youth several seats away, the one who'd taken his watch.

A flicker of hope pierced the gloom. Emma studied the boy. "Why? Does the watch have GPS—?"

Jeremiah silenced her with a kiss. Soft, sweet, steady pressure that reminded her of the rapture she'd felt that night on the balcony under the stars. *How long ago that seemed now.* If only she'd known how fleeting that moment of peace would be… she might've promised him the forever he'd insisted on.

Tomorrow is promised to no man.

The quote echoed through her mind, filling her with fresh regret. She should've seized that moment. She should've said yes.

The changing scenery outside caught her attention. Emma sat up straighter. Instead of endless wilderness, they were passing squat cinderblock and tin structures, an entire neighborhood of shanties. Ahead, taller buildings twinkled in the darkness, beckoning them into an urban jungle far more frightening than the wilderness behind them.

Jeremiah squeezed her hand apologetically, then released it. "I need to watch where we're going." He leaned forward, scanning both the road ahead and the window beside him with sharp, steady attention.

Emma peered out as well, but the maze of narrow streets all looked the same. Then, at an unmarked intersection, the combi squealed to a stop, the sound wrenching through the silence and rousing Sammy, who gasped and clung tighter.

"It's okay." Emma held her close. "We've stopped, that's all."

The other hostages murmured anxiously, tension thickening the stagnant air. Then, without warning, the combi's door swung open—and six of the guerrillas stood, filing out silently, weapons in hand.

"No, no, no."

Overhearing Jeremiah's words, it took Emma a moment to figure out the reason for his protest: The one he'd nicknamed "Chubby" was stepping off the bus. As he walked away with Jeremiah's watch, dismay tackled her.

My God. How much worse can this get?

Her answer came in the form of a fresh wave of young men bounding onto the bus and carrying their own weapons. As they moved down the aisle to ogle the victims, Jeremiah's head bowed and his shoulders slumped—not only to avoid their notice, Emma guessed. He had to be as devastated as she was that the watch, their only hope, had just vanished along with Chubby.

From up front, the leader snarled at the newcomers to take their seats. Once they were all seated and facing forward, Emma stretched out a hand and clasped Jeremiah's muscular arm to console him. He laid a hand over hers, shooting her a grateful look that she could translate, even in the dark. *We'll get through this.*

How bizarre that they should find themselves in this situation together. Never in a million years would she have guessed she'd wind up a hostage in Mexico with her favorite former student.

But thank God he was here, that she hadn't been thrust into this nightmare alone. She released a humorless laugh.

Life sure hadn't pulled any punches with her. From her parents' deaths in a car crash more than ten years ago, to Eddie's abandonment, to winding up kidnapped with her daughter when she was supposed to be on a fun-filled cruise—she had to be cursed. Maybe she'd done something awful in a past life and was paying for it in this one.

The bus lurched forward, continuing its tortuous route to an unknown destination. Five minutes later, it stopped in what was clearly an industrial side of the city. Ugly, squat buildings stood behind walls topped by barbed wire. A guerrilla clambered off the bus to unlock the steel gate and hold it open for the bus to enter.

Backfiring loudly, the bus crept fifty more feet into a parking area that fronted a cinderblock building. It backfired again as the driver cut the engine.

Looking out at the blacked-out windows of what appeared to be an abandoned two-story factory, Emma quailed. The building had once been covered in adobe, but much of it had fallen off, leaving bare patches that resembled open sores. The windows on the upper level had all been boarded with plywood. At least, the water tank perched on the flat roof suggested they would have running water.

How long would this prison be their home?

Sammy gripped her hand so tightly that she winced. "I'm scared, Mommy."

"Me too, baby. But Jeremiah will protect us."

The leader jumped to his feet brandishing his weapon. "*¡Arriba!*"

His fearsome growl caused one woman to break into tears. Emma rose on spongy knees, clinging to Sammy who hugged her from behind. Jeremiah stepped into the aisle before them. Grasping her hand firmly, he led them off the bus while the other hostages followed. The leader's eyes glittered like black sapphires as he watched Jeremiah move past him.

Once off the bus, the leader ordered them to walk in a single line into the building. They stepped through a large front door into a dark and musty building where their footsteps echoed off the cement floor. Their heads all swiveled as the door clanged shut behind them. They were still standing in an uncertain knot when, with a loud bang, the halogen lights overhead blinked on, blinding all of them.

While still blinking against the brightness, Emma took in her surroundings. Cement floors, exposed pipes, and rough walls all contributed to the inhospitable atmosphere. The guerrillas had made themselves as comfortable as possible, stringing hammocks between cinderblock pillars and erecting tables and folding chairs. The windows had been covered in a dark, but translucent film that allowed them to see out, while nobody could see in. Given the quantity of personal items strewn about, they had been living here for some time.

"*¡Arriba!*" one of the guerrillas shouted, pointing toward a run of rusty, metal stairs with his assault rifle.

With Jeremiah in the lead, the Americans marched obediently up the stairs and through a steel door at the top into a second-story chamber much like the first, with hammocks hanging from pegs on the pillars. But the windows at this level were boarded from the inside rather than blackened with film. The glimpse of toilet facilities at the back of the room heartened Emma.

"*Bienvenidos a su nueva casa.*" *Welcome to your new home.*

The pock-faced leader had climbed the steps behind them. Hitching a thumb through a belt loop with one hand, he pointed his semi-automatic at one captive at a time while talking. Emma kept Sammy behind her, just in case the man started shooting. "*Ju* will estay here until *jur* family pays *el rescate.*" His dark eyes landed on Emma and slid with oily interest toward Sammy's face as she peeked around her mother.

Emma pushed her daughter firmly out of sight.

"Tonight *ju* eat and *ju esleep*. Tomorrow *ju* tell me who will pay to see you *lif.* If *ju* are *estill jere* when the food is gone," he pointed toward a stack of boxes in the corner, "I will sell *ju* to someone else or kill *ju.*" He then turned toward two of his underlings issuing orders in rapid-fire Spanish.

Those men headed toward the boxes and began to empty one of them, unloading bottled water and stacks of home-baked tortillas, the scent of which brought an unexpected rumble to Emma's stomach. At least, they wouldn't be going hungry—not tonight anyway.

Told to start eating, the hostages formed a loose circle around their food supply, consuming their first meal together. Emma took a headcount. Of the roughly twenty-seven people who'd boarded the ferry that morning, only thirteen remained—the three of them, the elderly couple, three middle-aged sisters traveling with the teen who'd tried to run; the tattooed man named Joe, his girlfriend, plus a young couple who might have been on their honeymoon.

Too shocked to speak, they nibbled their rationed tortillas in silence and drained their water bottles while the head guerrilla orbited them slowly, taking stock of his prizes. His gaze slid repeatedly toward Jeremiah.

Seeing him through the leader's eyes, Emma could see why. Unlike the rest of the Americans, Jeremiah wasn't trembling or staring vacantly into space. Even with his gaze fixed on the floor in front of him, he gave off an air of silent resistance that the guerrilla leader had clearly taken note of.

"*Ju.*" He pointed his rifle at Jeremiah, causing him to glance up warily, then look back at the floor.

The leader swaggered closer. "*¿Cómo te llamas?*" *What's your name?*

"Jeremiah." He addressed the man's boots.

"*¿Y qué haces?*"

Jeremiah shook his head, pretending not to understand though Emma knew his Spanish to be better than hers.

"What *ju* do for work?" the leader translated.

"I'm a doctor," Jeremiah said without a second's hesitation.

Surprise widened Emma's eyes at his quick response. Of course, he couldn't tell them what he really did.

The leader looked him up and down. "*¿Un médico?*" He sounded skeptical.

Jeremiah nodded, and the leader stepped closer still, causing Emma's heart to thud painfully at the calculated look in his eyes. The man stretched out a hand, and Jeremiah visibly tensed as the leader lifted the sleeve of Jeremiah's green T-shirt, exposing the powerful contours of his upper arm.

"How *ju* get so *estrong*?" Dark eyes watched his captive's response carefully.

"Triathlon." Jeremiah's answer was immediate. "I swim, bike, and run."

"Hmph." The leader dropped his sleeve and stepped back. His expression, like his tone earlier, was doubtful. Turning toward his underlings, he addressed them in Spanish, which Emma managed to translate. *Keep an eye on this one. Kill him if he causes any trouble.*

"*Sí, jefe.*" They all eyed Jeremiah mistrustfully.

The tortilla Emma had just swallowed moved painfully down her throat as it tightened with fear. Without Jeremiah, she and Sammy were doomed.

The one who'd been limping pointed to the hole in his boot and the blood continuing to trickle out of it. "*Si es médico, me podría arreglar el pie.*" The man's pallor and the sheen of sweat on his face suggested he was suffering and hoped Jeremiah could help him.

"*Mañana,*" the leader decided. "*Ahora, tienen que dormir.*" *Right now, they need to sleep.* He pointed toward the back of the room. "*Hay dos baños, allí. Ju* all wash, *ju* keep clean, and no get sick. Then *ju esleep* here *en las hamacas*. Go." He waved them toward the bathrooms.

As a group, they trudged toward the two bathrooms where they lined the walls awaiting their turn. Emma could see that the locks on either door had been removed, but at least there was a door. With civility and consideration, the hostages took turns using the facilities, some of them in pairs.

Emma and Sammy went in together. Wanting to normalize their situation as much as possible, Emma instructed her daughter to brush her teeth with a finger. She bent over the sink splashing water onto her face and under her arms, grateful not to have to see her reflection, as the mirror had been taken down. She used the skirt of her yellow sundress to dry off.

As Sammy's red-rimmed eyes welled with tears, Emma turned and cupped her daughter's face. "We're going to be alright, baby." She kept her voice firm and hopeful.

But would they really? Worry gnawed at her as she considered how much the two of them relied on Jeremiah and that their captors already considered him a liability. If they knew what he did for a living, and if they guessed that the U.S. Navy would soon be out there looking for him, they'd shoot him where he stood.

As for herself, she had no idea where the money would come from to secure her and Sammy's release. Her parents had left nothing of any value behind when they'd died, except the home they'd lived in, which she and Juliet had sold to pay off their college loans. The best that she could hope for was that Jeremiah's SEALs found and rescued them before something irreparable happened.

Think positive. Jeremiah's faith in the power of positive thinking gave her something to cling to. Even now, help is on the way. For Sammy's sake, she willed that it be so, with all of her might.

"We're together." She pulled Sammy close for a reassuring hug. "We're going to get through this." Then she swept them out of the bathroom, eager to reunite with Jeremiah, whose presence was her only comfort.

CHAPTER 11

"I don't think I can sleep." Juliet glanced at the two double beds occupying most of the space in their affordable but meticulously clean Playa del Carmen accommodations.

The clock by the bedside read 2 a.m. With the *Escapade* locked down tight, they'd sneaked off the cruise ship through the employee entrance. Once on the pier, they'd found a boat in San Miguel to ferry them from Cozumel to the Mexican mainland. Their boat driver had been so inebriated that Tristan ended up taking the helm while the driver tossed his cookies overboard.

As they skimmed over the dark waves of the Western Caribbean, Juliet marveled at the detour her life had just taken. As fiercely self-reliant as she preferred to be, she silently thanked the stars shimmering overhead for pairing her with Tristan—who'd proven just as adept at maneuvering a boat as he was at racing his four-wheeler.

By the time they motored up to the pier at Playa del Carmen and jumped off with their bags, every shop, bar, and even the police station were shuttered for the night. Not a soul wandered the quiet streets of the small seaside pueblo. There was no way to rent a car or motorcycle, leaving them no choice but to find the nearest motel and stay put until morning.

"Nothing else we can do but sleep." Tristan stripped off his T-shirt, crossed to the sink, and pulled out a bottle of mouthwash from his shaving kit.

Juliet's attention shifted from the cutesy ocean-themed artwork on the bungalow walls to the screaming eagle tattooed across Tristan's broad back. A vision of something else to do besides sleeping made her heart trot. If sex couldn't take her mind off the fear of losing what little family she had left, nothing would.

Tristan, mouthwash tilted to his lips, caught her ogling him in the mirror and slowly turned. He must have read her thoughts—no doubt the desperate, want-filled look on her face—because he immediately stopped rinsing. Pivoting back to the sink, he spat and rinsed before facing her again.

He pointed at her. "You said you'd rather be my teammate than my rebound lover, remember?"

She had said it—and wasn't about to change her mind long-term. But this was different.

"I need a distraction." It was hard to admit. "It's the only way I'm going to get any sleep."

He drew a deep breath, his tanned chest swelling. His abs rippled as he slowly exhaled. Thoughts flickered in his dark-blue eyes—thoughts she couldn't begin to interpret. "I think I can help with that." He nodded slowly.

I'm probably going to regret this later.

Before she could talk herself out of it, Juliet crossed to Tristan, plucked the mouthwash from his hands, and rinsed her own mouth. Their gazes locked. Anticipation sizzled through her torso to the tips of her fingers and toes. She spat, rinsed with water, wiped her lips with a clean towel, then launched herself at him.

Absorbing her weight like it was nothing, Tristan pulled her close, lifting her off the floor and freeing her to wrap her thighs around his hips. She clung to him as their mouths fused. Their tongues tangled for the first time, shocking her with how fantastic it felt.

He turned with her, pinning her between the wall and his hard body.

Wallowing in the breadth of his shoulders, Juliet raked the smooth skin of his back with her short nails. His minty, clean-cut taste made her want to consume all of him. She kissed him with rising passion, reveling in the hard ridge pressing at the front of his jeans and riding the heated valley between her thighs.

He pulled their hips closer, fanning a flame that exploded inside her.

Primitive and powerful desires overtook Juliet, making her a creature of instinct. With whispered permission to let go, she gained her freedom. Sliding down his body until her knees hit the tiled floor, she tackled the button and fly that held his jeans in place.

He reached for the wall as if needing support. "You don't have to." His voice was a low growl.

But she'd already tugged his zipper down and peeled the elastic band of his boxer briefs away from his straining length.

Yeah, but I want to.

She bit back the shameless words.

"But I'm not going to complain," he added, groaning as she inhaled him, taking as much as she could in one desperate lunge. The more, the better. It was impossible to think of anything else with her mouth circling his sex. She liked everything—the size, the silky skin over steel, the ever-so-slight upward tilt that would ensure he hit her G-spot when he finally filled her. She couldn't wait.

"Okay." He pulled free of her lips a moment later, his voice a little shaky. "Now it's payback."

That was all the warning she got before he hauled her up off the terracotta floor and tossed her across the nearest bed.

His manhandling was exactly what she wanted—physicality without pain. Something rough, real, and completely absorbing to keep her thoughts from straying to the unthinkable.

Thank God, he seemed to get that. Leaning over her, his hands went to the waistband of her shorts. With a flick of his fingers, he undid the buttons and hauled them off—her panties, too—in one competent yank.

"Ah-ah. Me," he scolded as she started to pull off her top. He nudged her hands aside and, in two seconds, she lay there wearing just her white satin bra. He raked her body with eyes that saw everything. "Smoking hot."

Their caveman talk was exactly what she needed. *Fuck me,* she almost retorted, biting her lip to keep the unladylike command from escaping—because clearly, the words were redundant. He was about to do just that—except he ducked his head and buried his face between her legs first.

Oh God.

Her hips bucked as his warm mouth landed on the epicenter of her quakes. He lashed the leaping bud with his tongue, sparking rapturous sensations that escalated her toward climax.

She cried out with equal parts pleasure and disbelief. No lover in her past had ever brought her so swiftly to the brink. "Tristan!" she gasped as she tumbled over the edge.

She barely caught her breath before he was crawling over her, the head of his sex nudging her slick entrance. As he stretched and filled her, she flared into fervor again.

Oh, my God.

She was right—his sex slid against her G-spot over and over, surging and retreating slowly at first, dragging sounds from her she was sure she'd never made.

"God, you're tight." His voice sounded pained, but he had to like it because he kept going, increasing his tempo just enough to pull a whispered word of encouragement from her.

"You like it?"

She didn't answer—it had to be obvious. She raked his powerful shoulders with her nails, straining to meet every thrust.

"Yeah, me too. A little too much. Let's try this." With that scant warning, he pulled out, delved a hand under her waist, and flipped her onto her side to penetrate her from a new angle.

Juliet swallowed a moan of ecstasy.

Oh, that felt good too. More. More!

That was just the beginning.

Forty minutes later, Juliet draped herself along the solid length of Tristan's body, a little tender but feeling as sated and replete as she could remember. She'd never enjoyed sex so much in her life.

With the feeling of sinking into quicksand, she surrendered to sleep's pull.

How crazy was it that she was falling asleep when Emma and Sammy had probably been kidnapped?

What was more, she'd just had sex with a man who was going to be her colleague as long as they hunted for the missing passengers—and she had a rule never to sleep with colleagues.

On rare occasions when she'd brought a man home, he'd been a friend of a friend she'd met at a bar—someone she never had to see again. Having to see Tristan in the morning might feel confining—like being trapped in a car, unable to escape.

She fought to keep the memory from returning to her, but there she was: fifteen years old, stuck in the backseat of the family sedan while her parents lay crushed in the front seats. She'd listened to her father drawing his last breaths. A chill permeated her body.

To counteract it, she threw a leg over Tristan's and wriggled closer, conforming her body to his. His hand tightened where it rested on her shoulder, holding her so securely the ten-year-old memory vanished.

It feels so good to be held like this.

But how were Emma and Sammy feeling right now? Were they chained somewhere dark, terrified out of their minds?

Amazingly, she sank deeper into oblivion, too exhausted and too sated to ponder those questions now.

Come tomorrow, she would leave no stone unturned in her quest to find them.

Emma tried to get comfortable. Sleeping in the deep hammock might have been tolerable by herself, but sharing it with Sammy torqued her spine. There weren't enough beds to go around. Jeremiah had surrendered his claim to one, so every adult but him had a hammock. Instead, he slept on the cement floor directly beneath her and Sammy.

The steel door leading to the staircase had been shut and bolted from the outside. With a bang, the halogen lights went out, leaving nothing for them to do but sleep. Or try to.

But with plywood covering the windows, the darkness was too complete, too ominous. Feeling trapped, Emma was only grateful Juliet wasn't with them—claustrophobia would've sent her over the edge. Emma closed her eyes and willed herself to sleep despite the discomfort.

Sammy started snoring in her ear, and a burst of ugly laughter floated up from the lower level, stinging like salt in an open wound and keeping her from escaping into oblivion. Their captors were celebrating their subjugation and control of other human beings.

Craning her neck, Emma tried to peer through the hammock's weave at Jeremiah. Were those his eyes, glinting in the darkness below?

"Are you asleep?" she whispered. How could he possibly fall asleep on the unrelenting cement?

"Not yet. I'll be right back. I need to check on the old couple."

Hearing him roll out from under them, she swallowed the selfish urge to keep him close. This was what it would be like to be his partner. It took a special woman to ally herself with a Navy SEAL—and not just a SEAL but a medic and a man who protected everyone, not just those closest to him. Could she ever be selfless enough to fill the shoes of his other half?

Straining her ears, she heard him whispering to the others. The darkness kept him invisible. Beyond the cement walls of their prison, the sounds of the city—the buzz of a *moto*, the barking of a dog, sirens wailing in the distance—all reminded her that they were nowhere near Playa del Carmen, and even farther from their ship in Cozumel. She might never see her sister again.

Slamming a lid on that unbearable thought, she closed her eyes and waited for Jeremiah's return.

~

Jeremiah crept through the darkness toward the hammocks in the corner where he'd watched the old couple lie down.

"Bert." He alerted the husband to his approach.

"Who's that?" Suspicion sharpened the old man's voice.

"Easy, sir. It's Jeremiah. I'm wondering how your wife is doing?"

"Oh," Bert sighed. "Better now that we ate, but by morning, her blood sugar's going to bottom out."

"I'm fine," Joan insisted, but her voice wobbled feebly.

"I brought you half a *tortilla*." Taking it from his pocket, Jeremiah felt for Bert's hand and passed him the portion of his dinner he'd saved. The odds of Joan lapsing into a diabetic coma still seemed likely. "Make sure she eats it in a couple of hours."

"Thank you. Is it true you're a doctor?" Bert sounded hopeful.

Jeremiah sensed others eavesdropping nearby. Weighing the risks and benefits of revealing his true identity, he offered a half-truth. "I'm a field medic."

"Then you're military."

Jeremiah winced as the man's voice carried. "Yes." Now everybody knew.

"I fought in 'Nam," Bert volunteered on a patriotic note.

"Then you know what we need to do." He matched the man's tone so everyone could overhear—including Emma. Having seen no evidence of listening devices or cameras, he'd decided it was safe to speak aloud. Their captors were too busy partying to hear them, anyway. "If we all work together, we'll get through this. We keep our eyes open, and we protect each other."

Silence followed his assertion. Then a gruff voice he recognized as Bad-Ass Joe's spoke up.

"I'm a cop in Newark." His voice sounded disembodied in the darkness. "Name's Joe. You need my help, you got it." His humble tone suggested he wanted to make amends for resisting Jeremiah earlier.

"Same here," said a voice that had to belong to the honeymooner. "I'm Mike. I'm—uh—I'm an accountant." His meek tone carried a note of chagrin.

The rest were too shaken, too afraid to speak, except the teenage boy whose mother, Carole, hushed him.

But Jeremiah felt as though he had a team—small but solid—and that was enough. "Thanks, Mike. Joe. We'll talk tomorrow. Night, sir, ma'am," he added. "Don't forget to eat in about two hours."

Making his way back to Emma, he found her more by her honeysuckle scent than the sound of her breathing. As he stretched out on the ground beneath her, she reached out from the hammock to touch him. Pleased by her gesture, he caught her hand and held on, even though he couldn't sleep with his hand in the air.

Her whispered words reached his ears. "Do you have a quote for this unenviable situation?"

He had to smile at the question, which injected humor into their awful circumstances. Searching his repertoire of quotes, he found something inspirational. "'If you aren't in over your head, how do you know how tall you are?' — T.S. Eliot."

She managed a humorless chuckle. "I'm feeling pretty short right now."

Dismay pierced him. "You'll grow." Growth, by its very nature, was painful. Yet there was still an upside to every situation. Hardship brought out the best in people, tapping strengths they didn't know they had. The only downside was that survival wasn't guaranteed. And nobody who died could appreciate how they'd become stronger.

The scariest part of their situation was that their survival depended on the human decency of the Noriega look-alike downstairs. If that man was in any way associated with the ruthless drug lords infesting Mexico, the chances of them all surviving unscathed were slim at best.

But I'm not going to dwell on that negative thought. Jeremiah focused on the positive. *We're all still alive. We've got food and a toilet—everything we need… until the food runs out.*

Sometimes the good was so slight, hanging onto it was hard.

~

Juliet and Tristan looked up as a Mexican of Mayan descent stuck his head into the waiting room. No taller than five feet, with a sharp, slightly hooked nose that gave his face a look of quiet intensity and keen dark eyes, he appeared too young to be the lead detective they'd been told to wait for.

"Miss Rhodes?" His pronunciation of her name came clear and almost without an accent.

"Yes." As Juliet and Tristan stood, the man's dark eyes seemed to take a snapshot of them.

"Detective Canché. Follow me, please."

He disappeared from the door, leaving them to chase after his diminutive form, past the information desk where they'd asked for help initially, down a carpeted hallway in a building so new it still smelled of fresh paint.

Passing a plaque with Detective Canché's name on it, they promptly entered a corner office boasting floor-to-ceiling glass walls on two sides, both overlooking the ocean, which was just a block away. The detective pulled a gun out from under his shirt, dropped it in his desk drawer, and threw himself into a chair that had been jacked up to make him look taller—Juliet and Tristan exchanged a glance, noting the effort.

As they helped themselves to the seats opposite the desk, Canché roused his computer with quick fingers on the keyboard. He finally looked back at them. "I'm told you have family members who were on the missing tour bus?"

"My sister and niece." Juliet scooted to the edge of the woven cushion on her high-backed chair.

Canché regarded Tristan. "And you are?"

"Tristan Halliday." Coming out of his chair, he held out a hand to the detective, forcing him to shake it before sinking back into his seat. "My teammate was also on the bus."

Halliday. Juliet repeated the name in her head. She hadn't even known his last name before she slept with him, which was par for the course—her usual MO—though nothing about her feelings for Tristan felt ordinary. Not that her feelings mattered at all. Nothing mattered except finding Emma and Sammy.

"Teammate?" Canché repeated the word with a frown.

"We serve in the Navy together."

Canché stared at him a second longer, perhaps coming to his own conclusions.

"Have you found the bus yet?" In Juliet's opinion they didn't have time for small talk with the passengers still missing. That was why they'd arrived at the glittering new police station at 8 o'clock that morning, after getting very little sleep: to discover whether the police had found the missing tourists yet. No one at the information desk had given them an answer, though their darting gazes suggested they knew something. Instead, they'd been told to wait for the lead detective who, given the rumpled state of his collared shirt and the dark smudges under his eyes, had been up most of the night himself, though certainly not for the same reasons.

Canché ignored her pointed question, poised his fingers over his keyboard, and said, "Your name, please, and the names of your family members."

A pulse tapped at Juliet's temples as she spelled out her names and the names of Emma and Sammy, while identifying their relationship.

Canché took the same information from Tristan.

"What do you do in the Navy?" Self-assurance bolstered his soft-spoken voice, lending him the authority that his stature denied him.

"We're Navy SEALs."

At Tristan's confession, Canché's fingers froze. He flicked Tristan an inscrutable glance before typing that information into his spreadsheet.

"You should know that SOCOM is aware of the situation and plans to take action," Tristan warned.

Juliet took a wild guess at what the acronym stood for—Special Operations Command? Tristan had been in constant touch with his superiors since they'd sneaked off the cruise ship.

With a glance at the empty doorway, Canché released a sigh, then said in a voice that was soft and empathetic, "The bus was located last night."

Juliet braced herself for awful news.

"It was abandoned on a remote road in the Parque Nacional de Quintana Roo, twenty kilometers inland."

Her heart lifted briefly, only to plummet in the silence that followed. What was the detective not telling them? Dread pooled in her belly. "Where is everyone?"

Canché broke eye contact. "I'm very sorry to tell you this. It appears that the bus was boarded by bandits."

She stared at him, dumbfounded. His words confirmed what Tristan's master chief had claimed to overhear via Bullfrog's cell phone, but bandits?

"We found many bullet casings but not much else. The bus had been set on fire."

"What?" Panic sheared the single syllable she uttered. He could not have said anything more horrific.

Tristan reached for her hand and squeezed it tightly.

"Of the twenty-seven souls who ought to have been on board, not counting the driver," Canché continued, his voice fraying but determined, "approximately half that number were still there, burned beyond recognition. It will take a while to identify them."

"Oh, my God!" Juliet clapped a hand over her mouth, her stomach twisting in a sick knot.

"That's only half the people, hon." Tristan covered their clasped hands with his free hand. "The others are probably still alive." With his grip, he urged her to hold herself together.

"Then where are they?" This couldn't be happening. Emma and Sammy were the only two people in the world that she had left!

"We found footprints suggesting the rest were made to walk for some distance. Then they appear to have boarded a second bus."

"They've been abducted?"

Canché nodded. "It appears so."

Stomach acid burned her esophagus. "Why? For ransom?"

"If money is the motive, we will know soon enough."

"But why kidnap only half of the passengers if they're after money?" Tristan asked. "The more hostages, the more money."

"I don't know yet." Canché grimaced apologetically. Pulling an iPad from the bag by his feet, he roused it, then tapped and swiped several times, looking for something. "There were a few personal items that escaped destruction. Can you identify any of these?" He handed the iPad across his desk to Tristan. "Swipe left to right."

Scarcely daring to breathe, Juliet stared at the photo of a soot-covered necklace she had never seen before. At her headshake, Tristan swiped the screen to the next picture—the remains of a cell phone. She shook her head. Her sister had left her phone in their cabin. "I don't know."

Tristan panned through several more photos—a singed iPod, the frames of someone's glasses, and then—

"I think this is Bullfrog's cell phone." Tristan's jaw leapt as he eyed the burnt and melted device. Only one blue corner of the frame had been untouched by the fire. "I recognize the color."

"Bullfrog?" Canché cocked his head.

"Jeremiah. We call him Bullfrog because he's fast in the water."

"Ah." The detective gestured to Tristan to swipe the iPad again.

In the very next picture, Juliet gave a cry of recognition. "That's Sammy's pool bag." The words came out in a tortured whisper. The orange canvas tote was charred beyond recognition, but the metal etiquette identifying its designer was still painfully familiar.

Horror gripped Juliet's esophagus, squeezing so hard she could scarcely draw breath. The need to escape had her clutching her chest, then leaping out of her chair and heading for the door. Tristan said something to Canché that she couldn't hear.

Down the hall she fled, pushing through the closest door into the brilliant sunshine. Her gaze went straight to the ribbon of aqua blue ocean behind the hotel across the street. If she could just get herself into the wind, she'd be able to breathe again.

The blare of a car horn brought her up short. Jumping back onto the curb, she avoided being struck by a yellow taxi as it barreled past, the driver yelling obscenities.

"Juliet!" Tristan caught her by the arm and pulled her into his embrace, where he held her firmly, rubbing a hand up and down her spine. The sun's warmth on her back was a small mercy, grounding her in the midst of the chaos.

With her cheek pressed to Tristan's pectoral muscle, Juliet

listened to the steady thumping of his heart. Her own racing pulse subsided to match his. She sucked a shuddering breath into her lungs and kept her eyes closed. "They're dead." She said the words barely above a whisper, scarcely able to admit it to herself. Crazy how a tragedy could flatten her completely while the sun still warmed her back.

"No." He refuted her words with so much certainty that it dispelled her gloom. "No way."

She looked up to see him shaking his head. "Bullfrog's too smart to let that happen to them. They got off that bus, honey. I'm sure of it." His beautiful eyes shone with certainty, further encouraging her to believe.

"But that was Sammy's pool bag."

"So what? She left it behind. Don't kids do that all the time?"

She thought about it. "Yes." Especially Sammy, who forgot to take her homework to school at least one day a week.

Setting her at arm's length, Tristan held her together with his gaze. "I'm telling you, they're alive. Master Chief told me something just this morning that I haven't told you yet."

"What?" Her heart ached for something, anything she could pin her hopes to.

"I thought it was bad news at the time, but…" he released her to bring his handsome watch to her attention. "See this watch? Bullfrog has one just like it, and it comes with built-in GPS, so Uncle Sam won't lose us when we're on vacation. Bullfrog's watch went to Mérida last night. The bandits must have driven them there in the second vehicle."

"Mérida." The news baffled her. "Why would they have taken them all the way to Mérida?"

"I don't know. It's a pretty big city. Maybe it's easier to hide hostages there."

"We have to find them."

"Of course. Hey." He caught her face in his hands, his stare enjoining her to keep it together. "We will. Just keep calm, partner. This isn't the time to freak out."

"No," she agreed. "You're right. It's just…" Panic threatened to rise in her again. She tamped it down by sheer force of will and kept her sentence incomplete. Tristan didn't need to know how vulnerable she felt with her sister and niece in jeopardy. Weakness wasn't the impression she wanted to give him—not after last night. She was a strong and independent woman who didn't need a man to rescue her. Who didn't need a man. Period.

"So where do we start?" he asked her. "You and Canché are the detectives. This is your wheelhouse, not mine."

She considered the glittering police station for a moment. "We need to go back inside and find out everything Canché knows—every damn, gruesome detail, no matter how small. Like what happened to the bus driver and the tour guide? Were they kidnapped, too, or were they possibly in on it?"

"Let's go find out." With his muscular arm anchoring her to his side, Tristan escorted her back into the building.

CHAPTER 12

A chill swamped every inch of Emma's body as she strained her ears for the sound of Sammy's voice floating up from downstairs. *God, help us!* Her daughter was alone down there with their captors. Emma's pounding heart rocked her as she stood with her hands clasped by the open steel door, as seconds stretched into hours. If not for Jeremiah, who stood directly behind her, holding her together with his hands on her shoulders, she might have succumbed to hysteria.

Half an hour earlier, the lights had come on, and the steel door had swung open. They were told they could help themselves to something to eat from the stash in the corner. Joe, who had elected himself governor of the food supply, doled out a banana, a tortilla, and a bottle of water to each hostage.

"We've got enough here for two weeks," he assured them as he handed out their food.

What their captors intended to do with them if they were still here in two weeks, Emma didn't want to know. Either they would be rescued before then, she told herself, or their ransom would be paid, and they would be released. But where would Juliet get her hands on the kind of money being demanded for their return?

No sooner had Joe from Newark distributed their breakfast than he was summoned downstairs as the first hostage to be questioned. Ten minutes later, he returned to report that the leader wanted the email addresses of whoever would pay to see his hostages alive again. He also wanted bank account numbers and personal identification numbers to go with the bank and credit cards he'd stolen. Joe had advised everyone to give out false information.

"And then what?" asked Carole, the mother of the teenage boy. "They might kill us."

"If you give them money right away, they'll kill you anyway. Better to stall them and hope we get rescued first." He shot a meaningful glance at Jeremiah.

Joe's girlfriend, mascara and tears streaking down her face, had been summoned next, followed by the newlyweds, then the two sisters who had accompanied the teen boy, Carter, and his mother. They had all taken the cruise together, Emma had learned, to move past the death of the boy's father.

She shed a tear for Carter upon learning of his circumstances. Why did life have to be so cruel?

She had expected to be called next—not Sammy, who'd been ordered at gunpoint to face the leader alone. It made no sense why the guerrillas would want to question a twelve-year-old.

Overcome with helplessness, Emma swayed against Jeremiah, who released her shoulders to wrap his arms around her.

"They're almost done with her."

His words could only reassure her so much. "What are they asking her?"

Instead of answering, Jeremiah hushed her as snatches of Sammy's frightened voice reached their ears. A wave of ugly laughter followed, and Emma would have attacked the heavily armed guard standing on the landing if Jeremiah hadn't forcibly restrained her.

"It's okay. They're not hurting her."

The words murmured in her ear made her bury her face into his sky-blue T-shirt and inhale the faint trace of balsam underlying more manly odors.

"Count to fifty," he suggested. "She'll be back before you finish."

The alternative was to scream in helplessness, then break into sobs, so she counted. One, two, three . . . At twenty-seven, Sammy came flying up the stairs, past the guard, and into her mother's and Jeremiah's arms.

Emma hugged her close, vowing never to let her out of her sight again.

Jeremiah promptly drew them away from the stairs, toward the area of the room where their hammock hung.

Emma searched Sammy's pale face. "What did they ask you, sweetheart?"

A glance at the guard showed him looking down the stairs, awaiting orders.

Sammy divided her green gaze between Jeremiah and her mother. "They wanted to know if the two of you were married."

As Emma met Jeremiah's gaze, an electric shock seemed to arc clear to her toes. "What did you say?" She looked back at Sammy.

"I said yes."

Emma's heart gave an illogical skip of joy. "Why, honey?"

"I don't know. So they wouldn't hurt us?"

"That's fine, baby. That makes perfect sense." She stroked Sammy's dark hair before meeting Jeremiah's gaze again. *Please understand,* she sought to convey. Her daughter wasn't wrong to consider him their best hope for survival. But was lying to their captors a good idea? What if they had a way of fact-checking Sammy's answer? Beyond that, was it fair to Jeremiah to expect him to protect them? There was only so much a single man could do against eight armed foes.

"Sauers!" The guerrilla guarding the stairs repeated the name being called up to him.

The old man, Bert, who stood by the hammock where his wife had lapsed into a coma, pulled back his shoulders while gazing down at her, then swept his gaze over the rest of the hostages. Holding Jeremiah's gaze the longest, he began to march resolutely toward the stairs.

Jeremiah abandoned Emma and Sammy to intercept his path. "Don't trust them to keep their promises."

Bert stopped and regarded him without recrimination. "I told you Joan wouldn't survive this. She needs a doctor—now, not just a field medic," he added with tempered bitterness. "I'll do whatever it takes to get her one."

"They'll kill you anyway." Joe from Newark, who was obviously listening in, spoke out. "They'll take every cent you've got, and then they'll kill you."

Jeremiah shot him a quelling stare. "Quiet."

The cop scowled and turned away.

"I'm sorry, but he's right." Jeremiah's voice barely reached Emma's ears.

With his blue eyes blazing, Bert gestured toward his wife. "What choice do I have?"

"*Apúrate, viejo!*"

The guard's shout urged Bert to move faster.

"String them along," Jeremiah advised. "Right now, all you need is insulin."

Bert shook his head and continued toward the stairs.

Watching Jeremiah's face as the old man disappeared, Emma could tell Bert's desperation deeply concerned him.

She turned back to Sammy, holding the hammock still for her. "Honey, I need you to lie down for a while."

"But they might call you next." Under the halogen lights, Sammy's freckles stood out starkly against her pale skin.

"They may call me and Jeremiah together since you told them we were married. Either way, I'll be fine. Now lie down here, where you're safe." Hopefully, Sammy would believe that she had a safe place to lie.

As Sammy climbed into their hammock, Emma expelled a breath of relief, then went to join Jeremiah, who stood with his arms across his chest and a frown on his face, listening to Bert's slow descent.

Emma touched one of his arms and whispered, "You think they'll just take his money and…?" She trailed off, unable to finish.

He met her gaze but didn't answer. Perhaps, in contrast to Joe, he refused to articulate negative thoughts for fear that he would manifest them. He had stressed the importance of positive thoughts more than once. Even so, he was obviously concerned—and for good reason. Their captors wouldn't release anyone who could go straight to the authorities or the American Embassy.

What if we're next? The question popped into her head.

She whispered instead, "What should I tell them when they ask for my PIN?"

Her bank information would give the leader access to both her checking and savings, even to her CD—to everything she had saved for her and for Sammy.

He put his lips to her ear. "Give them a false PIN for now. We try to stall them until help comes."

She nodded, grateful for his feedback and welcoming his faith in his master chief's ability to find them. *Please let that be true.*

They stood there for what felt like mere seconds compared to when she'd waited for Sammy, when the sound of Bert's slow steps preceded him. But he wasn't alone. Two guerrillas followed closely on his heels.

Bert's refusal to look at Jeremiah suggested he'd struck a deal with their captors—but what sort of deal?

Holding a collective breath, the hostages watched as the trio crossed to Joan's hammock. With Bert hovering worriedly on the fringes, the two narcos lifted the unconscious woman and toted her toward the stairs. Bert followed right behind them. Before stepping through the open door, he threw a look back at the remaining captives, lifted a hand in farewell, then stepped through the door and disappeared.

The guard at the top of the stairs followed him, shutting the door behind him, which suggested the interviews were over, at least for the moment. As the metal door clanged shut, the remaining captives regarded one another in shock. Emma suffered a deep-down certainty that she would never see Bert and Joan Sauers alive again. The old man must have promised their captors thousands of dollars in exchange for his and Joan's release. If he'd given them everything they wanted, would the leader really release them as he'd promised, or would he kill them the instant the money was wired?

Going by Jeremiah's grim expression, the latter was more likely. Emma closed her eyes and swallowed the sob in her throat. *This can't get any worse.*

Catching herself thinking such a negative thought, she revised the statement into a positive one. *Things can only get better.*

~

They needed more options than to wait.

Pivoting on the balls of his feet, Jeremiah stalked toward one of the boarded windows at the front of the building. There, he curled his fingertips over the top of the plywood hammered to the frame and gave it a determined yank. The board gave a sharp crack. He tugged again, and a piece of the corner broke off, just enough to allow him a view outside as he rolled up on tiptoe.

Sunlight stung his eyes as he took his first look at their surroundings by daylight. The people in the yard below tore his attention from the neighboring buildings. There was Bert, stooping to slide into the back seat of a rust-colored Corolla. The two guerrillas carrying his wife passed her into the car for him to hold. One of them jumped behind the wheel while the other went to unchain the gate.

With a heavy heart, Jeremiah watched the car back into a one-point turn before pulling through the chain-link gate. The second man shut the gate and locked the padlock there before slipping into the front seat of the Corolla, which then drove away.

When the car disappeared, leaving a small dust cloud in its wake, Jeremiah attempted to remote view, hoping to catch its trail—probably straight to a bank. But his mind was clouded, blinded by emotion, and he couldn't hold the image for more than a few seconds. A tightening ache banded his chest as he considered Bert and Joan's fate. Would anyone ever hear from them again?

Shifting his attention back to the view outside, he discovered that Mérida reminded him of Comitán, where Echo Platoon had stormed El Cuchillo's compound the previous year. This, too, was a larger city. A palm tree here and there betrayed its proximity to the coast—in this case the Gulf, not the Western Caribbean. Run-down buildings, trash in the street, and the stray dog sniffing at the gate all testified to a socio-economic situation that gave rise to thugs like El Cuchillo and Craterface in the first place.

The worn Fanta sign, abandoned in the dirt yard below them, suggested the building they were in may have been a bottling plant back in the day. The sign lay propped against a wall that was made of cinderblock, like the building they were in, only it was topped with barbed wire to keep intruders out. Just one taller building stood within the vicinity, but it was too far down the street to offer a decent vantage point for snipers.

A sudden noise made him freeze.

"Someone's coming," Emma warned him from a few feet away.

Jeremiah quickly jammed the bit of plywood back into place and spun around. He'd seen enough to realize that a staged rescue would pose several challenges.

"*Médico.*" Their guard, resuming his stance at the door, waved him over. "*Tú y tu señora abajo. Ahora.*"

Jeremiah nodded. As expected, they were taking him and Emma together. It was clever of Sammy to tell them they were married. He waited for Emma to offer her daughter a swift hug before taking her hand in his. Together, they descended the iron steps to face their captors.

"*Quién es?*" The male voice from behind the locked door wobbled with fear. *Who is it?*

Tristan regarded Canché, who had jumped to one side of the door after knocking—clearly trying to avoid any bullets that might fly. On the flower-covered patio, Tristan planted himself on the other side of the door, keeping Juliet behind him and blocking her movement with his arm.

"Inspector Canché, *Policía.*" The detective's authoritative voice conjured the image of a much taller man.

A bolt grated back, and the door cracked open. Dark eyes pinned the detective with mistrust, then darted toward Tristan and Juliet as they edged into view.

The home belonged to Nacho Nuñez, an employee of Yucatan Tours who should have been driving the missing tour bus. According to Canché, Nacho had called his employer at seven that morning to tender his resignation. Whether he'd been on the bus when it was overrun by bandits was still unknown, but his actions suggested he knew something about the incident. This had to be Nacho speaking through the four-inch opening.

"What do you want?" His darting gaze betrayed guilt.

Canché held his stare. "I think you know."

Nacho hung his head for a moment, then pulled the door open and stepped back. *"Por favor, entren. Rápido."*

As they all slipped into the humble dwelling, the homeowner peered anxiously up and down the street before shutting and locking the door.

They found themselves in a minuscule living room. Tristan heard a woman humming and rattling pans in the adjacent kitchen. A baby babbled happily. Why would Nacho quit his job when he had a young family to support?

Young and wiry, the former bus driver gestured toward the only piece of furniture—a pink sofa still covered in plastic. "Sit, please. Do you want something to drink? Water? Juice?"

"No, thank you. We won't be here long." Canché sat on the sofa, prompting Juliet to do the same. Tristan stood at Juliet's right shoulder, taking in every detail as the nervous man wrung his hands.

Tristan gave Nacho a thorough once-over. Jeans, sleeveless T-shirt, dark hair sticking out in every direction—he looked like he hadn't slept the night before.

Nacho tucked his hands under his armpits. "Then how can I help you?"

Canché's voice softened. "I'm investigating the hijacking of the tourist bus you accompanied to Tulum yesterday."

Nacho's Adam's apple bobbed.

"You know it vanished," Canché pressed, unblinking.

"Yes."

The detective gestured to Juliet. "This is the sister of one of the missing tourists. And this man's colleague was also on the bus."

Nacho nodded, looking thoroughly nonplussed. Tristan wanted to grab him by the collar and shake the truth out of him, but instead, he shoved his fingers in his jean pockets and waited.

"Why weren't you on the bus when it left Tulum, Señor Nuñez?" Canché's gentle tone invited confidence.

The former bus driver's chest rose and fell as he chose his words carefully. "Because I knew it wasn't safe." His voice stumbled over the admission.

A chill ran up Tristan's spine. He glanced down at Juliet, whose hands curled into fists.

"I knew something bad was going to happen," Nacho added, voice hoarse.

"How did you know?"

Nacho's dark eyes took on a distant look. "I was sitting at the bar near the entrance to Tulum while my passengers explored the ruins when César Salvador walked up to me."

Canché's expression sharpened—he recognized the name.

Juliet asked, "Who is César Salvador?"

That was Tristan's question too.

"A bad seed," Canché muttered. "How do you know him?" he demanded of Nacho.

The man wet his lips. "We went to school together, here in Playa del Carmen." He wiped his palms on his thighs. "César was a troublemaker. He never finished school. Went to jail for selling drugs. I heard he got out last year, and now he's worse than ever. When he told me to drive my bus into Quintana Roo with my passengers, I told him no— not even for the five hundred pesos he offered me. Another man at the bar, a taxi driver named Paolo, said he would drive the bus for me. All I wanted was to get away without César slitting my throat, so I gave Paolo the keys."

Tristan lowered himself onto the arm of the couch, laying a

heavy hand on Juliet's shoulder in case she sprang up and attacked the man. Through her cotton T-shirt, he felt her heart pounding like a bass drum.

"Why didn't you call the police?" Canché sounded frustrated.

Nacho looked down at the tiled floor, then at the wall separating them from his wife and baby. He stepped closer. "If I tell you what I know, then you have to help me." His dark eyes pleaded with Canché. "If not, César will send someone to kill me. He'll know that I talked." The quiver in his voice was real fear.

Canché considered the man's plight a moment. "Deal." He stood and held out his hand. "The police will protect you, Señor Nuñez. Please, tell us what you know so we can find these people and save them."

Nacho nodded and quietly spilled everything he knew.

Minutes later, Tristan, Juliet, and Canché sat inside of the detective's car, deciding their next move. If Nacho was right, César Salvador had taken his victims to Mérida, where—according to Canché—he had connections to a larger drug ring.

Tristan pictured exactly what kind of man Salvador was: one who killed innocents and cared only about squeezing every peso out of his victims. If Bullfrog was still alive, he was surely trying to find an escape plan for himself and the other hostages.

Canché banged his palm against the steering wheel, clearly frustrated. "Here's the problem: Mérida's outside my jurisdiction. Worse, the police chief there is corrupt. Half his people are involved in narcotics. No one can be trusted to help you."

Worse and worse. Tristan flicked a worried glance back at Juliet, who sat silent and rigid in the back seat. Now they faced a foreign land without police help.

She finally spoke. "We need to leave for Mérida now."

Tristan's phone chimed signaling a new text. "Excuse me." He teased the phone from his pocket and scanned the update, heartened by the news. "It's a message from my master chief. He's putting a search and rescue team together now. They'll fly into Mérida tomorrow." He shot his two companions a hopeful look.

A touch of color returned to Juliet's wan face.

Canché heaved a sigh. "I'm glad to hear it."

So was Tristan. A coordinated rescue effort was finally underway. Perhaps by this time tomorrow, Bullfrog would be safe—and Emma and Sammy reunited with Juliet—if they weren't among the tourists brutally killed.

Tristan kept that caveat to himself. Juliet seemed tough enough to withstand life's cruelties, but lately, her behavior suggested she was far more vulnerable than she let on.

"We'd better find our way to Mérida, then." He jutted out a hand to thank Canché for his help. "You have my phone number. Please keep us apprised of any further updates."

The detective pumped his hand with vigor. "That goes both ways. Miss Rhodes—" releasing Tristan's hand, he twisted in his seat to shake Juliet's hand next. "My thoughts and prayers go with you. Now—" He faced forward again—"I assume you will want to rent a car, so let me take you the best rental agency in the area."

~

Sweeping an eye around their prison's lower level, Jeremiah's blood ran cold. Last night, the room had been swept clean and tidy. The state it was in that morning—littered with broken glass, chicken bones, and reeking of urine—made it clear their captors weren't just greedy kidnappers. They were drug dealers who lacked discipline and valued nothing beyond the fulfillment of their addictions and greed.

Most of them still lounged in their hammocks, too hungover to rise even at this hour. As he and Emma neared the table where Craterface sat, the man lifted bloodshot eyes to them, his torso wreathed in cigarette smoke. He had spread out their stolen credit cards and ship passes on the table as if playing solitaire.

An old laptop sat within arm's reach with an unfamiliar browser open, suggesting the man had Wi-Fi. As they paused before him, Craterface tipped his chair back on two legs and regarded them coolly.

Emma's grip on Jeremiah's hand told him she was stronger than she looked.

"Señor y Señora Winters?" The leader sent them a crafty smile.

"Yes," Jeremiah affirmed, taking small pleasure in the sound of her name linked with his, even if it was only make-believe.

Dropping the front legs of his chair to the floor, Craterface plucked up three of the ship's cards—theirs and Sammy's. He made a show of comparing Emma's photo to how she looked now: white-faced with fear and her auburn hair in need of a comb. He then tried to say her name, butchering it with a Mexican accent.

"*Ju* no change *jur* name?" he asked.

"We just got married," she replied, her voice hoarse with fear. "I haven't had time yet to update my credit cards or IDs."

Craterface showed her a bankcard with her name on it. "How much money *ju haf?*" He squinted up at her.

"About a thousand dollars."

As Jeremiah asked himself whether she was lying, Craterface tsked his tongue and shook his head. "I need fifty thousand dollars. *Ju* have a *pariente* who can pay me? A relative?" he translated.

As far as Jeremiah knew, Emma's only family was Juliet. The sisters had lost their parents to a tragic car accident years ago.

"I think so." She didn't sound at all certain.

Craterface indicated the pad of paper and pen on the table in front of them, where the hostages before them had jotted down email addresses. "*Escribe tu correo electrónico.*"

She bent over the notepad and, fighting the tremor in her fingers, printed out Juliet's email address. Jeremiah took advantage of the leader's distraction to inventory possible escape routes.

He made out a back door at the rear of the open space, bolted shut like the front with multiple deadbolts. Opening either door from the inside would take only a couple of seconds, but he wouldn't have that long—not with seven armed guerrillas at his back.

"Jerónimo," Craterface called him, modifying Jeremiah's name so he could pronounce it. "*Eres médico, eh?*"

Jeremiah nodded. "*Sí.*"

"*Ju haf* no bank card, *ninguna tarjeta de crédito?*"

He shook his head. "No, I left them on the ship."

"Hmph. Who will pay *el rescate* for you?"

"My father." His answer drew a sidelong glance from Emma, who knew his parents owned a horse farm in Loudoun County. Though he was certain his folks would happily part with fifty grand to secure his release, he wouldn't dream of putting them in that position.

"Write his email." Craterface gestured for Emma to give him the pen.

Bending over the list, Jeremiah read the Gmail address Emma had put down for Juliet. In crisp, clear script, he wrote beneath it Master Chief Kuzinsky's private email, with its "Never-Forget" alias. If Craterface sent ransom emails on the laptop in front of him, maybe the Navy could trace them straight to this building using the IP address. The thought heartened him.

"*Mira.*"

As he put the pen down, Craterface directed his attention to the man with shrapnel in his foot. That morning, he lay groaning in his hammock, his bloody boot propped up on the higher side of the woven fibers.

"*Es mi hermano,*" Craterface added, watching Jeremiah for a trace of comprehension. "My brother, Sergio. If *ju e-fix* his foot, I no kill *ju* today."

Emma's sharp inhale told him she believed the leader's threat.

The injured man spoke up from across the room. "*Me va a operar hoy, César?*"

Without meaning to, Sergio had just given up his brother's name. Jeremiah squeezed Emma's hand reassuringly. "I can help him," he confirmed.

"*Ahora.*" Now. Shutting his laptop with a snap, César pushed back his chair.

"Right now?" Jeremiah glanced down at his own filthy hands.

"*Sí, ahora,*" the man repeated. "*Vete, mujer.*" He waved Emma back up the stairs.

She started to turn away only to swing back around and plant a fervent kiss on his lips, her eyes wide open and staring into his. *Be careful.* He felt the words as clearly as if she'd said them.

He would have given anything to reassure her—and to steal another kiss—but she whirled away and ran up the stairs without a backward glance.

With reluctance, Jeremiah turned toward the matter at hand. Saving a murderous narco from dying of his self-inflicted wounds wasn't exactly his cup of tea. The threat of being killed by Craterface—aka César—if he didn't save Sergio was his only incentive. But returning to Emma so he could bask in her rising attachment to him—that was his real motivation.

He had pulled more shrapnel out of his teammates than he cared to remember, so this would be nothing new.

Easy day, he assured himself.

CHAPTER 13

Sitting in the passenger seat of the tiny Nissan March they'd rented, Juliet craned her neck to better view the speedometer as Tristan pressed the accelerator to the floor. The little Nissan gave new meaning to the phrase *compact car.*

Yet for its petite size, it was capable of gratifying speed—at least with Tristan driving.

A wilderness of thorny trees and sandy soil streamed past them, keeping her from relaxing. They were snaking through *El Parque Nacional de Quintana Roo* on a road riddled with potholes, making it less than safe for travel. But it was still the fastest way to hit the highway for Mérida.

When she finally spied the needle on the speedometer, she gasped. "You're going over a hundred!"

His baritone laughter eased a portion of her tension. "Kilometers per hour, honey. We're only going about seventy."

Oh. She eased her grip on the armrest and reassessed their speed. Maybe this wasn't as dangerous as it felt. Tristan avoided the potholes with ease. He even swerved around an armadillo that scuttled into their path, leaving it unscathed as they sped around it.

"Please don't call me honey." She couldn't let the meaningless endearment pass this time.

In her peripheral vision, she caught him sliding her a puzzled look. "Not even after last night?"

Her eyes sank shut. Of course he would bring that up. The memory of what they'd shared sent a tide of bliss rolling through her.

"Last night doesn't count," she said through her teeth. "I was out of my mind with worry, and I needed a distraction."

The silence that ensued drew her gaze to his somber profile. Oh, that had come out sounding less than kind.

"So that's what I am." He nodded several times, lips pressing into a tight line.

"No, that's not what I meant." Turning slightly toward him, she spent a moment contemplating his arresting profile—the high forehead, Greek nose, sensually shaped lips, and strong jaw. "If you want to know the truth, you're amazing."

He glanced at her briefly, a spark of optimism in his deep-blue eyes.

"I can't imagine going through this without you. But last night should not have happened." She forced herself to be honest. "I can't be in a relationship, Tristan. I'm not that kind of girl. I need my space. Plus, you just got out of a relationship. And I told you—I'm not interested in being your rebound lover."

A humorless smile touched his lips. He nodded as if agreeing with her. "Well, you can't blame me for tryin'."

She frowned, taken aback by his easy acceptance.

"But don't let my history and your own prickly nature blind you to what we have now."

Her eyes narrowed. "Oh, and what's that? Chemistry? A common bond born out of a scary and tragic situation?"

Her edginess seemed to have no effect on him. He darted her an admonishing look. "You keep forgetting something, honey. We're a team. When we work together, we get better results. Don't sabotage that."

His patient reprimand had her swallowing a retort. For the time being, he was right. What had started out as a joint effort to throw Emma and Bullfrog together had morphed, out of necessity, into a partnership of sorts. Right now, she needed him for his level-headedness and his connection to the SEALs. He needed her because Detective Canché couldn't go with them to Mérida, and she knew how to hunt down missing people.

It dawned on her that he'd called her honey again. "I said not to call me that. Look, the ramp to the highway's coming up." She had just caught sight of a tiny little road sign.

"Yep."

They would arrive in Mérida in two hours, around three in the afternoon. And then what? Would the GPS in Bullfrog's watch lead them straight to their loved ones? How long before the SEALs could enact a rescue?

The thought of enduring another nerve-fraying night alone with Tristan prompted Juliet to gnaw on the inside of her lip. Could she get away with claiming him as a distraction two nights in a row? That wouldn't be fair to him.

But if she'd desired him before they'd had sex, now her body clamored for more. As Tristan took the ramp on two wheels, she admired his competent grip on the steering wheel. Just the sight of his hands, with their handsome knuckles and long, dexterous fingers, reminded her of how skillfully those fingers had coaxed her toward climax. Hidden muscles deep within clenched with the desire to do it all again.

Stop it!

The sex had been amazing—so what? Repeating the experience would only confirm in Tristan's mind that they were a couple now—which they weren't. They were simply teammates, like he'd said. Colleagues of a sort. And she never, ever dallied with a colleague. One-night stands with friends of friends—that was her modus operandi. It kept her independent and unattached, which was how she intended to stay.

Just keep telling yourself that. No, better yet, *tell him.*

"Look. We're not going to have sex again." If he were the

gentleman she believed he was, he'd keep his distance, and she'd find the strength to do the same.

He shot her an inscrutable glance, saying nothing.

"I mean it," she added more firmly. "That was a one-off for me."

He kept silent a minute longer, shrugged carelessly, and said, "Whatever you say, boss." After a pause, he added, "Technically, we did it twice. Or was it three times?" Then he chuckled.

Suspicious of his indifference, she studied him out of the corner of her eye while trying to stay aware of her surroundings. Did he really not even care one way or another? Unexpected hurt accompanied the thought.

Sealing her own lips shut, she fixed her gaze on the passing landscape. Intermittent buildings on the side of the road told her they were approaching civilization. Every person she glimpsed as they flew by—a mother carrying a baby in a sling, an old man fixing a chicken pen—they all seemed to be living on the edge of poverty.

Maybe Tristan was used to amazing sex. Maybe last night hadn't been anything special. *Hell, he might have had it better with Mariah than with her.* The thought soured her stomach.

See? That's why you should never be somebody's rebound.

Fine. Lesson learned, and she wouldn't make the same mistake twice. Whatever circumstances they encountered in Mérida, she was going to cope on her own without turning to Tristan to distract her. Despite her assurances to the contrary, that was all he'd been—and all he was ever going to be.

"*Aquí.*" Sweeping an arm across the table at the front of the room, Craterface designated it the operating table. Chicken bones, a plastic ashtray, and several paper cups toppled to the floor.

Eying the stained tabletop, Jeremiah quelled a shudder. "*Agua?*" He made washing motions with his hands—although with the table already a breeding ground for bacteria, what difference would it make if he disinfected his hands first or not?

The leader ignored him, going to help his brother from the hammock. Sergio had risen on his elbows to toss back a handful of pills. Grimacing with discomfort, he chased down the narcotics with a swig of tequila.

Jeremiah focused on the pill bottle. Were these men trafficking opioids, fentanyl, or something worse?

With an arm around his brother, César brought him to the table and helped him lie back onto its surface. The legs of the spindly table groaned beneath his stocky frame. Holding up a finger, César indicated for Jeremiah to wait while he crossed to the corner to pick up an old carpetbag stowed there. After bringing it to Jeremiah, he gestured for *el médico* to help himself.

Opening the bag, Jeremiah found an assortment of first-aid supplies, a bottle of peroxide, a dull scalpel, needles and thread, and a pair of dirty tweezers. With a wave of longing, he thought of his medic's kit stowed in his locker in the Team building.

"Towels?" He asked this in English, not wanting to betray how much Spanish he knew. But César understood, barked at an underling, and seconds later, a wad of semi-clean towels was dumped on the table by Sergio's foot. The man's eyes, meanwhile, were rolling back in his head as he succumbed to the narcotic cocktail he'd just consumed.

Jeremiah drew a deep, centering breath and slowly exhaled. First, he spread the largest towel under Sergio's heels. Then he tackled the laces on Sergio's ruined boot before pulling it gently off his injured foot—no reaction from Sergio. The smell of infected flesh layered over the stink of unwashed socks had Jeremiah holding his breath. He removed the sock next, snipping off bits of thread coated in blood and stuck to Sergio's wound.

With the sock finally off, he assessed the damage. A chunk of metal had embedded itself in the narco's big toe. It had gone straight through the toenail and might have broken the bone, but in and of itself, it wasn't a lethal injury.

The infection that ballooned the toe with pus and turned his whole foot red might yet kill him, however. Karma was unforgiving. Recalling how this man had slaughtered the foreigners on the bus and then doused them in gasoline and lit them on fire, the empathy Jeremiah normally would have felt was tepid at best.

Sergio might deserve to die a slow and painful death, but it served Jeremiah's interests to keep him alive a little longer. With the remaining narcos looking on, he bathed the wound in hydrogen peroxide, drained about sixty ccs of pus from the toe, and set about removing shrapnel.

Practice under fire kept his hands steady. César's unblinking scrutiny testified that the leader wasn't squeamish either, which meant he'd probably seen more gore than an emergency-room doctor. Jeremiah's blood ran cold at the thought.

Twenty minutes later, without a peep from Sergio, the metallic souvenirs from the bus had all been removed. Jeremiah sewed the wound as cleanly as he could, given the thickness of needle and thread. He then wrapped the toe in gauze and secured it with electrical tape, which was all anyone could find.

Wiping his sticky hands on the last towel available, he spoke directly to the leader.

"His toe is still badly infected. Without antibiotics, your brother could die."

César studied him through mud-colored eyes. "*Antibióticos?*"

"*Sí.*" Jeremiah nodded. "Penicillin."

"Ah, *penicilina.*" Craterface looked back at his brother, then shook his head. "*Ay, no. Tiene alergia a la penicilina.*"

Terrific. The man was allergic. "You can try Cephalosporin." Jeremiah doubted the man had ever heard of the drug.

César scratched his jaw while frowning with concern at his brother. Taking Sergio to a clinic or a hospital was apparently out of the question.

"*Si se enferma, te corto los dedos.*" Pretending to hack off his own fingers, César illustrated what he would do to Jeremiah if his brother died. "*Basta.*" Enough. With a jerk of his head, he gestured for his hostage to return upstairs. "*Vete.*" *Go away.*

All too happy to retreat, Jeremiah headed for the stairs. He hadn't gone halfway to the second level when the sound of booted feet outside the building made him freeze. A pounding at the door reverberated through the old factory.

Who was this? Please let it be local law enforcement arriving to arrest the drug traffickers. Hope buoyed his heavy heart.

But the narcos didn't seem the least bit alarmed, least of all César, who ordered one of his men to let the visitors in.

Jeremiah withdrew just far enough up the steps to avoid potential gunfire while maintaining his line of sight into the room below. The door swung wide, and in swarmed six men—the same who'd been replaced by these men the night before.

His hopes took a nosedive. Duty rotation, he realized, searching the faces of the young men streaming into the room for any sign of Chubby. In lieu of the military-style clothing they'd all worn the day before, the young men were dressed like ordinary youths, scruffy and unkempt. They fussed at the current occupants for the condition in which they found the place.

Chubby was the last man to enter. As Jeremiah's gaze went to his left wrist and then his right, his disappointment tripled.

He continued his ascent with gathering gloom. He had assured Emma that the SEALs would rescue them soon. But, given that his watch could be anywhere by now, how would Master Chief even know where to find them?

On feet that had turned leaden, he reached the top of the stairs, only to be shoved into the room by the guard standing guard there.

"Jeremiah!" Emma, who stood just inside the door, rushed up to him and hugged him fervently. "Are you okay? Did you do it?" He could feel her heart hammering against his chest.

"Yeah, it went fine, but I really need to wash my hands." He took care not to touch her with them. Mostly, he needed a minute alone in the bathroom to reshuffle his plans and rebuild his resolve.

"Be right back." Pulling away, he spun toward the men's washroom, where he shut himself inside. For five minutes, he scrubbed Sergio's gore off his hands, but he couldn't seem to chase away the stink of infection lingering in his nostrils.

It took every ounce of his willpower not to let negativity crowd his mind.

Yes, their situation was a bad one. His Special Ops tactical watch was God-knew-where, sending their rescuers on a wild goose chase. But at least he'd made inroads into securing César's trust and confidence. Their captors all thought him a doctor. If for no other reason, they would keep him alive while waiting for his ransom money.

The next time someone asked him for treatment, he could try to get his hands on Sergio's pills. If he found a way to slip them into the tequila that the men drank, he might even debilitate them to such a degree that he could steal a weapon and escape.

Once out of the building, he could locate a telephone and contact his master chief in person. But that meant he would have to leave Emma and Sammy behind to fend for themselves.

His heart balked at the thought. Ultimately, he might not have much choice but to abandon them. Without the watch providing their coordinates, no one was going to find them here. They had simply vanished, making rescue impossible. The only recourse he had, then, was to break away in search of help.

"Are you sure we're in the right place?" Juliet swept her gaze up and down the city block as Tristan parked along the curb of a narrow street.

In contrast to the pink and white colonial buildings on the nicer side of town, they'd driven to a section of Mérida devoted to industry—at least it had been back in a better economic era. Idyllic parks and quaint, cobbled streets had yielded to rundown houses, slums, and abandoned factories. Picturing her sister and niece here made Juliet's skin crawl.

Tristan checked the compass on his own watch. "The watch is within fifty feet of the coordinates Master Chief gave me—as long as it hasn't been moved," he qualified.

Considering the graffiti-covered facades of cinderblock and stucco buildings around them, Juliet quailed at the number of windows fronted by wrought-iron grills. Was that an indication of the crime here or just a common architectural detail? Her gaze snagged on a store sign written in English—Pawn Shop—and the top of her head tingled.

"Oh," she said.

Tristan followed the direction of her gaze. "What?"

"What if it's in there?" She pointed out the shop.

Dismay wreathed his face. "Crap. That wouldn't be good."

"You said it's within fifty feet of us. I think we'd better check."

"Yep." He shook off his seatbelt with a grimace. "I've got a bad feeling about this."

Heat rose off the concrete as they crossed the street together. She could feel people watching them, even though she couldn't see a soul. Aside from a cat licking itself on a door stoop, the area stood deserted. If criminals ruled this side of town, the inhabitants probably knew it wasn't safe to walk around.

Bells jingled on the door as they pushed it open. Juliet trailed Tristan into a musty, poorly lit room filled with display cabinets. Everything from pistols to jewelry sat under a sheet of glass, while an ancient suit of armor drew her gaze to the corner of the room where it stood. Staring at it, Juliet tried to determine if it might be a relic of the conquest of Mexico, until a man as short as Detective Canché edged around a red curtain coming from a recessed area. Eying them warily, he didn't bother to greet them.

Tristan headed straight for him. "Hello. Do you speak English?" Gaining a curt nod, he extended his wrist. "I'm looking for a watch just like this one."

Juliet looked over in time to see recognition flicker in the shop owner's eyes. Still, he shook his head. "No." He started retreating toward the area from which he'd just emerged.

Juliet caught up to Tristan. "He's lying."

A wide counter made up of display cases separated the two men. Tristan couldn't just grab the smaller man and shake the truth out of him. "Wait. You're sure you don't have a watch like this one? Someone would have brought it in here last night."

"No, no watch." The man waved them off and headed back behind his curtain.

"I have money," Tristan called while digging into his front pocket.

The shop owner looked back, his deep-set gaze sliding toward the wad of bills Tristan withdrew. "Four hundred dollars—" He held the cash out to the old man. "—to buy the watch back from you. More money if you can tell me who sold it to you."

Well done. Juliet hid a satisfied smile. She'd have made the same offer, but coming from Tristan, it sounded like a smart deal.

The shop owner retraced his steps, then stretched out a hand to take the money.

"Show me the watch first."

Tristan's cool tone brought a sheepish expression to the older man's face. Moving to a glass display, he unlocked it with a key strapped to his wrist and pulled out a watch identical to Tristan's. It had been sitting in plain view the whole time, camouflaged by the sheer number of watches, bracelets, and rings crowding the case.

He extended it to Tristan while holding out his other hand for payment.

Tristan made the swap, strapped Bullfrog's watch onto his right wrist, then showed it to Juliet, who could tell it was worth way more than four hundred dollars.

He looked back at the store owner. "Someone brought it to you last night?"

The little man firmed his lips and glanced down at Tristan's pocket.

The latter sighed audibly and pulled out another wad of bills, before laying a fifty on the countertop. The man went to snatch it up, but Tristan slapped a hand over it first. "Who brought it to you? Do you know him?"

The shop owner nodded. "*Se llama Manolo,*" he said with contempt he didn't bother hiding.

"Manolo. What does he look like?"

"*Gordo.*" The shop owner held his hands out to indicate Manolo's girth.

"Old or young?"

"*Joven.*"

"Young then." Tristan let him take the money. He laid another fifty on the counter and pinned it there with his fingertips.

"Where can we find him?"

The shop owner bit the inside of his cheek, deliberating. He finally pointed toward the north end of the block. "*Por allí. En una casa amarilla.*"

Tristan kept his fingers on the bill. "In a yellow house up the road. Is he there now?"

The shopkeeper just stared at him.

"Does he work?" Tristan rephrased. "*¿Trabaja?*"

The old man averted his gaze. "*No sé.*" He shrugged.

"Does he work for César Salvador?" Juliet had grown tired of the cat and mouse.

The small man startled back a step, his gaze darting wildly, as if expecting César to walk in the door right then and shoot him.

"We'll take that as a yes." Tristan held up the fifty. "*¿Dónde está César Salvador ahora?*" His Spanish was rudimentary at best.

But the shopkeeper just shook his head. "Go," he commanded, proving capable of speaking English and waving them toward the door while backing toward his curtain. "I don't want your money."

Grabbing Juliet's arm, Tristan towed her toward the exit. "*Ya vamos, señor,*" he called in an easy voice. "*Gracias.*" He snatched the door open and pushed Juliet out of it, back into the blinding sunshine.

CHAPTER 14

"Well, that was a jackpot." Juliet marveled at their luck as Tristan hustled her along the uneven sidewalk. "You really are a golden boy."

He shot her a grin but kept glancing over his shoulder, eyes sharp with mistrust.

"I hate to admit it," she added, "but you'd make a decent detective."

"Thanks. All SEALs are trained in interrogation."

But as they moved up the block, the pawn shop owner became the least of their worries. This was a rough neighborhood. The vulnerability prickled over her skin, making her long for the familiar weight of her nine-millimeter. "I wish we'd bought one of those pistols he was selling."

He glanced at her and shook his head, half in disbelief, half in admiration. "Figures you'd know how to shoot." A smile teased his mouth. "Don't worry. My teammates will be loaded for bear when they get here."

She stopped short, forcing him to halt. "Wait. Are you saying they're going to take over and I won't get to shoot Salvador myself?"

He stared at her like she'd grown a second head. "You're joking, right?"

Hands on hips, she squared off with him. "Do I look like I'm joking?"

A laugh burst from him, incredulous. "Trust me—it's not that easy to take down a *capo*."

"A what?"

"*Capo*. It's what they call drug lords." His gaze swept the area, always calculating. "You can't just blaze your way into his hood and expect to walk out alive. A *capo* has no scruples. He'd kill every hostage and himself before he gave in."

A wave of nausea rolled through her. "So how do you do it?"

"Stealth." His lashes cast shadows on his cheekbones as he looked down at her. "That's why we're the ones going in when the time's right. Okay?"

Anger flared hot in her chest. "No, it's not okay. We're talking about *my* family. I want in on the rescue."

"You *are* in on it." His hands landed on her shoulders, steady but firm. "You're helping us *find* them. But don't let your ego get in the way of their safety."

That stung. She shrugged him off and started walking again. "Let's go find this yellow house."

But this street didn't have any yellow houses.

"Next block," she muttered, refusing to slow down. Even if they found the hostages, how many hours of planning would the SAR team need?

As they headed north, businesses and shops appeared, scruffy storefronts lining the cracked sidewalks. Then Tristan caught her elbow.

"Check it out."

A sprawling yellowish tenement stood at the next intersection. Its tiled roof sagged. Wrought-iron grilles sealed every window. It looked exactly like the kind of place that might house a petty thief named Manolo.

As they neared, a middle-aged woman stepped outside, beating a rug against the railing.

Manolo's mother? His landlady? Juliet paused. "Let's talk to her."

"Hell no." Tristan hustled her past the tenement toward a tailor shop. "I know what you're thinking." He spun around, pinning her with his blue stare. "You want to grab Manolo, drive him out of town, and make him spill everything he knows. Right?"

She lifted a shoulder. "Something like that."

"Bad idea. If César gets word that gringos are sniffing around, he'll relocate. Then how do we find our family?"

She frowned. "Bullfrog's related to you?"

"Not by blood. But my teammates are as much my family as your sister and niece are yours."

That gave her pause. She arched a brow. "So what's your brilliant plan?"

"We wait for Manolo to show up and tail him. Sooner or later, he'll lead us to César."

"*Eventually*?" Even to her own ears, the word sounded thin with panic.

"Honey, this can't be rushed. Failure is not an option."

Panic rose, tight and suffocating, but she got the message. She'd been on stakeouts before. She knew how they worked.

"Wait where?" Scanning the opposite side of the street, she noticed locals watching them, curiosity sparking in their eyes. No way tourists came to this side of town. And what if Manolo didn't show up for days? Another night like the last one might break her.

Tristan looked as unsettled as she felt. "I don't know yet. We need to walk the area, get a feel for it."

Exhaustion swept over her like a wave. "How about *you* walk around, and I'll keep an eye out for Manolo."

"I don't like leaving you alone."

"I'll be fine." She pulled her phone from her pocket. "I'll give you fifteen minutes, and I'll stand here like a *patient* woman."

The phone buzzed unexpectedly in her hand. "Hah! I've got service! Three bars!" Finally. She'd been in a dead zone since leaving New Orleans. "I can use my phone!"

"Sweet. Call mine first—I'll give you the number."

As he rattled it off, she punched it in and pressed call. His phone rang, and she hung up.

"Perfect." Then, without warning, he bent and pressed a swift kiss to her cheek. "Sit tight. Stay out of sight if you can. I'll be right back. Call me if you need me."

As he strode off, she checked her notifications, heart skipping with hope for news of Emma. Nothing.

Then her eye snagged on a message from an unfamiliar alias.

Spam, probably.

But on impulse, she opened it—and scanned it once, then again, her heart rate rocketing until her knees went weak.

"Tristan!"

She whirled, searching for him. Gone. Panic surged, but she had his number now.

Fumbling with the phone, she redialed. He answered on the second ring. "What's up?"

"I just got a ransom note." The words felt foreign coming out of her mouth.

Silence. Then, "I'm on my way. And I think I found a spot to watch Manolo's place."

Click.

The call ended.

She slid the phone back into her pocket, her heart pounding. If things kept moving at this pace…maybe they still had a chance.

~

Emma watched the lone figure sitting by the boarded windows, removed from the others. Enough daylight slipped through the edges of the clapboards to reveal Jeremiah's silhouette. He sat cross-legged, his shoulders relaxed, forearms resting loosely on his knees, eyes closed as if at peace.

But she knew better. Something was bothering him, something deeper than their terrifying predicament.

Thunder rumbled beyond the walls, heralding a storm. Their captors had finally sealed the steel door and switched off the halogen lights to spare them the heat. Darkness crept around them like another enemy.

"They let Bert and Joan go because he paid them off," Carole muttered, drawing Emma's attention to the knot of sisters murmuring in the shadows.

"The leader wants fifty thousand dollars per person. I have just enough left from Jeff's life insurance to pay for all of us."

"Don't do it." Joe's voice cut through the gloom. He swung his legs from his hammock and sat up. "They didn't let the Sauers go. They took the money, drove them to some abandoned warehouse, and blew their brains out. They're dead. Trust me."

Emma flinched. Instinctively, she checked on Sammy, still dozing beside her. Please let her stay asleep.

She glanced at Jeremiah, hoping he would counter Joe's fatalism like he had before. But either Jeremiah hadn't heard—or worse, he agreed.

"You know what? Shut up," Carter's mother hissed, rising to her knees, ready to storm across the room. "Don't you dare talk like that. There are children in here."

"She's right," Cheryl murmured, her voice dull with exhaustion.

"Your son's not a child," Joe snapped, his gaze cutting toward Carter's hunched shoulders. "And he knows I'm right. Kid, you were smart to run when you got the chance."

Carter flinched but didn't meet Joe's eyes.

"Don't talk to him," Carole ordered Joe in a sharp voice. "You don't have permission to speak to him."

"Listen to us," Emma interrupted on a pleading note. "We're not enemies. We're all in the same nightmare, and we all want the same thing—to survive this and go home. The best way to do that is to stall for time. Rescue *is* coming. The Navy knows where to look for us."

Silence followed. Then, in the shadows, she realized Jeremiah's eyes were open, fixed on her with a gaze that sent a chill sliding down her spine.

Help was coming… wasn't it?

Driven by a sudden need to understand him, she left Sammy's

side and crossed the room. Folding down in front of him, she reached for his hands. "What is it?" she whispered.

He gave her a faint smile. "What do you mean?"

"Something's bothering you."

He gave a low chuckle. "How could that be? I'm in paradise with you."

Paradise.

The word conjured that glorious morning on the ship's prow, sunlight sparkling on the waves as he quoted Wordsworth. Her stomach twisted with regret.

We were in paradise. And she hadn't even realized it. How had they gone from that fleeting perfection to this? Locked inside an abandoned factory with ruthless killers, waiting to die.

A terrible truth struck her: she'd never fully embraced life, even when it had been handed to her. Even when Jeremiah had offered her everything—romance, companionship, love—she'd held him at arm's length, afraid.

What if this was it? What if this filthy, stifling prison was her last chance for love? For life?

Their captors were killers. Joe wasn't wrong about that. They would take the money, drain their accounts, and kill them anyway. People like her—people without a rich uncle or fat insurance policy—had zero chance.

The thought of Sammy's small body crumpling under a bullet shattered her composure. A sob broke loose, and she pressed her hands to her face to contain the flood of grief.

"Shh." Jeremiah was beside her in an instant, one strong arm sliding around her shoulders, pulling her close. Her face pressed against the soft cotton of his T-shirt as she tried to suppress the sobs tearing from her throat.

Regret poured through her—more bitter than the day she'd discovered Eddie's betrayal. This was worse. This was everything she'd ever done wrong crashing down on her.

I blew it. I'll never get the chance to make it right.

Jeremiah's hand combed gently through her hair, rocking her, grounding her. Gradually, the ache in her chest eased enough for words to escape.

"I wish we'd had more time," she whispered, choking on the words.

His lips brushed the top of her head. "We will."

The soft certainty of his voice planted a fragile seed of hope in the wreckage of her despair. She sniffed and lifted her tear-streaked face to his. "Promise me."

In the shadows, his dark gaze locked on hers. "Absolutely."

For the first time, she almost believed him.

Why did I ever push this man away? Love, romance, all of it—it wasn't just chemical reactions. It was him. Jeremiah. Steady. Loyal. Real. Unlike Eddie, this man would never betray her. She knew it in her bones.

If she got another chance, she would seize it with both hands.

"I'll never send you away again, Jeremiah," she vowed, voice breaking on the words.

He stilled, his gaze searching hers. "Will you promise?" he echoed softly.

"With all my heart." She gave him a watery smile and sealed it with a trembling, desperate kiss.

From the tiny balcony of a third-story apartment ideally situated across the street and a block down from Manolo's place of residence, Juliet kept watch, confident that nightfall kept her unseen from curious eyes.

During his reconnaissance earlier, Tristan had located the perfect vantage point—a third-floor apartment for rent. Together, they'd made inquiries, pleased to find the landlord, who lived on the first floor. Not only had he spoken English, but he'd agreed to lease them the apartment for a week at double the usual rate. Within five hours of arriving in Mérida, they were ensconced in a humble but furnished apartment.

When they'd toured it, Juliet's gaze had fallen on the single bed, a spike of concern piercing her. How was she supposed to resist Tristan tonight as she'd sworn she would? Until now, that worry hadn't mattered—they were taking turns keeping watch on Manolo's house. Besides, the narrow balcony with its wrought iron bars gouging her back kept her from drifting off.

I can't believe I'm here right now.

Two nights ago, she'd been enjoying a carefree cruise, flirting with the hottest guy on the ship. Now, she was in a strange city in northern Mexico, torn apart from her sister and niece. If she didn't have Tristan for company, she'd be frantic with grief by now.

A warm, sultry night had stolen over Mérida. With the fading light, the streets had gone from busy to eerily quiet. Only an occasional car broke the silence. Salsa music drifted out of an adjacent building—the lone soundtrack to lawlessness. Now and then, scruffy-looking men wandered the sidewalk below, likely why the neighborhood's residents had locked themselves indoors.

For the dozenth time, Juliet touched her phone, reassured by its weight in her front pocket. That phone—and the email app on it—was her lifeline. Somewhere at the other end, Emma and Sammy waited. *Please, God, let them still be alive.*

As soon as they'd gotten situated, Juliet had looked up the U.S. consulate in Mérida and apprised them of the kidnapping, stressing that the captives were likely being held right here in the city. While Tristan moved their rental car to a secure lot behind the building, she'd stayed on the line. By the time Tristan brought up their bags—and dinner from the only restaurant their landlord deemed safe—she'd done all she could.

They'd sat down at a tiny table in the kitchenette, eating quietly. Watching him, Juliet had felt a flush of gratitude. Not only could Tristan drive like a maniac, interrogate like a cop, and sing like Garth Brooks, he could find food in the middle of a crisis. If he did one more thing right, she might scream.

Speak of the devil. The glass slider rumbled open, and Tristan stepped out wearing nothing but boxer briefs.

Good grief. Juliet wrenched her gaze away from him, forcing her attention back to Manolo's house. Apparently, her watch was over.

"Still no sign of him, huh?" Tristan offered her his hand.

With her backside aching, she accepted. He hauled her effortlessly to her feet, his grip steady and sure. The scent of soap and clean man filled her nostrils, making her knees wobble.

"Nope. There's a light shining by the back door, like someone's expecting him. But all the windows went dark by ten. What time is it now?"

"After midnight. I'll take it from here."

When Tristan released her hand, she suffered the ridiculous urge to cling to him. But that was exhaustion talking. She'd already done all she could today—alerted the consulate, coordinated with Detective Canché, and set the CIA after the ransom note's IP address. Now everything hinged on finding César Salvador—and that meant keeping eyes on Manolo.

Overwrought, she rubbed one eye with her fist. When she dropped her hand, Tristan's abs filled her vision.

"Are you seriously going to stand out here in your underwear?"

"Who's going to see?" His tone was maddeningly amused.

I am.

Before she could stalk past him, the sound of footsteps on the sidewalk had them both peering over the railing.

A bulky shadow moved beneath them. "Could be him," she whispered, noting the man's girth.

"Sure looks like it," Tristan agreed, as the figure crossed the street and approached the tenement.

Young and rotund, Manolo unlocked the back door, stepped inside, and shut off the light behind him. Seconds later, a lamp blinked on in an upstairs bedroom where Manolo promptly tugged the blinds closed.

"Damn it." Frustration prickled Juliet's scalp. "He's going to bed." She clenched her fists.

Tristan turned to her. "Might as well get some sleep yourself."

Sleep? How could she possibly sleep knowing that one of her family's kidnappers was snoozing peacefully down the street? "I'd rather break in and interrogate him."

"Trust me, we'd get shot. At least we found him." He guided her toward the slider. "We'll get up early and follow him. Maybe he'll lead us straight to Salvador."

"We'll get up?" She wheeled to face him—and regretted it instantly. They stood inches apart, and he was practically naked. "You're going to sleep, too? You're not keeping watch?"

"There's not much point, is there? Don't worry. I'll wake up before he does. Come on." He slid the door open and gently nudged her inside.

Suddenly, all Juliet could think about was how many hours stretched between now and daylight—and how she'd possibly survive them. She spun to face him, acutely aware of the heat thrumming between them. Not by having sex with Tristan.

But it would pass the time like nothing else.

"I can tell you're beat," he murmured.

As he reached past her to lock the door, his chest grazed hers, and her nipples pearled against her bra. Sensation rippled through her, sending liquid heat to her core. Her lips tingled for his. She swayed toward him.

"I think I'm too wound up to sleep," she confessed, her voice husky with need.

"I know what you could do."

"What's that?" *Please say take me to bed.*

"You could take a hot bath," he said mildly. "That's what I do when I can't sleep."

She blinked. A hot bath? Alone?

He patted her cheek. "I put your bag in the bedroom. You'll have everything you need. I'll be sleeping here."

Wait. What?

Her fantasy shattered like glass underfoot. She glanced at the couch—a pillow and sheet already arranged. "Sweet dreams," he murmured, brushing his lips over her cheek before turning away.

Shock held her immobile. He dropped onto the couch with a groan of relief and stretched out. "Figured if I slept out here, I wouldn't tempt you."

Her face burned. "You don't tempt me."

His grin lit up the whole room. "You just keep telling yourself that, honey."

Honey. Juliet's hand twitched toward the nearest lamp, but she clenched her jaw and whirled toward the bedroom, slamming the door behind her.

In the tiny en suite, she snapped on the light and stared at her flushed, frustrated face in the mirror. *You let him get to you. Again.*

In one week, Tristan Halliday had worked his way under her skin like no man ever had. And now—now—he was pushing her away.

"Suit yourself," she muttered, spying his shaving kit beside the sink. A bottle of cologne tucked inside caught her eye. She uncapped it and inhaled. The scent was pure him—and pure torment. Bliss, bottled.

She jammed the lid back on. She could handle this. After all, she'd survived four hours trapped in a car while her parents bled to death in the front seat. After that, she could survive anything.

Anything but losing her sister and niece.

The color drained from her face as that terrifying thought landed like a gut punch. *Dear God—anything but that.*

CHAPTER 15

The sound of the lock grating open yanked Jeremiah out of a light slumber. Stygian darkness confirmed that dawn was still a long way off. Above him, Emma and Sammy slept in the hammock, unaware that someone was stealing into the upper level of the old factory with foul intent.

Heart thudding, Jeremiah rolled silently to his feet and darted behind the nearest cement pillar.

The door grated shut. Two men whispered in Spanish.

"Who's there?" Joe called, betraying his awareness of the danger.

Jeremiah peeked around the pillar. A bright beam sliced through the dark as one intruder activated the flashlight on his phone. Behind the glare, Jeremiah recognized two of César's men—members of the night shift—clutching pistols as they prowled toward the sleeping hostages. Their jittery movements screamed drugs, sending a jolt of fear through him.

Did César even know they were up here? Surely he hadn't given permission for his men to prowl upstairs, looking to slake their lust on the captives.

Not Emma!

Pivoting, Jeremiah checked on her. Awakened by Joe's voice, she lifted her head, looking beneath the hammock, searching for him. To his relief, she didn't call out. The flashlight beam swept over her, and the men snickered, muttering crude intentions.

"Go back downstairs." Joe's voice was low, menacing.

The beam swung to Joe and his girlfriend—a busty blonde clinging to his arm. Something in Joe's posture made them hesitate. After a tense beat, they turned away, casting their light over the three women traveling with Carter. Carole, Katherine, and Liz were awake now, watching with wide, terrified eyes.

Carter jerked upright, his expression fierce despite his youth. They dismissed him as harmless, but Jeremiah saw the steel in the boy's stare.

The larger of the two narcos holstered his Glock and withdrew a switchblade. Opening it with a snick, he flashed it at the women, hissing at them to stay silent, or he'd slit the first throat that made a sound. His companion cocked his pistol in reinforcement.

Jeremiah's blood went cold. César would never approve of this. He wouldn't risk his ransom by allowing harm to come to the hostages. The men's furtive behavior proved they were acting on their own.

As they closed in on Carter's youngest aunt—unmarried, pretty, and petite—Jeremiah and Joe acted at the same moment. Joe lunged from his hammock and tackled the one with the switchblade while Jeremiah pounced on the gunman. The startled narco fired, but Jeremiah jerked his arm up. The round cracked into the ceiling, and the phone tumbled to the floor, casting its beam crazily across the scene.

His opponent was stronger than expected—drugs, no doubt—or was Jeremiah weaker than he'd realized after days of deprivation? Teeth gritted, he swept the narco's legs out, slamming him face-first into the floor and wrestling the weapon from his grasp. He drove the pistol hard into the man's skull, knocking him out cold.

Meanwhile, Joe wrestled the blade from his opponent's hand—and turned it on him. With ruthless efficiency, Joe gutted the man, leaving him to collapse in a spreading puddle of blood, the hilt protruding obscenely from his belly.

Breathing hard, Jeremiah palmed the Glock. Could he keep it?

Joe crouched by the other narco's corpse, confiscating his pistol. Their gazes met over the carnage.

"What now?" Joe asked grimly.

The pounding of boots on the stairs answered that question. Without hesitation, they broke for cover in opposite directions.

"Everyone down!" Jeremiah hissed, ducking behind his pillar, Glock in hand.

His heart hammered as he calculated their chances of escape. They weren't good—but at least they were armed.

The overhead lights blinked on, stabbing at his vision. He shut his eyes, dropped the magazine, and checked the Glock. Damn. Just two bullets left. He reinserted the mag with a soft *snick*, opened his eyes, and waited.

Everything now depended on how many rounds Joe had—and only Joe knew that. Even with full mags, pistols were no match for the semi-automatics wielded by their captors.

More men stormed into the room, shouting for their leader.

"*¿Qué pasó aquí?*" *What happened here?*

César's furious bark silenced the chaos. Elbowing his way through the crowd, he emerged with an assault rifle balanced in the crook of his arm, his finger resting on the trigger.

Jeremiah's stomach dropped. He could already see the scene—César unleashing bullets on the helpless hostages. If Joe fired first, César would retaliate without hesitation.

Acting fast, Jeremiah lowered the Glock and kicked it toward their captors. Then, moving into view with his hands raised, he found himself staring straight into the barrel of César's weapon. A narco darted forward to seize the surrendered pistol.

Out of the corner of his eye, Jeremiah searched for Joe. Nothing.

Then Emma rolled from her hammock and stepped in front of him. "Don't shoot him!"

Jeremiah yanked her behind him. "Everyone put your hands up. Show them we're unarmed."

Their best hope was to look defenseless—to show that the dead narcos had been the aggressors.

One by one, the hostages raised their hands.

Cheryl's terrified gaze fixed on something behind the narcos. Jeremiah followed her line of sight and understood—Joe was hiding in one of the bathrooms, behind the approaching men. If he came out shooting, César would mow him down before Jeremiah could intervene.

But Joe didn't move.

A tense silence filled the chamber. César stared hard at Jeremiah, then glanced at the man Joe had gutted. He gave a wet gasp, then went still.

The quiet deepened.

It was hard to tell who was more shocked—the captives or the men who'd taken them hostage. Noting the empty holster on the fallen narco, César stepped over the dead man and crossed to his unconscious companion. Nudging him with his foot, he elicited a groan. The man stirred, reaching up to feel the welt on the side of his head and groaned again.

César bent low, grabbed him by the shirtfront, and shook him hard.

"*¿Quién mató a Jorge?*" he demanded as the man's eyes blinked open. *Who killed Jorge?* "*¿Y dónde está su pistola?*"

The recovering narco searched the room, clearly looking for the man who'd attacked his friend—but couldn't find him. "I don't know. He's not here," he muttered in Spanish.

Straightening with alarm, César counted his captives. Realizing someone was missing, he spun around, threatening the lot of them with his rifle before bearing down on Cheryl.

"*¿Dónde está tu novio?*" *Where's your boyfriend?*

The other guerrillas spread out, searching the open space for any sign of Joe.

Cheryl shook her head, trembling. "I—I don't know. I think he's using the bathroom, maybe."

As César ordered his men to search, one of the bathroom doors opened—and there stood Joe with his hands in the air, no pistol in sight.

"Easy, easy!" he protested as several men tackled him at once. Flung against the wall, he was patted down while another searched the bathroom and came out shaking his head.

César marched back to the stunned narco, who had managed to sit up. Pointing at Joe, he demanded, in rapid Spanish, if Joe had been the one to kill Jorge.

"*Sí, sí, sí.*"

Next, César asked if Joe had taken Jorge's pistol.

Looking confused, the injured narco seemed to think before shaking his head. "*No sé. No recuerdo.*"

The fact that he couldn't remember heartened Jeremiah. Maybe they'd get lucky and get to keep the pistol Joe had evidently hidden in the bathroom.

César raked a withering glare over his men. "*¡Pongan atención!*" *Pay attention!* For the next two minutes, he raged at the young ruffians in Spanish, telling them that no one was ever to touch his captives without his permission.

An expression Jeremiah had seen on the faces of radicals all over the world slid over César's face as his ire grew. When the narco leader pointed his assault rifle at the wide-eyed young man still sitting on the floor, Jeremiah barely had time to cover Sammy's eyes before César pulled the trigger—four rounds slamming into the man's torso, flinging him prostrate onto the floor and killing him instantly.

The captives screamed—all except Jeremiah and Joe, who exchanged a look of grim understanding.

An instant later, César swung around and fired another bullet—straight into Joe's right leg.

With a roar of agony, Joe crumpled to the floor. Jeremiah lurched forward, then stopped himself. He could probably take out the drug leader, but he'd be set upon by all the others at once. He couldn't help Joe—or anyone else—if he got himself killed.

As Cheryl flew across the room and dropped to her knees beside Joe, Jeremiah held his breath, praying César was done shooting.

At last, César lowered his rifle. "This is a warning to all of *ju*." He turned slowly in a circle, making eye contact with every captive. "Especially *ju*," he added, pinning Jeremiah with a long, lethal gaze. "*Me causas problemas*, I will injure you, too." Then, barking rapid-fire instructions to his men, he stalked toward the steel door and watched his underlings carry out his orders.

Two bright trails of blood bisected the floor as the corpses were dragged by their feet to the door before being lifted and carried down the stairs. The last to leave, César stood watching Cheryl sob hysterically over a writhing Joe.

Her blonde head whipped toward Jeremiah. "Do something!" she raged.

Conscious of César's dark gaze pinning him anew, Jeremiah crossed cautiously toward the couple. Dropping to one knee opposite Cheryl, he examined Joe's wound. The kneecap had been shattered by that one bullet. Bits of cartilage and bone peeked through the blood spilling from the gaping hole.

Jeremiah glanced up, meeting César's smirk. The man's look said plainly, *You are mine to do with as I please.*

Before Jeremiah could ask for the carpet bag with the medical tools, César withdrew, shutting and bolting the steel door behind him.

He looked back at Cheryl's tear-filled eyes. "We need something to slow the bleeding."

"Take my belt," Joe growled through clenched teeth. As Cheryl fumbled with the buckle, the lights blinked out, plunging the room into darkness.

Working by feel and with others murmuring words of comfort around them, Jeremiah and Cheryl fashioned a makeshift tourniquet from the belt.

"I'll check back in an hour or so. Let's pray that it clots and we can loosen this without much bleeding. I wish I could do more. I'm sorry."

"I'm fine," Joe insisted, though his gravelly voice told a tale of misery. "Just help me back to my hammock."

Accountant Mike stepped forward to help Jeremiah lift Joe off the floor and guide him to his hammock. As Joe collapsed into its folds with a grunt of agony, he seized Jeremiah's sleeve and pulled him down to whisper in his ear.

"Check in the toilet tank."

That's where Joe had hidden the pistol. Smart thinking.

Sensing Emma hovering nearby, Jeremiah sought her in the dark. "Stay with Sammy. I need to go wash my hands."

Inside the dark bathroom, he shut the door and felt his way to the toilet. Lifting the ceramic lid, he balanced it in one hand and plunged the other into the tepid water.

Satisfaction bloomed as his fingers closed around the weapon. He lifted it from the tank, letting water trickle from its cracks and crevices, savoring its weight for a moment. Then he checked the magazine. One, two, three rounds.

Damn. If only he'd emptied the magazine of the other pistol before surrendering it, they'd have five rounds. Too late now. Still, a gun with three bullets was better than nothing—and Joe had sacrificed himself to get them even this much.

Sliding the magazine back into place, Jeremiah debated hiding it elsewhere but could think of no better place. The Glock could tolerate immersion for a while. Lowering it back into the water, he gingerly replaced the lid.

He flushed the toilet to conceal the sound of his movements, washed his hands, and made his way back to Emma and Sammy. As he passed Joe's hammock, he heard Cheryl softly soothing Joe while he issued a low grunt of pain.

"Jeremiah." Emma's outstretched hand groped for him as he reached their hammock.

Gratitude filled him at the strength of her grip. Hovering over her and Sammy, he was assaulted by protective instincts. Thank God no one had been killed but the two narcos who'd been up to no good. Sammy's frightened voice wavered in his ear.

"We're going to die here, aren't we?"

Emma replied before he could. "No way." Her confidence lifted his spirits. "Aunt Juliet's good at finding people, remember? She found that runaway teen last year. I bet she's almost found us already."

"I hope so," Sammy murmured, ending on a sob.

"I *know* so, baby."

The urge to hold them both overwhelmed Jeremiah. "We'll be fine," he promised, stroking Sammy's soft hair. With reluctance, he released them. "Now try to sleep."

As he stretched out beneath them, Jeremiah took comfort in Emma's growing confidence. She was becoming braver by the hour. By the time they gained their freedom, he had to believe she'd be willing to link her life with his. After all, she'd promised him with all her heart that she would never send him away again.

Closing his eyes, he willed that promise into manifestation.

"Do you see him?" Juliet whispered.

Pressed between Tristan's bigger body and a stucco wall, she watched the vein pulsing gently in his muscle-corded neck as she waited for his answer. It was all she could do to focus on their pursuit of Manolo with Tristan leaning into her to peer around the corner.

They'd been so careful not to be seen that they'd lost sight of him barely three blocks from the yellow tenement. The young thug had risen late, thwarting their hopes for an early start. Now, with the sun directly overhead, scant shadows remained for cover as they tailed him through winding intersections. One minute he was buying a churro from a street vendor, the next he'd turned a corner—and vanished.

Turning her own head, Juliet scanned the empty plaza. Every house had painted its front door a different color. Manolo could've ducked into any of them. How had such a bumbling, half-witted youth given them the slip?

"Let's try that alley over there."

Following Tristan's gaze, she spotted a narrow opening between two buildings. Hope flickered as he grabbed her hand and led her across the plaza.

What's with the handholding?

She debated calling him on it. Partners didn't hold hands, and it grated on her professional instincts to overlook it. But after last night's rejection and a sleepless, fear-filled night, she lacked the will to pull away. After Sammy and Emma were safe, she'd assert herself.

Tristan slipped into the alley first, only to backpedal abruptly, pushing her with him.

"What?" she demanded.

"I just saw him glance back. He might've seen me."

"So? We can't lose him. Go." She shoved him into the alley and followed close behind. Together, they crept forward, straddling the trickle of water between their boots, dodging broken bricks and litter.

Tristan's gaze lifted to the clotheslines crisscrossing overhead. Sheets and garments fluttered under a slight breeze, obscuring their view of the rooftops. "This feels like a trap," he muttered.

Juliet agreed, but they couldn't afford to lose Manolo. With her nerves humming, she followed Tristan through the maze of alleyways. The sudden bark of a dog made her flinch. Through the bars of a window, a mongrel lunged at them. Aromas of meat roasting with garlic made her stomach cramp—she hadn't eaten breakfast.

Abruptly, the winding alleys spat them onto an abandoned road, cracked with weeds and scattered trash. A refrigerator lay on its side in the broiling sun. Fifty yards away, Manolo approached a gate where several other young men waited. Tristan yanked her back into the alley.

"Let's wait here."

She nodded and leaned against the wall, peeking around the corner. The boys stood around, looking impatient. "I sure miss my nine-millimeter."

"I'll get one of my teammates to loan you one."

She glanced back at him, recalling the SAR team's arrival in

Mérida that morning. Once Tristan handed over the hostages' coordinates, the team would sweep in—and she'd become a third wheel. "What for, if you won't even let me use it?"

Her grumpy tone drew his attention from the street. "Didn't sleep much, did you?"

No doubt his close inspection revealed the same bloodshot eyes she'd seen in the mirror. Resisting the urge to stick her tongue out, Juliet poked her head out again. The thugs were finally entering the gate.

"Let's go." She stepped forward, only to be caught by the elbow and dragged back.

"Not so fast, hotshot. There could be others coming."

As if summoned by his words, male voices echoed from the alley behind them.

"Like them." Tristan pulled her swiftly in the opposite direction. With long-legged strides that forced her to trot, he hustled her past derelict buildings, scanning for cover.

As the new group spilled onto the street, Tristan yanked her into the recessed doorway of an abandoned building, pressing her flat against the door to shield her blonde hair from the sun.

Adrenaline surged through Juliet's veins. The thrill of danger had drawn her to investigative work in the first place. The other reason—discovering whether her parents' deaths had been murder—had long been laid to rest.

But it wasn't just adrenaline heating her blood. With Tristan's body molded against hers, she could feel his heart thudding, the solid wall of his chest, and—oh, yes—the undeniable hardness pressing into her pelvis.

So he wasn't immune after all. She couldn't help goading him. "Do you always get turned on in dangerous situations?"

His gaze met hers, amused. "That'd suck for me, considering I work with sixteen guys. No, it's just that I'm just finding *you* a *distraction*."

Touché.

Footsteps neared their hiding place, cutting off their exchange.

One glance their way would give them away. Unless the door behind her just happened to be unlocked…

Juliet tested the latch—and the door swung inward. She dragged Tristan with her into a foul-smelling stairwell. He eased the door shut just as one of the boys passed by, oblivious.

They exhaled together, then looked over at the elegant, dust-cloaked staircase that ascended to the upper floors.

CHAPTER 16

A chill chased down Juliet's spine as she stared up at a dusty, dark stairwell. "What is this place?"

"No idea. Let's find out." Catching her hand again, Tristan led her deeper into the building. Graffiti and bullet holes marred the walls. The only sound to greet them was the flutter of what sounded like paper coming from a floor above them. Perhaps out of curiosity, they climbed the stairs, finding a corridor of gutted offices. Doors hung broken or were missing altogether, leaving hollow frames. Trash, broken furniture, empty liquor bottles—they crunched through the wreckage on dull, sticky parquet floors.

"Nice place to work, huh?"

"It was once," she murmured, noting the remnants of grandeur—high ceilings, crown molding, ornate but peeling wallpaper. In another time, this had been beautiful.

"Let's find a bird's-eye view of the gate."

They climbed to the highest floor, where an inner office led to a front corner room. Two wide window frames gaped open to the air, casings gone. A tropical breeze fluttered the yellowed pages of an old newspaper on the floor.

As Tristan crossed to the nearest window, Juliet stooped to pick up a cracked picture frame. Inside, a family beamed at her—mom, dad, and six kids. Where were they now? Still together? Still alive?

"Juliet." Tristan beckoned her over.

Carrying the photo, she stepped up beside him.

The window afforded them a clear view of the street. Behind the closed gate loomed an old factory—two stories of crumbling adobe and cinderblock. A reservoir tank squatted on the flat roof, likely their water source, and a single door led into what looked like a stairwell leading down into the building. Apart from that, the place was sealed. Boarded windows. Cinderblock walls topped with barbed wire. Surrounded on all sides by smaller buildings, it resembled a fortress.

An uneasy chill tightened her scalp.

Tristan watched her reaction. "What do you think? Are they in there?"

The icy dread expanding in her stomach told her exactly what she didn't want to admit. "Yes."

Tears stung her eyes—part relief, part horror—as she imagined Emma and Sammy trapped inside. *Alive*, she assured herself. The ransom note suggested they were still alive.

Tristan stepped away, pulling out his phone. She drifted closer, overhearing the low rumble of his voice.

"Hey, Red. Screaming Eagle here. I've got the coordinates for the nest. You ready?"

Screaming Eagle. Instantly, that tattoo flashed across her mind. Seriously? Did he have to be that hot? Why couldn't he be average? Maybe talk with a lisp? Or have a small—no, of course not. He looked like the hero of a summer blockbuster. Muscles flexed as he read coordinates off his watch. His butt alone deserved its own movie trailer. And as for his other attributes… Yeah. She knew those intimately, too.

"What's your ETA? Over." He caught her staring and winked.

Ugh. Juliet turned away, pretending the butterflies didn't exist.

"Roger that. You'll find us one klick southwest in an abandoned office building. We've got eyes on the facility."

A pause. "Hooyah. Out."

He tucked his phone away and met her gaze. "They'll be here within the hour."

Weariness tugged at Juliet. More waiting. Staring hard at the factory's boarded windows, she pictured Emma and Sammy trapped inside—hungry, despairing, terrified. The tears that had threatened for nearly forty-eight hours finally spilled, a deluge she couldn't blink away. With so little sleep in the past two days, she let them fall, lacking the will to fight.

"Hey, hey." Tristan's soft, compassionate tone made her face crumple. Crossing the room, he gathered her into his arms. His big, beautiful body anchored her as she proceeded to soak the front of his T-shirt.

"I hate waiting." The explanation probably told him nothing since she'd yet to share the story of being trapped in her parents' car with their bodies.

He smoothed his hand up and down her spine. "Me too. Trick is—don't think of it as waiting. We're scoping sniper positions. Gathering intel. Watching for patterns. Failure's not an option. We get one shot."

"Right." She tried to pull away, but his arms tightened.

"I know ways to pass the time."

Even with her heart aching, her body betrayed her with a hopeful quiver. She wiped her face, met his gaze. "Like what?"

"Twenty questions."

She stared at him. "A game?"

"Come on. It'll be fun."

"Maybe I already know as much about you as I want to know." Shrugging free, she marched over to the second window, even though the view wasn't as good.

"That's not how the game is played, but why not? You afraid of questions, or something?"

She kept her gaze fixed on the factory. "If that's your first question, the

answer is no. I'm only afraid of cockroaches."

"It's not. Okay, we'll play it your way. I ask twenty questions, then you ask twenty questions. Here's my first: Are you attracted to me or not?"

She rolled her eyes. "I wouldn't have slept with you if I wasn't."

"Well, duh." He gestured for her to go. "Your turn. Ask anything."

She thought for a moment. "Okay, what's the longest you've been celibate, not counting your first twenty years?" She watched his reaction from the corner of her eye.

He frowned, notching his thick arms over his chest. "What kind of question is that?"

"Oh, you don't like the game now?"

He gritted his teeth, then seemed to give her question consideration. "I don't know," he finally answered. "Like a month maybe."

"A *month*?" The answer told her everything she needed to know.

He showed his palms as he dropped his arms. "I mean, I can't really help it. Women throw themselves at me."

"Really? That's your excuse? Do you even *want* me to like you?"

"Well, yeah. That would be nice."

She shook her head, trying to wrap her thoughts around his astonishingly active sex life. *A month.*

"You act like sex is the most important thing in the world to me," he protested. "It's not, you know."

"Oh, it's not. Okay, then do this: Go celibate for six months. Prove to yourself and to me that you don't *have* to be in a relationship to be happy. Then I might even date you."

He visibly winced, like she was asking for the world. "Brutal."

"Sorry. Did I strike a nerve?"

He didn't answer. With a deep scowl between his eyebrows, he seemed to consider her ultimatum. "Okay, you're on. For the next six months I'll be celibate."

She scoffed at his assertion, looking back outside.

"And just for the record, I think *you're* the one with issues."

"Hah!" Juliet wheeled back to face him. "Me?"

"Yeah. You're afraid of getting close to people."

She opened her mouth to argue, realized he was right, and promptly shut it.

"That's why you're prickly," he continued. "It's your defense. Keeps people at a distance. I'm probably the only one who can tell you're a softy on the inside." He sent her a slow, devastating smile that melted her resolve like the sun melting an ice cube.

Feeling self-conscious, Juliet spun toward a broken desk and set it upright, brushing dust off her palms. When it seemed stable, she retrieved the framed picture from earlier and placed it on top, a small gesture of misplaced sentimentality. "This isn't the time or the place to talk about that."

Tristan stepped up behind her, brushing her bare arm with his fingertips, raising goosebumps. "Who said anything about talking? I was thinking we could let our bodies do the communicating. After all—we've got the place to ourselves."

Her pulse spiked. She considered the ruined room in a new light. But then she remembered *why* they were here. *Emma. Sammy.*

"Not here." She sidestepped him, returning to the second window. "Plus, you just said your celibacy starts right now."

He shrugged at the reminder. "You're right. I did say that."

With easy acceptance, he returned to the first window, where he studied the factory like she hadn't just turned him down. His coolness irked her. He couldn't want her that badly.

As he leaned against the sill, her gaze slid down his indolent body and her body responded to the thought: *Sex would pass the time.*

"Check it out."

His low exclamation had her rushing over to see what he was looking at. A group of young men were straggling out of the same gate the youths had entered.

She furrowed her brow. "What's going on?"

"Looks like a duty rotation. The night watch is clocking out." He checked his watch. "Noon. I guess they keep late hours."

"So…they come back at midnight?"

"I guess we'll find out."

She blinked and stared at him. "What do you mean we'll find out? I thought SAR was showing up in an hour. We sweep that building the minute they get here."

He straightened, grimacing. "Sorry, honey. That's not how this works. Hostage rescues depend on *knowing* everything—the terrain, the guards, their routines. Twenty-four-hour surveillance is standard operating procedure. We don't jump blind."

Her brain knew he was right. Her heart didn't care. The thought of *still* standing here twelve hours from now while Emma and Sammy suffered across the street broke something inside her. Sagging, she slid down the nearest wall until her butt hit the floor, forehead dropping to her knees in utter defeat.

"I'll take first watch," Tristan murmured in a sympathetic note.

She'd done stakeouts before—waited eight days once for a suspect. But this wasn't just a suspect. This was *her family*. Planning for success might save them—but the waiting was going to kill her.

"Thank you," she whispered, forcing the words through a tight throat. Closing her eyes, she let exhaustion take her.

On the heels of the prior night's violence, none of the captives stirred that morning. The lights blinked on, and noises floated up from below. Only Jeremiah rose, crossing the room to check on Joe.

"How's he doing?" Emma asked when Jeremiah returned to the hammock she shared with Sammy. Her soft blue eyes searched his face, no doubt seeing the stress that kept his jaw muscles jumping.

"He's suffering." Jeremiah closed his eyes, betraying his own suffering by rubbing them. "I wish I could get him some pain medication." Feeling other people's pain was as much a burden as it was a blessing.

Emma caught his hand and squeezed. "Maybe you could ask César for some—after all, you saved his brother's life."

He opened his eyes and managed a smile. "That's the plan, just as soon as someone opens that door."

But the door remained shut. Carole, who'd taken Joe's place rationing food, handed out their breakfast—more corn tortillas, bananas, and water. With the hours stretching endlessly, Jeremiah wandered to the windows again and peered through the small opening he'd created earlier.

Apart from two pigeons pecking at the dirty yard, the scene outside was as quiet as it was inside. He replaced the plywood and lowered himself to the floor to meditate.

After half an hour of unsuccessfully seeking serenity, he gave up and got to his feet. A mix of jujitsu and Thai kickboxing provided an outlet for his frustration while keeping Emma and Sammy entertained as they watched from their hammock.

"He's like a dancer. It's pretty," Sammy whispered, her voice floating to his ears.

He prayed her innocence would remain intact through this ordeal. What she saw as dancing were strikes meant to debilitate and kill. *Let her only see what a child should.*

~

"It does look like a kind of dancing," Emma agreed. But picturing the invisible man Jeremiah was fighting, she recognized just how lethal his "dance" really was.

"Is Joe going to die?"

At Sammy's soft question, Emma regarded her daughter, then glanced at Joe. Concern pricked her at the sight of his pallor, visible through the weaves of his hammock, where he suffered in silence. Cheryl had opted to sleep on the floor to avoid jostling him.

"No, honey. Of course not. He's just hurting, that's all."

The sound of the steel door being unbolted had her grabbing her daughter's arm even as she sat up straighter. A quick glance toward the windows showed Jeremiah lowering his arms from a defensive posture.

A young man leaned into the room. "*Jerónimo, ven.*" Sweeping his gaze around the space, he finally spotted Jeremiah making his way cautiously toward the stairs.

"*¿Sí?*"

"*El jefe te necesita.*"

The boss needs you. Emma's heart began to thud. God only knew what craziness might unfold on the heels of last night.

At the door, Jeremiah shot her a look—steady, reassuring—

before ducking under the lintel and following the narco down the steps. The metal door clanged closed behind him. The bolt grated.

A whimper escaped Emma's lips. *I can't do this without him.*

Sammy hugged her from behind. "He'll be back."

Her daughter's innocent faith only deepened Emma's dread. At one time, she'd believed in positive outcomes, too. Her parents' deaths had destroyed that forever. "Of course," she whispered.

But what if he doesn't return, just like my parents never made it home…

Catching herself before she spiraled, she remembered Jeremiah's confidence in the power of positive thinking. *He'll be back. Just count the seconds and believe in his return.*

Falling back into the hammock, she stroked Sammy's hair as she silently counted. *One, two, three…* She focused on her blessings. She and Sammy were still alive. Even better, they had Jeremiah. What more could she ask—except for his safe return?

She'd reached more than three hundred before giving up. Counting took too much concentration, and she was straining to hear anything through the cement floor. The distinct bark of the guerrilla leader was discernible—but not Jeremiah's softer replies.

Dread sat like a stone in her stomach. Her lips shaped the only thing that gave her strength. *Please, God—keep him safe.*

Twenty minutes might have passed before footsteps sounded on the iron staircase. Emma held her breath, eyes locked on the steel door. When it swung open and Jeremiah ducked through, she scrambled out of the hammock and ran to him. Without intending to make a spectacle, she threw her arms around him.

"You're back." Her voice cracked with relief as tears blurred her vision.

"Of course, I'm back." His eyes danced as he held her at arm's length, studying her flushed, tear-streaked face. "Would you do that every time I come home?"

Her heart skittered at the deliberate reference to a future they could share. *Could I handle being the wife of a Navy SEAL?* "Only if you promise to always return."

He gave her a slow smile. "Greet me like that, and I'll always come home."

It felt wrong, under the circumstances, to be suddenly giddy with joy. But when Sammy clambered out of the hammock and wrapped her arms around them both, Emma's happiness tripled.

"What'd they want from you?" Joe's growl shattered the blissful moment.

Drawing a deep breath, Jeremiah gestured for the others to join him as he moved toward Joe's hammock. "We need to talk, everyone. And we need to do it quietly."

A needle of concern pricked Emma's contentment as she hovered close, joined by the other hostages. Whatever Jeremiah was about to say sounded like a potential game changer.

With hopeful looks on their haggard faces, the others gathered around Joe's hammock.

Jeremiah's low-pitched voice carried confidence. "Our captor is worried about his brother. His foot's badly infected. Without antibiotics, he could die. And he's allergic to penicillin and needs a substitute called a cephalosporin. César doesn't trust his men to grab the right meds if they hit up a pharmacy, so he's ordered me to go with them."

Emma's blood ran cold. "No." She grabbed his arm and clung to it.

"This is good," he promised gently, pulling a pill bottle from his pocket. "For agreeing to help, I got this for Joe." He handed the bottle to Cheryl. "Two tablets now. Two more in eight hours—with food."

"He can have the other half of my banana. I didn't finish it."

As Carole spun away to retrieve the banana, Emma searched Jeremiah's calm, resolved expression. Hope thawed the fear locking her heart. This had to be the break they needed. If she knew Jeremiah, he wasn't about to fetch medicine and return meekly to captivity.

"You're planning something. What is it?"

He drew a visible breath before answering. "I'm going to break away and go for help."

As the others reacted with hope and encouragement, fear squeezed Emma's heart.

"But you could get hurt," she protested.

Joe spoke up, voice raw with pain. "He doesn't have a choice. If you want to get out of this place, let him go. He's our only hope."

In other words, she had no choice but to be brave.

"Don't worry about me," Jeremiah assured them all. "I won't be the one getting hurt."

"You're going to kill them, aren't you?" young Carter asked.

"Carter!" His mother elbowed him sharply.

Jeremiah didn't ignore the boy's question. "My job is to protect the rest of you, and, to that end, I'll do whatever it takes to get us out of here."

"How?" Mike the accountant looked skeptical. "Where are you gonna find help?"

"My teammates can't be far away. They're waiting to hear from me. Soon as I send the signal, they'll come fast. All I need is a phone. And when I come back, I won't be alone."

Emma's heart went into free fall. Breaking away, evading killers, finding help—none of that would be easy.

"Listen carefully now." Jeremiah's urgent tone cut through her spiraling fears. "From here on out, sleep with one eye open. If you see purple smoke or hear gunfire, head for that wall by the bathroom. Make yourselves small. And if anyone approaches you, tell them immediately that you're American. This could all be over soon—if not tonight, then tomorrow."

Several people spoke up, peppering him with questions. Jeremiah answered each one with unwavering patience. Emma barely heard the words. All she could hear was the steady resolve behind his voice. He was determined to make the most of this opportunity. Didn't he realize what he was asking of her—leaving her and Sammy here, alone?

Dismay shredded the contentment she'd felt earlier.

I can't do this without him. I'm not strong enough.

But what choice did she have? She'd fallen in love with an extraordinary man. Jeremiah didn't sit idly by and let evil rule unchallenged. He was a game changer—a knight errant standing against darkness.

I love him so much.

The realization swept through her like an unstoppable tide.

Oh, my God. This isn't limerence. That was fleeting, a temporary madness. What she felt for Jeremiah had begun years ago—maybe the very moment he'd stepped into her office asking questions about Wordsworth. Six years apart hadn't dimmed those feelings one bit. In fact, the one thing that might outlast both of them was her love for him.

And that love would give her strength.

The realization let her breathe again. She *would* get through this—because of him. Because of *them.*

"Hey, you okay?"

Jeremiah's gentle voice pulled her from her thoughts. The others had drifted into smaller clusters. Sammy was talking to Carter.

"They'll be okay for a minute." Jeremiah cupped her elbow. "Can I talk to you in private?"

"Sure."

He guided her to the back of the building—straight into the men's restroom—before shutting the door behind them and flicking on the light.

His gaze held hers. "Tell me what you're thinking."

She couldn't stop the trembling, not with him standing this close. "I'm thinking…I've been wrong all this time."

His brow furrowed. "Do you understand why I have to do this?"

The lump in her throat made it impossible to speak the words *I love you,* so she nodded instead.

With a sharp breath, he gathered her to him, holding her like something precious. Tears burned her retinas, but she held them back, trying to stay strong for him.

At last she managed to force the words out. "I love you, Jeremiah."

He pulled back slightly, delight flashing across his lean features. His hazel eyes smoldered.

"I'm sorry it's taken me so long to realize it."

Moisture rimmed his lashes. "You have no idea how long I've waited to hear that."

She smiled shakily. "Oh, I think I do."

He huffed a laugh. "What happened to limerence?"

She shook her head. "I've been such an idiot. I'm so sorry."

His thumb traced her cheekbone. "No, Professor. You've been protecting your heart. But you don't have to protect it from me. I've loved you since the moment I walked into that Romantic Lit class and saw you consulting your notes. You looked nervous."

She laughed softly at the memory. "That was only my second year of teaching." Then a raw fear bubbled up from inside her. "Jeremiah, what if you don't make it back?"

"I will."

The certainty in his voice, the steadiness of his gaze, calmed her panic. "Promise me?"

"I promise." Ducking his head, he pressed a tender kiss to her lips.

Desire sparked wildly, catching her off guard. Parting her lips, she kissed him back as though her life depended on it. Passion that had smoldered for years ignited with volcanic force. This might be their last chance to be together.

Jeremiah broke the kiss, breath ragged. "This isn't how I wanted to make love to you," he muttered against her throat, tracing kisses along her collarbone.

The romantic balcony scene he'd once described flashed through her mind. "My fault." Four stark walls. A bare lightbulb. A commode. None of it mattered now—only the pulsing need demanding release.

"Not your fault. It wasn't right then." His gaze burned into hers. "Now?"

She nodded. "Now."

Backing her firmly against the door, his solid frame pressed into her softer one. One hand tangled in her hair as he kissed her again, his other hand cupping her breast, teasing her nipple into a peak. Emma slid her hands beneath his T-shirt, reveling in his taut, hot skin, tracing the scars she'd always wondered about. Trembling, she cupped his backside and drew him against her, needing him with a wild ache.

The world dissolved into sensation.

He gathered the hem of her dress, pushing it up to reveal her curves. Sliding his hand between her legs, he stroked her through the damp fabric of her panties. With a desperate whimper, she thrust her hips forward, maddened by the barrier.

Dear Lord. She was going to explode.

Her legs gave out beneath her. Heat bloomed across her skin, feverish and urgent. "Please," she whispered.

With a growl, he lifted her, and she wrapped her legs around his hips. Pressing her against the door, he worked his zipper down, freeing himself. With one tug, he shifted her panties aside, positioning himself at her slick opening.

Their eyes met.

"I don't have a condom."

For a heartbeat, she hesitated. "I'd love to have your baby."

He groaned, laughing roughly. "Why is that such a turn-on?"

"Now, please." She dug her heels into his thighs, urging him forward.

He slid into her. White-hot pleasure bloomed through her entire body. She bit her lip, barely containing her cry as he withdrew and thrust again, sending her soaring.

It was *him*—finally *him*—filling her, touching her, completing her, and *that* sent her spiraling over the edge almost instantly. The climax consumed her like nothing she'd ever experienced before.

And this was how it felt in a dirty bathroom, in the middle of a hostage crisis. She might've laughed if she hadn't been floating in the haze of afterglow.

Jeremiah groaned as he pumped his seed deep inside her, his face buried in her hair. His heart pounded against her chest, wild and beautiful, and she marveled at how profoundly they had touched each other. Slowly, his grip eased, and he lifted his head, giving her a dazed, utterly wrecked look.

"Sorry that happened so fast," he murmured, sounding breathless.

"I'm not sorry." Yet as the future loomed uncertain again, she wished it had lasted longer.

As always, he read her mind. “Next time.”

“There *will* be a next time,” she said, her voice thick with sudden tears. “You promised.”

“I did.” His voice roughened with emotion. He bent to kiss her again, but not before a flicker of doubt clouded his eyes.

CHAPTER 17

Since the SAR team had joined Juliet and Tristan, the third floor of the abandoned office building swarmed with seven additional SEALs. Juliet, having been introduced to each man by name, could recall their unique monikers—each one as distinct as Tristan—and as close to demigods as mortals could get.

They answered to two leaders—Lt. Sasseville, a tall, swarthy officer who could've passed for some Puerto Rican heartthrob she'd seen on TV, and Master Chief Kuzinsky. The latter was the only SEAL who didn't fit the stereotype. Auburn-haired and not even as tall as she was, what he lacked in stature, he made up for in presence. His dark brown—nearly black—eyes carried an unsettling authority, making it difficult not to squirm under his gaze.

The others were Cougar, whipcord thin, from Colorado; Teddy, a hulking Black man; Haiku, of Asian descent; Bronco from Montana with bright blue eyes; and Hack, the tech guy, who immediately began setting up their gear.

Juliet was used to alpha males playing games of dominance. But these SEALs were different. They worked with the kind of quiet, efficient competence that only came with absolute trust in one another. Within minutes, they'd transformed the windowless inner office into a temporary command center.

Hack propped up a two-legged table with stacked garbage cans and spread his equipment across it. Soon the cold glow of his monitor pushed back the surrounding gloom. Moments later, Hack and his leaders were conferring with an OGA operative—*other government agency*—whom Juliet deduced was their CIA contact, the one who had housed them the previous night.

Leaving Hack and Haiku to operate the technology, the others moved into the front room to study the factory through the windows there. As she eavesdropped on their low conversation, Juliet noted something unusual. Whenever someone spoke, the others *listened*—giving due consideration to even the youngest's input.

Bronco had set up a device called a Xaver 1000, aiming it through the window at the old factory. From the terse exchanges, Juliet gathered that the device allowed them to see through walls, even cinderblock ones. She inched closer to the glowing screen, desperate for a glimpse of her sister and niece.

"I think I see them."

As the lieutenant and the master chief rushed over, Juliet edged closer too. Over Kuzinsky's shoulder, several green blobs glimmered on the screen.

"If those are the recovery targets," Lt. Sasseville murmured, "they're not moving at all."

The words chilled her. Was he implying they were dead?

"Agreed." Kuzinsky rubbed his jaw as he stared at the display. "I count maybe ten or so. You?"

"Yes. At least ten."

The low number dropped like ice in Juliet's bloodstream. There ought to be at least thirteen. Her heart started to pound. "May I look?" Maybe she'd recognize Emma, and the fear clawing at her would ease.

Kuzinsky turned his head, meeting her gaze. Compassion flickered in his dark eyes. Stepping aside, he gestured for her to take his place.

Juliet stared at the screem. The glowing outlines of the building sharpened into focus. She was looking into the second story, as if the wall didn't exist—but the blobs didn't look remotely human.

"How do you know those are people?"

"Heat signatures," Kuzinsky replied. "Heads are the easiest to identify." He pointed to a vaguely oval shape, and suddenly she saw it too.

"Oh. Yes." Her pulse leapt. *Emma*. It could be Emma. But there was no way to tell who she was looking at.

"Haiku." Kuzinsky turned, issuing a crisp order. "Advise HQ we've fixed the targets' location. Hack, let the OGA know."

Relief surged through Juliet, rushing and ebbing like a wave. It was too soon to rejoice, but, at last, the rescue effort had officially begun. *Emma and Sammy could be freed tonight.*

Leaving the Xaver 1000 to Lt. Sasseville and Bronco, Juliet scanned the dim room for Tristan. There he was, standing apart, cloaked in shadow. The sunlight outside had faded, but not so much that she missed the slow, encouraging smile he sent her.

She jerked her gaze away, forcing down the rush of affection—and gratitude. *How could she have done this without him?* She couldn't. But the time had come to assert her independence. He wouldn't be available to her once she went home.

Illogically dismayed by the thought, she drifted toward the doorway, where she overheard Hack telling Kuzinsky there were no floor plans for the factory across the street—but he'd found some old photos.

That brought every SEAL but Bronco crowding into the inner office. Though Juliet was gently nudged aside, she managed to find a gap and slip back into the circle, straining for a glimpse of Hack's monitor.

In a halting, New England dialect that made him hard to follow, the tech wizard explained what they were seeing. "Building went up in 1917, right after the Mexican Revolution. Became a bottling plant for Fanta in '56. These are the best I've got—old black-and-white photos. Plus a satellite view."

A hand curled gently around Juliet's elbow. Tristan pulled her forward so she could see better.

She flicked him a grateful glance.

Master Chief pointed at two grainy images displayed side by side. "Both of these are taken on the lower level, facing the back of the building, I believe. Stairs run up the eastern wall—see how the light's falling on the floor?"

Lt. Sasseville nodded. "Same perspective."

Juliet studied the photos. The assembly-line equipment. The thick cinderblock walls. The squat support pillars. It looked impregnable.

"Pretty safe to assume the building hasn't been remodeled since these were taken," Lt. Sasseville murmured.

"Yes, but is the second story one big room like this one?"

"Looked that way on the Xaver."

Master Chief folded his arms. "We need men on that roof tonight to confirm the layout."

"I'll take First Squad," Lt. Sasseville volunteered.

Juliet glanced between the two leaders. They worked together with seamless precision.

"Let's see the satellite."

Hack clicked a key, and a colored photo replaced the black-and-white ones. Every head strained forward as he magnified the view. Juliet realized they were staring straight down at the rooftop.

Master Chief pointed again. "This small structure's probably a stairwell. Be a hell of a lot easier to take stairs down to the hostages than rappel through boarded windows. And if that roof's sturdy enough, we could land a helo up there. Extract the hostages fast."

Juliet's heart thudded. *Please, yes.*

"First Squad will check it out tonight," Lt. Sasseville promised.

Scanning the team, Juliet wondered who First Squad included. Hopefully not Tristan—not that she needed him to stay.

"We'll have to go over the wall, cut the barbed wire," the lieutenant added casually, like he was planning a picnic.

Tristan's voice rumbled behind her. "We picked up some intel today. Witnessed a duty rotation at twelve noon. Might happen again at midnight."

Master Chief consulted his watch. "First Squad moves out as soon as it's dark. Take the Xaver. You'll get a better reading if you lay it face-down on the roof. And when the night shift arrives—count tangos in, count tangos out."

"You want us to take rations and hunker down?" Lt. Sasseville asked. "Save us from having to climb back up."

Juliet frowned. Why would they need to return?

Kuzinsky shook his head. "No. You'll roast when the sun comes up. Come back here at oh-two-hundred."

Juliet's heart lurched. "Wait—you're not going to rescue them tonight?"

Eight pairs of eyes turned to her. She locked her knees to keep from shrinking under their scrutiny.

Master Chief shot Tristan a questioning glance—*Why is this woman here?*

Tristan's hand landed firmly on her shoulder. "I told you, Juliet. We recon first."

"Right." She dug her fingernails into her palms and turned away, holding on to her dignity with both hands. *Don't cry. Don't you dare cry.* They were being professional. Methodical. She should be grateful they were here.

Blinking back the tears, she crossed to the far window in the front office. Bronco gave her a fleeting glance before focusing on his equipment again. Across the street, faint light glowed behind the tinted windows on the factory's lower level. But the rest of the structure had succumbed to darkness, like a tide rising against its walls. She could only imagine what Emma and Sammy were feeling, trapped in that place.

Reconnaissance made absolute sense. She knew that. In her own job, she gathered every piece of evidence before making a move, ensuring airtight cases that sent criminals to prison. But tonight, for the first time, she *understood* how hard it was for her clients to wait.

From now on, she'd be more compassionate when they begged her to act.

Closing her eyes, she tried to send her family a silent, kinetic promise. *Hang in there, Emma and Sammy. We're coming for you.*

Thank God for these intrepid warriors willing to walk into the belly of the beast.

~

The steel door swung open, admitting light into the dark, quiet upper room.

"Jerónimo." One of the *jefe's* men summoned him from the lit stairwell.

It was finally time. Jeremiah had been pacing the length of the second story, shaking off his awareness of Emma's worried gaze as she watched him from her hammock.

He'd needed to focus—to envision every step required to secure his liberation from the *narcos*, then to contact his SEAL team. They were somewhere nearby—he could sense them—unable to pinpoint his exact location, but waiting, hoping, for the least sign from him.

"Un segundo." Stopping first by Emma and Sammy's hammock, Jeremiah bent over them to offer quick assurances. "Everything will be okay."

Emma's fingers dug into his shoulders as he drew her into a fierce embrace.

"Please, be careful," she whispered in his ear.

"Always. Sammy, stay close to your mom." He ruffled her hair.

"¡Jerónimo! Apúrate." The guerrilla swung the muzzle of his rifle into the room, urging haste.

Emma's warm lips pressed a feverish kiss against the corner of his mouth, reminding Jeremiah of their passionate union. He'd promised her it wouldn't be their last—and he intended to keep that promise.

Before he could straighten, Sammy threw an arm around his neck in a quick, unexpected hug. Heartened by the show of affection, he gently extricated himself. "I'll be back soon."

As he crossed toward the exit, he spared a thought for the Glock still immersed in the toilet tank. *Better in there than on me.* The risk of being caught trying to carry it out of the building wasn't worth the added insurance. Besides, unless his escorts numbered more than four, he didn't need a pistol to turn the tables on them.

Stepping into the bright stairwell, Jeremiah cast a backward glance at his fellow hostages, identified only by the whites of their eyes. The door clanged shut between them, severing their gazes. With a tightening of his ribcage, he preceded the *narco* down the stairs into an area reeking of cigarette smoke and tequila.

Craterface sat in the same chair he'd occupied earlier that day, only now he was surrounded by his men—and they were playing poker, by the looks of it. At Jeremiah's descent, they paused to regard him with varying degrees of hostility. When he realized he'd have to wait for them to finish their game, he crossed to Sergio's hammock to check on the patient.

The leader's younger brother lay coated in sweat and lost to hallucination. His infection had progressed so far that it was doubtful any kind of cephalosporin could restore him to health.

A collective groan broke over the table as César produced a winning hand. Pushing back his chair, he ground out his cigarette and ordered two of his men to go find the *medicamento* they needed—and to take *Jerónimo* with them. Two of the biggest, meanest-looking youths swaggered toward him.

"This is Hércules and Toro," César announced in heavily accented English. "*Ju* go *a la farmacia* with them."

Jeremiah assessed his escorts. Both were aptly named—hefty in the shoulders. Both carried assault rifles, along with a second weapon: a pistol for Hércules, a machete for Toro.

In rapid-fire Spanish, César told them not to steal anything aside from the *medicamento*—something about the police chief forgetting their agreement if they destroyed another local business.

Jeremiah made a mental note: local law enforcement was in bed with the narcos. Good to know.

Hércules stood there scowling at him. "*¿Qué si intenta correr?*" he asked his leader. *And if he tries to run?*

César responded in English so that Jeremiah got the message.

"*Ju* shoot him if he runs," then in Spanish added what sounded like, "But only in the leg. I need him alive."

Without warning, César patted Jeremiah down, feeling for weapons, making him glad he'd left the Glock upstairs. "See? He has nothing on him. He's harmless. Go now. I want that medicine by midnight."

While Toro went to open the door, Hércules clapped a hand on Jeremiah's back and propelled him through the exit. In the next instant, Jeremiah was stumbling off the stoop and crossing the dark yard toward the gate. Fresh air—cooler in contrast to the sweltering building—carried the scent of the nearby Gulf. He drew a cleansing breath, clearing the cigarette smoke from his lungs. Freedom had never smelled so good.

How far they had to walk before reaching the pharmacy was anybody's guess, but he hoped it wasn't close. The farther away it was, the more opportunity he'd have to catch his escorts by surprise.

Only the thinnest thread of worry stitched through him at the thought of taking them both down at once. Jeremiah had envisioned every conceivable scenario in his mind and planned accordingly to avoid injuring himself. But luck still played a hand in the scuffle.

Lifting his gaze to the hazy night sky, he spied a few pulsing stars high above them.

Here I am, Universe. Look down on me with favor.

~

"Heads up, Master Chief. We've got movement in the arena."

Lt. Sasseville's warning crackled through the radio, snatching Juliet out of a light slumber. Jerking awake, she realized she'd fallen asleep with her back against the wall between the inner command center and the room with the windows. Her pulse quickened.

The lieutenant, Bronco, Teddy, and Cougar had snuck away to reconnoiter the roof and had reported in twice before: First, to say they'd breached the wall and scaled the building without coming across a single soul. Then, to report that they'd located the recovery targets on the floor below them. While the door providing access to a stairwell was locked, it could be blown open. Assuming the stairs were sturdy enough, they could evacuate the recovery targets to the roof, which appeared solid enough to support a helicopter.

At that second report, Juliet had bitten her tongue to keep from begging Kuzinsky to initiate the rescue immediately. The fact that the SEALs intended to wait twenty-four hours was killing her. When the team fell silent, watching and waiting for the night shift to appear, exhaustion had finally dragged her under.

But now she was wide awake. Lt. Sasseville's warning had Kuzinsky lunging for the radio. "Sit rep?"

"We've got three men exiting the gate."

Those words sent Kuzinsky and Tristan racing into the front room, snatching up helmets before dashing to the windows. As they jammed the headgear on, Juliet rolled to her knees and followed. The helmets, she realized, held night vision goggles, which they flipped down to peer into the street below.

"*Demonios*," the lieutenant muttered, his voice floating from the inner room, edged with disbelief. "I think that's Bullfrog, leaving with two tangos."

What? Juliet lunged for the far window, vying for a view. Only Bullfrog? Where was Emma?

Taking note of her, Tristan tugged her in front of him and pointed. "They just stepped out of the gate, walking away from us. Lean way out. You might see them."

Juliet leaned so far over the sill that a faint breeze lifted a tendril of her hair—but all she could make out were three shadows slipping away into the night.

"I'm sure that's him," Lt. Sasseville insisted. "Send two men in pursuit."

Juliet gripped Tristan's arm. "Ask if they see Emma."

But Kuzinsky had already spun around to dish out orders, and her request disappeared in the commotion.

"Tristan and I are going after them. The rest of you, stay put. And that includes you, ma'am."

Juliet suffered Kuzinsky's pointed stare, then grappled with envy as Tristan checked the inter-team radio on his headset before snatching a rifle from their stash. A terrible thought sliced through her as she watched him swap his white T-shirt for a black one, followed by a tactical vest: Was Bullfrog the only survivor? Were Emma and Sammy already dead?

She swayed on her feet, nausea rising.

As Tristan headed for the door, she snapped out of her stupor and chased after him. Grabbing his arm, she swung him around. "Where's the pistol you promised me?" The words flew out, the first thing that came to mind.

He patted her hand. "Later, Juliet. I need to move before Bullfrog disappears. Stick with Haiku if you want updates."

Be safe. The words jammed in her throat as Tristan joined Master Chief and rushed down the stairs. Their footsteps faded almost instantly.

Taking Tristan's advice, she ducked into the inner office, hoping to overhear him on the radio. Hack and Haiku hovered over their respective stations, focused and silent. No sound issued from the comms.

"Why aren't they talking?" she demanded.

Hack didn't even glance up. Haiku cast her an enigmatic look. "No transmission unless they tab their mics."

Terrific. Torn between watching the street and hovering by the radio, Juliet chose the former. Returning to the front room, she lowered herself onto the nearest sill and stuck her head out the window again. A fleeting shadow caught her eye on the street below—Tristan and Kuzinsky? In the next instant, the street was deserted again.

After ten minutes of nothing, she drifted back to the makeshift command center, certain something would break soon. Hack's steady clicking made her wonder what he was doing. Walking behind him, she stared at two luminous dots drifting across what looked like a spider's web.

"Wait, is that a map? Can you see them?"

He answered her this time. "Yes, ma'am. GPS puts them five blocks northeast of our location."

Holding her breath, Juliet stared at the glowing dots. Tension pinched her shoulders and the back of her neck. But nothing happened—just dots creeping across the screen.

"Will you call me if something happens?"

"Sure." One word, uttered in his peculiar New England accent.

"Thanks." Juliet stalked back to the window, struck by the unnatural silence. The cops she'd performed stakeouts with were noisy by comparison—belching, scratching, sighing heavily. Not these warriors.

At last, Kuzinsky's hushed voice floated out of the inner office, and Juliet dashed back in time to hear Master Chief's report.

"We're ghosting Bullfrog now, about six blocks northeast of the factory. Destination unknown."

"You waiting to find out?"

Lt. Sasseville's voice, chiming in from the rooftop, made Juliet realize all nine SEALs, including Tristan, were wired in, listening. Of course they were.

"Leaving that up to Bullfrog. He doesn't know we're here yet, but that's about to change. Stand by."

"Roger that."

Juliet's pounding heart nearly rocked her off her feet. Even if this wasn't the rescue she'd prayed for, at least Jeremiah would know whether Emma and Sammy had escaped the bus inferno.

They had to have escaped. They *had* to. Being the last surviving member of her family would break her.

Now or later?

Jeremiah queried his gut. The chill pooling in his stomach had kept him docile so far, but his window of opportunity was closing. Where the streets had been deserted, signs of life cropped up as they ventured into better neighborhoods. A motorcycle zipped past. Lights glowed in windows. Somebody out here had a phone he could use, improving his odds of success.

One last time, he rehearsed it in his head: Roll left. Heel-strike to Toro's back while ripping Hércules's rifle away and smashing the butt into his nose. Then finish off Toro before he recovered.

A soft twitter nearly broke his stride. Chills prickled his arms. Tristan's signature whistle. *Hooyah!* The team was here—they had eyes on him!

Toro cocked his ear toward the sound, frowning slightly but continuing to walk. Hércules, oblivious to everything but his own muttered threats, jabbed Jeremiah between the shoulder blades again.

Raising a hand to the back of his neck, Jeremiah gave the signal.

An infrared dot flared on Toro's head. Another, no doubt, glowed on Hércules. Then—*pop-pop*—two suppressed shots. Toro crumpled. Hércules folded with him.

Jeremiah spun and bolted toward the gunfire, adrenaline fueling his malnourished body. A man stepping from his car gaped at him. Jeremiah veered into a side street—and collided with a solid wall of muscle.

Hands shot out, steadying him. The blackened face, helmet, and grin were unmistakable.

"*You're here?*" Jeremiah gasped, pulling Tristan into a hug.

"Got you, brother," Tristan murmured, clasping him tightly. He swung him toward a faint light at the alley's far end. "Let's go."

Jeremiah sagged into a crouch. "Haven't eaten much," he rasped.

Tristan tore open a wrapper and handed him a power bar. "Eat."

Jeremiah obeyed between breaths. "How'd you find me?"

"Your watch. Juliet and I tracked it to a pawn shop. You owe me four hundred bucks."

That casual jab grounded him. If they'd found his watch, the team was close. Sure enough, boots crunched behind them, and Master Chief materialized out of the darkness, waving them deeper into the alley. "Move."

Fifteen minutes later, Jeremiah was staggering up the stairs of an abandoned building. By the third floor, he wasn't sure if his legs would hold—until a female body launched into him, hugging him so fiercely he thought of—

"Emma?" His heart twisted. But it was her sister, Juliet.

"You're here," she whispered fiercely, digging her nails into his arms, wild with fear. "Tell me they're alive."

Emotion broke over him. He gripped her arms tightly. "They're alive. Emma and Sammy are fine."

But a darker certainty churned in his gut. They were alive *for now.* Something evil was coming. He could feel it like a storm surging ever closer. But he wouldn't say that to Juliet.

"They're going to be okay. We're going to get them out."

Lt. Sasseville's voice crackled on the radio, calling for Jeremiah. With Juliet still clinging to him, he towed her toward the handset Haiku held out and took it.

"Welcome back, Bullfrog," the lieutenant greeted. "Start talking."

With four SEALs gathered around, Jeremiah summarized the entire story: their capture, Joe of Newark's injury, César Salvador's volatility. "We have to go in tonight," he urged.

Suddenly, a vivid vision crashed over him. Chaos. Blood. *No!*

He gripped his forehead.

"What is it?" Tristan's voice cut through the haze. "What do you see?"

The room quieted. Even Lt. Sasseville went silent on the line. Whenever Bullfrog got a hit, they listened.

Jeremiah glanced at Juliet. He didn't want to scare her, not with what he'd seen. Instead, he offered the next best reason. "If César's men don't come back by dawn, he'll know something's up. He might try to move the hostages—or kill them, like he did the others on that bus."

Juliet's gasp filled him with remorse. There was no gentle way to say it.

Feeling Emma's pull like a tether, Jeremiah broke free of everyone and walked into the adjoining office. Two windows stared down at the factory across the street. He picked it out easily, his fists curling with urgency. *Hold on, Professor. I'm here.*

Kuzinsky joined him. "You know I hate being rushed," the master chief growled, but his tone held grudging acceptance.

"We have to go tonight," Jeremiah whispered.

Kuzinsky exhaled hard. "Hooyah. Get back on the horn. You knkow more than any of us."

Hope kindled. They were doing this. The hostages would soon be free.

Jeremiah rejoined his teammates with a plan formulating. "What time is it?"

"Thirty-three minutes to midnight."

Not much time left. "The next shift appears in half an hour. What if we show up wearing their jackets, posing as them? If we can't get in that way, then we force our way in. First Squad blows the roof access just as we're at the door. With two entry points, the narcos will flee out the rear where Haiku and Hack will clean house."

"Yes, do it," Juliet urged, her voice so like Emma's that it made his heart ache.

Lt. Sasseville's voice broke through the headset. "Happy to oblige… wait. What the fuck now?"

Bronco's voice cut in, tense. "We've got company."

Every SEAL except Haiku bolted for the front room, vying for a view out of the windows.

Jeremiah froze at the sight three vehicles idling at the factory gate. A shadowy figure hopped from the truck bed, bolt-cutters in hand. The chain hit the ground. The convoy rolled inside the walls, winding up beside the factory like a snake.

Panic hollowed Jeremiah's chest. *No. Not now.*

Kuzinsky's voice rasped over the comms. "How many?"

"Seven," Lt. Sasseville answered grimly.

"Shit," Tristan hissed.

From behind them, Juliet made a choked sound of despair.

"Heavily armed," Lt. Sasseville added. "They might be here for César—or not. Wait… isn't that—?" A pause. Then: "No fucking way. One of them's El Cuchillo. Or his twin."

Silence gripped the room like a vise. El Cuchillo. The narco lord who'd escaped prison last year. Their white whale.

Kuzinsky moved first, pivoting on his heel and storming back into the office. "Hack, call the OGA. Find out if El Cuchillo's got a presence in Mérida. If it's confirmed, I want ten more shooters here within the hour. We're not letting that bastard slip away again."

Jeremiah's knees buckled. He slid down the wall, heart pounding, bile burning his throat.

This wasn't a rescue mission anymore—not for the brass. Not for the CIA. It was about El Cuchillo now.

He dropped his head into his hands. *I'm so sorry, Emma.*

CHAPTER 18

At the sound of vehicles pulling into the yard, César Salvador glanced up from his brother's waxen face, a splinter of alarm sliding beneath his skin. Hércules and Toro should have been the ones showing up with the medicine, but they hadn't left in a vehicle. So who was that outside?

"*¿Quién es?*" He waved one of his men to the window to check. Only a few loyal men held keys to the gate, and none of them owned vehicles.

Manolo, who'd imbibed a fifth of rum over cards, rolled out of his hammock and staggered to the window. Peering through the adhesive tint, he stared for a moment, then turned back with a look of alarm. "*Es El Cuchillo.*"

The dreaded words thinned César's blood. He swung a panicked gaze around the filthy lower level of the building. Of all the times for El Cuchillo to drop in unexpectedly—this was the worst. Not only had his soldiers made a mess of their living space, but most of them were wasted, sleeping off their last hour as they waited to be relieved of duty.

What did El Cuchillo want with him at this hour? Surely not his fealty money. He had to know it was too soon for that.

A crisp knock at the door left César no time to conceal the steel safe standing conspicuously against the wall. On leaden feet, he crossed the room, summoned a wide, plastic smile, and threw the door—and his arms—wide open.

"*¡Jefe!*" It was best to make El Cuchillo feel welcome. After all, without the overlord's protection, the police chief would have chased César out of Mérida months ago. Beckoning the older man inside, he embraced him with as much warmth as he could pretend to feel for a man who would just as soon kill him as look after his interests. "Come in, all of you."

All but one man, who turned his back to guard the entrance, tramped inside.

The much-feared *capo* stopped just inside the threshold and looked around. Envisioning the room through his bespectacled eyes, César cringed.

"You must forgive the filth my men have made, *jefe*. Manolo, secure the door. Pedro, Suturo, clean off the table. Get El Cuchillo a chair. *Rápido!*"

Fussing and clucking, he escorted the *gran capo* to the table as his men worked desperately to clear it. For his part, El Cuchillo remained stoically silent. Disdaining to sit, his gaze fell upon Sergio, lying half-dead in his hammock.

"What's wrong with your brother?"

The question speared César with grief. "An infection," he admitted. "Some of my men have gone to fetch medicine for him. Please, sit," he added, gesturing to the chair he had pulled out. "Can I get you something—tequila?"

El Cuchillo refused to sit. His hair—it had turned silver since César had last seen him, when they were together in prison—glinted under the halogen lights as he stared at César with a faint frown. It dawned on César that this wasn't a social visit. Worse, El Cuchillo's men had positioned themselves throughout the room, surrounding his inebriated narcos in a menacing semi-circle. Every one of them bore sneers of contempt and scars to prove their mettle. An assortment of weapons bristled from their bodies. César's greatest ambition was to become one of them.

"I have come for my fifty percent."

César gulped. Sure enough, this wasn't a social visit. "Of course. Of course, *Tío.* But you must know it's too soon." He spread his hands in a gesture of appeasement. "It's only been a few days that I have held these *gringos.* Not all of the ransom money has been paid—in fact, very little."

The spectacles that gave El Cuchillo such an intelligent demeanor magnified the chilling ruthlessness in his muddy-brown eyes. "How much do you have?" He fingered the knife at his waist while asking the question—a reminder of how he'd come across his fearful nickname.

César glanced toward his safe with dismay. Every last dollar he had stolen from the tourists—the money he'd made pawning their jewelry, and every withdrawal he'd managed to get from the captives' bank cards—would be taken from him tonight. His heart broke at the thought of parting with it.

He would have to comfort himself with the sum he'd forced the old couple to transfer to his secret bank account.

"All that I have is yours." He managed to sound sincere, though his men gaped in astonishment. Please, even in their sotted states, they ought to realize the reason for his charity. El Cuchillo would just as soon slaughter them all as put up with any competition. If they wanted his protection, it would have to be on *his* terms.

Crossing to his safe, César toggled the lock, swung it open, and gathered up the contents before carrying them to the table, where he spread the bills to make his booty appear greater than it really was. He gestured to it while facing his boss. "Help yourself, *compadre.*"

Without any outward expression, El Cuchillo finally sat down and proceeded to count the bills.

"Suturo," César hissed, "get him a drink!"

As Suturo laid out two shot glasses, filling them from a bottle that trembled in his hands, César slipped into the chair next to his overlord.

"How is your wife?" Determination to engender feelings of

camaraderie in the formidable older man made him bold. Back in jail, they had gotten to know each other rather well.

El Cuchillo had counted the fifty-dollar bills already. "She is sick." He began to count the twenties.

"Don't tell me!" César professed his dismay. "I'm so sorry to hear it. Give her this money. Tell her it is from her husband's most loyal friend."

With a snort of disbelief, El Cuchillo kept right on counting.

Hack looked up from his computer monitor. "OGA says they've secured the perimeter, Master Chief. They've already picked up two of César's night shift and plan to snag the rest. With the gate open, we're cleared to approach the building. No need to disguise ourselves."

In the muted light of the temporary operations center, Juliet's heart thudded painfully as she watched Kuzinsky jam three spare magazines into the loops of his webbed belt. What was supposed to be a simple rescue had turned into an inevitable firefight—one where the primary objective was to capture or kill a high-value target. No one had even mentioned her sister and niece since El Cuchillo arrived on the scene. She wallowed in dismay.

"Bring all the firepower you can carry," Kuzinsky ordered his underlings. "You remember what happened in Comitán."

The comment wreaked havoc on Juliet's imagination. El Cuchillo had obviously put up a fight the last time they'd taken him. The fact that Kuzinsky expected a similar outcome now left her reeling.

"The OGA wants access to our radio frequency," Hack said.

Kuzinsky froze.

"Oh, come on," Tristan protested. "We don't need them meddling in our operation."

Kuzinsky gestured to Hack. "Give it to them. Don't forget who we're dealing with."

Haiku, who hadn't said a word until then, muttered under his breath, "Only the biggest, baddest *capo* in Mexico."

A shiver traced Juliet's spine. Hack shut his laptop, and the room went dark. As he began sliding it into his pack, she realized he was leaving, too. Wait—were they all going to jump into the fray and just leave her here?

She blocked their path toward the stairs. "What about my sister and niece?" Her voice shook with emotion. "Who's going to protect them when the bullets start flying?"

With an apologetic glance at Kuzinsky, Tristan quickly made his way to her.

"Listen." He pulled her back to the front room so the others wouldn't overhear. "No one's forgotten about your sister or the other hostages. We've got this covered. You don't need to worry."

She gasped in affront. "I don't need to worry? Did you really just say that to me?" Tristan's face, slathered in camo paint, looked so different from the man she'd spent the past week with. He sounded like a stranger now—like a soldier doing his job, with no emotional connection to her or her family.

Curling her fingers into fists, she dug her nails into her palms, fighting to stay calm. "You're already outnumbered. You know El Cuchillo is heavily armed, and he's going to resist. Who's going to protect the hostages if you're all busy shooting each other?"

"We'll protect them." To her relief, he gripped her upper arms and gave her a reassuring shake. "We've done this a million times. We know what we're doing."

"Let me help." Unwelcome tears surged into her eyes. "I really want to help."

He shook his head, grimacing. "You can't help us, Juliet. I hate to say this, but you'd only be a distraction."

That word again. She wished she'd never used it in the first place.

"Here. Take this." He pressed cool metal into her palm.

Recognizing the contours of a nine-millimeter, her fingers closed instantly around its reassuring weight. Finally, Tristan was keeping his promise. The thought of using it to kill the men who'd stolen her family instantly dried her tears.

He caught her chin between his thumb and forefinger. "Only

use it to defend yourself." His tone turned stern. "You're going to be up here alone—for a while, anyway. If anyone tries to join you, shoot them."

Like hell I'll be up here. Releasing the clip stealthily, she was heartened to find it full of bullets.

"Let's go," Kuzinsky barked from the other room. "We're moving out."

Tristan still gripped her chin. "Don't do anything stupid." He held her gaze, as if sensing her private thoughts.

She knocked his arm away, suddenly angry with him. "You promised me we'd get Emma and Sammy back."

"Hey." Her vehemence clearly surprised him. "We will. It's all good, honey. Everything's going to work out. You'll see." He went to hug her, but she pushed him away.

"Go."

With a sigh and a searching look, he turned and disappeared out of sight—and seconds later, out of hearing.

"And don't call me *honey*," she muttered, but no one was left to hear her.

Right then, it was crystal clear that despite the camaraderie she'd enjoyed with Tristan, despite his ability to make things seem better than they were, and even in the face of her devastating attraction to him, they had no future together. Even if she were the kind of woman to indulge in a long-term relationship—which she wasn't—she could never do it with a man who answered to orders before he followed through on personal commitments.

She'd thought they had an understanding. She'd thought Tristan could be counted on to ensure Emma and Sammy emerged from this nightmare unscathed.

But he couldn't. She would have to make sure of that herself.

~

"Two thousand twenty-three." El Cuchillo laid the last dollar bill down on the pile he'd created while counting the money. Helping himself to a second shot of tequila, he leaned back in his chair and sighed.

To César's hopeful eye, he appeared slightly more relaxed.

But then the *capo* shook his head. "This is not nearly enough money to ensure my protection. You will have to give me more. Much more."

César's chest hurt. "And I will, *Tío*. I will." He rushed to reassure his boss. "Soon the ransom money will come flowing in. I will give you fifty percent on top of all this. Please, it's yours. Buy something special for your wife."

Hmph. By the glint in El Cuchillo's dark eyes, César could tell the *capo* saw straight through his generosity to the fear that inspired it. "I tell you what." Without warning, he slammed his shot glass down on the table, making César jump. "I will take three female hostages with me now, and leave you with all the ransom money."

On the surface, the offer struck César as a good deal. The ransom notes had all been sent. Money would be transferred into his secret account whether the captives upstairs lived or not. On the other hand, he'd gone to a lot of trouble to capture those Americans. They were all his—especially the women.

"It will cost you less to feed them," the *capo* added.

Yes, but César had planned to sell them to a pimp after the ransom came in. Now El Cuchillo would do that instead, profiting from the price they commanded. White women had to be worth more on the black market than he'd realized.

Regret warred with greed. For a split second, César weighed his odds of overcoming El Cuchillo and his posse—keeping both the money and the women for himself.

But in his peripheral vision, he caught the *capo*'s henchmen tensing, anticipating a backlash. Given their superior firepower and fighting experience—versus that of César's wasted, good-for-nothing hoodlums and his unconscious brother—he stood zero chance of winning such a battle.

"Of course, *jefe*. You should have asked me for the women earlier. All that I have is yours." He spread his arms convincingly. "Come, *come*." Pushing back his chair, he gestured for the *capo* to rise and join him. "Inspect the women for yourself and pick any three who please you."

El Cuchillo's dark gaze slid over him, searching for weapons, but César carried none. After calling two of his most trusted men to join them, the *capo* rose and followed.

On the way up the stairs, César turned and called down, "Manolo, turn on the upstairs lights!"

~

The lights blinked on unexpectedly, so glaring that Emma flinched and threw up a hand to shield her eyes.

She'd been lying with Sammy in her hammock, wide awake, listening with apprehension to the voices penetrating the cement floor. The fear that Jeremiah might come to harm and never make it back kept her from falling asleep. People had entered the building recently—could *he* be one of them? Maybe he'd brought the local police with him. The voices she could hear were authoritative, spoken in *Spanish*.

But there'd been no sign of the purple smoke Jeremiah had mentioned, nor of the Navy SEALs who were supposed to rescue them.

The sudden grating open of the steel door filled her with relief. She rolled carefully out of the hammock, loath to wake her daughter. But the men stepping into the room didn't include Jeremiah. The breath backed up in Emma's lungs, and she froze, petrified, as the guerrilla leader entered, accompanied by three strangers.

As they swaggered into the midst of the groggy, blinking hostages, Emma glanced back at Sammy, who was also waking up. *Oh, God.* "Don't move," she whispered, pressing a hand to Sammy's shoulder to keep her still.

Emma focused on the man in glasses, and a fingernail of fear raked her spine. Unlike the thugs who'd held them for days, this man wore a lightweight trench coat over slacks and a dress shirt. His silvery hair and spectacles made him look older than his smooth complexion suggested. *This is a capo,* she realized, recalling the

Spanish word for a drug lord. Behind his lenses, his soulless gaze touched on her unkempt hair and yellow dress before sliding away to inspect the others.

His attention snagged briefly on Joe, recognizing him as potentially dangerous, until he noticed the injury that kept him helpless in his hammock. Joe's grim expression confirmed Emma's worst fears.

Shifting, she tried to block the *capo's* view of Sammy, who lay as still as a statue pretending to sleep. But the newcomer took note of Emma's protective stance and, turning back, dropped a considering gaze on the sleeping girl. Emma's hands curled into fists as she willed him to move away. Casting her a smirk that turned her heart to ice, he turned and ventured deeper into the room, César right behind him, the frightening thugs still guarding the door.

Fear-filled silence had fallen over the hostages as they no doubt realized the extent of their helplessness with Jeremiah gone and Joe debilitated. All of them except Sammy had sat up when the lights came on. Some, like Emma, were now on their feet, driven by sheer survival instinct.

As the *capo* approached Carter's family, the youth edged protectively in front of his womenfolk, his eyes wild, his chest heaving like he'd just run a mile.

The *capo* strained to see over Carter's head and caught sight of pretty Katherine, his youngest aunt. He pointed her out to César. "*I'll take her*," he said in *Spanish*. Then, as if as an afterthought, he swung around and added, "plus the redhead and the sleeping girl."

"*Claro*," César agreed, with only the slightest hesitation.

The twist of events froze Emma where she stood. She willed herself to wake up from what had to be a nightmare. Jeremiah was supposed to be here. He had *promised* he'd be back tonight.

With a jerk of his silvery head, the newcomer signaled for his henchmen to collect the women he'd selected. As they moved forward, Joe tried to climb out of his hammock, only to fall back with a roar of helplessness and pain.

"No!" Emma threw herself over Sammy, who stopped pretending to be asleep.

"Mommy?"

Across the room, instead of holding his ground to protect his aunt, Carter clapped a hand over his mouth and fled for the bathroom.

Hands like iron bands clamped around Emma's arms and lifted her off Sammy, who screamed in protest.

"It's okay. It's okay, baby." Emma's hoarse voice sounded like a stranger's. But she knew it wasn't okay. She and Sammy were about to be carted off to God knew where. They'd be sold to some pimp in the slums of Mérida, pumped full of narcotics—and then her precious baby girl would be forced to endure the perversions of adult men.

With a surge of superhuman strength, Emma wrested free of her captor's grip. Issuing a cry she'd never made before, she backhanded him. Her knuckles struck his hard skull with a satisfying *thwack*, but the blow scarcely fazed him, even as it sent pain streaking up her arm. He grinned at her protest, revealing a mouthful of gold teeth. And then he retaliated, slapping her so hard she sprawled across the floor.

"No!" Sammy screamed, fighting to get to her mother.

César and his vile friend chuckled in amusement as Emma lifted a hand to her ringing ear.

With a vitriolic curse, Joe lurched out of his hammock again, but the thug who'd struck Emma decked him too. The cop staggered into Cheryl's arms, and they both collapsed onto the floor, where Joe lay limp and unconscious. He must have passed out from the pain.

Sammy, managing to break free of her captor, dropped to her knees next to her. "Mom!"

Emma clutched her daughter close, but the brute who'd hit her was already coming to snatch Sammy again. Across the room, Katherine's two sisters fought like wildcats in her defense, while the *capo* chuckled at their furious struggles.

Suddenly, the bathroom door burst open. Carter emerged with something in his hands.

Emma glanced—and gasped.

Crack! A circle of red blossomed on the chest of the goon right in front of Emma. With a look of stunned surprise, the man with the gold teeth pitched face-first onto the cement floor.

César and the *capo* whirled toward the unexpected threat, the latter producing a weapon from beneath his trench coat. Carter fired again. This time, it was César who hit the floor, sprawling at the feet of the stranger, who—with a ruthless snarl—squeezed the trigger of his wicked-looking pistol.

The third discharge rang in Emma's ears. Carter staggered back, his weapon skittering across the floor. Striking the wall behind him, he slid down its length with a stunned expression, leaving a streak of scarlet in his wake.

"Carter!" his mother screamed, running for him. The third goon took advantage of her absence to catch Katherine in his burly arms.

The bespectacled newcomer turned his cold gaze on Emma. The instant their eyes met, she knew his intention.

"No!"

But it was too late. He was already crossing toward them, and with strength that belied his age, he snatched Sammy from her grasp, lifting her off the floor, out of reach. Emma scrambled after them, managing to seize Sammy's ankle.

"Mom!" Sammy wailed as the *capo* yanked her foot free and headed for the door.

Heedless of her own bare feet, Emma rose up like a tigress and chased them to the stairs—where they ran into the rest of the guerrillas, who had swarmed up the steps after hearing the gunfire. At the sight of César splayed dead on the floor, Emma's young captors hesitated just long enough for her to push past them, pursuing the silver-haired devil down the stairs to the lower level.

No way in hell was he taking her daughter—not without taking her, too.

Jeremiah stood on the stoop of the factory, poised to rap on the door. The quiet emanating from the lower level kept his adrenaline pumping. What the hell was happening in there? Why was light leaking around the plywood windows on the second floor? Were César and El Cuchillo gloating over their captives? He was about to find out.

Blowing out a breath, he lifted his hand and issued a swift, hard knock.

If only he were coming down off the roof with First Squad. Then he could be the first to reach Emma and Sammy, who would need protection the moment the door opened and chaos erupted.

César Salvador was anticipating *Jerónimo's* return, so here Jeremiah was, clutching a smoke grenade under the pretext of bringing back the cephalosporin, while El Cuchillo's man—who'd stood in that same spot moments earlier—now lay dead, courtesy of Tristan's broken-neck handiwork.

Heart galloping, Jeremiah counted the seconds. *Come on.* As soon as the door opened, he would toss the smoke grenade, blinding the occupants in a haze of purple smoke. Then Tristan and Master Chief, stationed at either corner of the building, would come in blazing. Tristan would hand him a weapon, and together they would take down everyone inside, while Hack and Haiku picked off squirters trying to flee through the rear door.

Simultaneously, First Squad would blow the lock off the roof entrance and surge down the stairs, shooting anyone in their path. Half would split off to locate and protect the hostages, while the others pressed forward, aiding second squad in wiping out the narcos.

The element of surprise was theirs. They'd rehearsed similar hostage scenarios dozens of times. *So why am I standing here in a cold sweat with my heart about to jump out of my chest?*

No one was answering his knock, for one thing. The ominous quiet suggested the key players were all upstairs, and that could not be good.

He lifted his hand to knock again but froze at the sharp *crack* of a gunshot.

The hell? He whipped his head toward Kuzinsky, crouched with Tristan behind El Cuchillo's van. *What now?* he gestured.

Crack. A second shot. Then a third—distinctly different weapon.

What in blazes was going on up there?

Jeremiah signaled again. *Blow the door?* Shouts of alarm floated from the second floor. A woman screamed in denial.

Jesus. That was Emma!

Kuzinsky motioned for Jeremiah to join him behind the van. Loath to move away from Emma instead of toward her, Jeremiah forced himself off the stoop and dropped beside his leader on the far side of the vehicle. "We need to get in there, Master Chief. All hell's breaking loose."

"I know. But you're not dressed for a fight. Suit up." He shoved a bag of gear toward Jeremiah and tabbed his mic. "Moving to Plan B. Plan B," he repeated for the benefit of the others.

Riskier for the hostages, Plan B entailed First Squad coming down from the roof and driving the tangos out of the building while second squad ambushed the enemy on their way out. With First Squad outnumbered three to one inside, the hostages would have to fend for themselves.

Raging inwardly at the unraveling of Plan A, Jeremiah yanked on a tactical vest and helmet, then snatched up his semi-automatic rifle. He sprinted toward the alley flanking the right side of the building while Tristan peeled off to cover the left. Master Chief stayed put, coordinating.

The weight of Jeremiah's rifle offered modest comfort. As he switched on his inter-team radio, Master Chief's order echoed in his earpiece. "First Squad, blow the door."

A faint *pop* sounded above as the hinges detonated. Seconds later, semi-automatic gunfire ripped through the building. *Come on, guys.* Exclamations of surprise gave way to return fire as the narcos fought back.

Squeezing his eyes shut, Jeremiah pictured a dome of protection forming around Emma and the other hostages.

He wasn't surprised to hear the front door burst open as César's youths fled the ambush. Jeremiah snapped his eyes open, raised his rifle, and swung around the building's corner, ready to aid Tristan and Master Chief in cutting down the squirters. Three young men—including the fat youth who'd stolen Jeremiah's watch—fell hard to the dirt, their sprint toward the gate abruptly over.

Haiku's soft voice came through his earpiece. "Two more squirters down in back."

Jeremiah processed that. So far, only César's green recruits were among the casualties. El Cuchillo's men—hard-bitten criminals used to fighting with their backs against the wall—would likely dig in and fight to the death. *Terrific.*

The lights in the building blinked out without warning. Darkness swallowed the structure, the yard, everything. The front door slammed shut, a bolt grinding home. Tense silence followed, broken only by the raw, terrified sobs of two women.

The hair on Jeremiah's forearms prickled as Emma's voice rose above the cries. *Holy hell.* What were they doing to her? And why was her voice coming from the lower level? Had the captives been moved downstairs?

"First Squad, sitrep," Master Chief's calm voice filtered into Jeremiah's ear.

Holding his breath, Jeremiah waited, dreading confirmation of his worst fears.

Lt. Sasseville answered grimly, "We've secured seven recovery targets up here. One's been shot—a teenage boy. We've also got the wounded police officer. Could use your help, Bullfrog. The kid's bleeding bad."

Carter had taken a bullet. Jeremiah's stomach lurched, even as his brain did the math. Seven targets secured. He tabbed his mic. "Is Emma there?" The raw edge in his voice turned it to sandpaper.

"Sorry, Bullfrog. They tell me the *capo*'s got her downstairs. Her daughter too. And somebody's sister."

Shock hit Jeremiah like a gut punch, paralyzing him where he stood. Emma, in the hands of the most ruthless *capo* in Mexico. El Cuchillo wouldn't hesitate to kill her to save his own skin. *No. God, no.*

"Haiku, call in that helo. We need a medevac for the kid and the cop," Kuzinsky said, steady as ever, dispelling the worst of Jeremiah's paralysis. "Lieutenant, have Cougar stabilize the boy while we re-evaluate this op."

"Copy that, Master Chief."

Bronco's voice broke in. "We can still blind them with smoke grenades, but we won't be able to tell who's friendly. If they use the hostages as shields, we might shoot one by mistake."

"I realize that. We need a new strategy. All right, men. Think. I want to hear all our options."

CHAPTER 19

Juliet scraped the tender skin on the undersides of her arms as she slid, back pressed against the stucco wall, toward the open gate.

The sudden burst of gunfire from inside the factory had driven her out of the nearby office building and into the dark street, where she blended into the shadows in the oversized, dark clothing left behind by the SEALs.

As she tiptoed through the darkness, a stubborn tendril of her hair escaped the cap she'd jammed over her head to conceal her hair. With the CIA crawling all over this neighborhood, somebody had to have caught sight of her by now. She could get shot at any second.

The thrill of courting danger kept her heart racing—almost as fast as it had two nights ago, when Tristan had her writhing, panting, begging him to let her come.

Stop it. This was *so* not the time for that memory.

Remarkably, she reached the open gate unimpeded, peeked into the yard—and froze.

A chill swept up her spine.

If Hollywood needed a ready-made set for a horror film, this was it. The dark factory resembled an abandoned insane asylum, its barred, boarded windows exuding menace. Bodies lay scattered across the dirt yard, surrounded by ten-foot walls topped with barbed wire. The number of dead narcos told her the SEALs were hard at work.

But the gunfire had stopped. Now the building stood silent. *Was it over?* Had they rescued the hostages?

Then she heard it—a woman's wail penetrating the thick walls.

I know that voice. Cold dread tightened her throat. *Oh, my God. It's Emma.*

Movement near the van parked out front caught her eye. Juliet jerked her head back behind the wall, pulse roaring—until she recognized the shape protruding from the figure's helmet. Night vision goggles. The shadow was a SEAL.

Even so, he might mistake her for the enemy and shoot on sight. On the other hand, if she didn't make her move now, she'd be stuck here—exposed, vulnerable, unable to help Emma.

Her choice was clear.

The *capo* dropped Sammy onto a chair in the dark, downstairs chamber. Katherine, identifiable by her grimy white shirt, was already there—curled into a fetal position on the floor, her back pressed to the wall.

Emma skidded to her knees beside the chair, wrapping her arms around Sammy. "I won't let you go. I won't let you go." Clinging to her daughter, she flinched as the cold barrel of a pistol gouged her scalp, the scar-faced criminal pressing the muzzle against her skull.

"Don't let them move." The *capo*'s harsh order was directed to someone behind her. With that, he removed the pistol and stalked toward a window by the door, where a layer of dark film blocked his view—until he peeled it back with impatient fingers.

Think! You have to protect Sammy. But her brain was sluggish, numb with terror, while her heart hammered against her breastbone, beating so hard she thought it might tear free.

And then—*Jeremiah.* The firefight she'd heard upstairs could only mean one thing. His SEALs were here. Coming down from the roof... Hope surged through her, piercing the fog of panic. Carter might live now. The others—they might all be saved.

But for her, for Sammy, for Katherine—it was too late.

Their lives now hung in the hands of half a dozen ruthless killers who melted into the shadows of the room, dark shapes taking defensive positions all around them.

In the inky darkness, she could hear them better than she could see them—some slamming fresh magazines into their rifles, others peeling back the tinted film to sneak glances outside. Surrender wasn't in their vocabulary. They would fight until the last round was spent or until they fell. And the hostages—they were nothing more than collateral, trapped in the crossfire.

A harsh voice dragged her attention back to the *capo*. He stood by the window, barking into his phone.

"Apúrate," she heard him snarl before pocketing the device—*hurry*.

A realization struck like a blow. *He's got reinforcements coming.*

Cold dread crushed her, stealing the breath from her lungs. She stared at the *capo*, shocked by the depth of his evil. Just then, his attention shifted to the hammock where César's brother lay comatose, succumbing to infection.

Emma barely had time to grasp his intent before the *capo* chambered a round and, without hesitation, fired point-blank into the man's chest. The limp form jerked once inside the hammock and then sagged like a broken doll.

Sammy whimpered at the sharp report, and Emma instinctively blocked her daughter's view, turning her face away, even as shock drained her strength away. *God.* The *capo*'s utter depravity defied comprehension.

A high-pitched ringing filled her ears. Spots danced before her eyes. *Not now.* She fought the rising blackness. *This is no time to faint.*

But *doom* pressed down, thick and suffocating. How could this end any other way but badly? Jeremiah's counsel to stay positive was a cruel memory now, easily swallowed by the tidal wave of despair crashing over her.

Positive thinking can't touch evil like this. No mantra, no mental trick could alter the reality of this nightmare.

Life was a gamble. Always had been. From the moment her parents died to Eddie's betrayal, Emma had learned that lesson the hard way. Hope was just another lie the heart told itself to survive.

But one plea burned through her soul, fierce as a mother's love.

Not Sammy. Please, God. Take me—but not my baby girl.

"Master Chief!"

Hack's urgent voice cut through their brainstorming like a blade. Jeremiah straightened off the wall, adrenaline igniting in his bloodstream.

"Go ahead, Hack," Kuzinsky snapped.

"OGA reports two armored police trucks just smashed through their checkpoint. Headed your way!"

A beat of ominous silence filled Jeremiah's earpiece. His heart spiked, galloping in his chest.

"It could be the law responding to the gunfire," Kuzinsky offered, but even he didn't sound convinced. "Could use the backup."

"Doubt that's gonna happen," Tristan broke in, his voice dark with dread. "The detective in Playa del Carmen said the police chief here is dirty."

Jeremiah cut in. "Confirmed. I overheard one of the narcos say the same thing. Local law's been helping these bastards."

As if on cue, sirens began wailing in the distance—closing in fast.

"Sonofabitch," Kuzinsky muttered. "I think El Cuchillo's about to get sprung by the local police. Hack, tell OGA to move in closer. Don't they have eyes in the sky that can stop those trucks? Second squad, fall back to the rear. Tristan, cover me."

Jeremiah obeyed, starting toward the rear of the building—but paused, glancing back. What the hell was Master Chief doing?

Kuzinsky was rolling from vehicle to vehicle, slashing tires, crippling every getaway car in sight.

Smart. They won't get far, even if the cops break through.

The sirens screamed louder, closer, closing in like wolves on the hunt.

"They're almost here, Master Chief," Jeremiah warned into his headset, his voice tight.

Then—silence.

The sirens cut off, replaced by the deep-throated roar of approaching engines. Heavy. Armored. The cavalry had arrived. But they weren't here to save the good guys.

~

Oh, shit.

Two emergency vehicles barreling up the road turned Juliet's mouth to dust. If she stayed where she was, she'd be caught in the glare of their headlights. But if she darted into the yard, she'd risk getting shot by the SEALs. The only chance she had was that they'd recognize her before pulling the trigger.

Ripping the cap off her head, she sprinted through the open gate, veering hard toward the nearest cover. No gunfire. No shouted warning. Nothing.

She dove into a narrow crevice between the wall and a propped-up steel sign—rusted, sharp-edged, just big enough for a child—or a desperate woman—to hide behind.

Headlights bloomed across the street, twin beams sweeping over the factory walls as one armored vehicle, then another, roared through the gate and skidded to a halt.

Out of the corner of her eye, she caught motion—the SEAL she'd glimpsed earlier rolling out from under the van and disappearing around the far side of the building.

Juliet's breath hissed between her teeth. *CIA? Please be CIA.*

A harsh *clang* broke the air as a pair of mounted searchlights blazed to life, their beams slicing across the yard, pausing on the sprawled, broken bodies, searching for survivors—or shooters.

"*¡Policía!*" a voice barked over a loudspeaker, killing her hope on the spot.

Not CIA. Local cops. And Canché had warned them—the police chief here was dirty.

Another burst from the loudspeaker. Juliet strained to decipher the rapid Spanish. The police were ordering those inside to surrender or die. Simple terms. Brutal terms.

Her heart climbed into her throat. *Please don't see me.*

Curling tighter behind the rusted metal, she shrank into the shadows, a silent prayer locked behind clenched teeth.

Jeremiah heard the armored truck doors clang open. Booted feet hit the ground in the front yard. The police had arrived in force to help El Cuchillo escape. It was only a matter of time before they rounded the building, where his four-man squad had two options—go up and over the formidable wall or use the lines First Squad had climbed to get to the rooftop.

"First Squad," Master Chief spoke in his quietest voice, "drop us a couple of lines."

Yes, the second option made more sense.

"I'm on it." Bronco's drawl was unmistakable.

A second later, the end of a black nylon rope slapped the ground next to Jeremiah's boots. He could sense the police advancing cautiously around the building. He'd have to shimmy up quickly, taking the rope with him to avoid being spotted.

A sudden *Ka-BOOM* of a grenade detonating in the yard spiked his adrenaline.

Where the hell had *that* come from? No time to look. It could only be their OGA counterparts arriving—per their request—just in time to hamper the corrupt police chief's rescue efforts. Yes, please. The thought of El Cuchillo getting away with hostages was unthinkable.

Haiku materialized from the darkness, startling him. Jeremiah handed him the rope. "You go first."

With spider-like agility, the Japanese American SEAL ascended, hand over hand, not even using his legs. Jeremiah watched him hook a knee over the ledge and disappear.

Now it was Jeremiah's turn. But he couldn't bring himself to retreat—not when El Cuchillo was poised to leave the building, possibly with Emma and Sammy.

"Bullfrog, let's go." Lt. Sasseville peered down at him from the rooftop. "The kid's bleeding out. We need you up here."

Torn between helping Carter and protecting Emma, Jeremiah shook his head. "I'm sorry, sir. If El Cuchillo's got Emma, I have to protect her. Pack the kid's wound with more gauze and start an IV."

"Copy."

Lt. Sasseville's curt answer gave Jeremiah permission to stay. But he'd need their best sniper's help to make it work.

"Bronco, can you put eyes on me? I'm on the east side of the building, directly under the ropes."

A short silence. Then: "I see you."

"Good. Cover me, brother." Leaving Haiku to pull up the rope, Jeremiah slid along the wall toward the front yard.

"Don't do anything stupid, Bullfrog," Master Chief warned. "Two cops headed your way!"

Thoop. Thoop. Before Jeremiah spotted either man, Bronco laid them out with two quick shots. Heart pounding, Jeremiah stepped over their bodies and slid toward the factory's corner, heartened to see the police caught between the SEALs and the CIA.

Ka-BOOM! Another grenade lobbed from the street detonated in the yard. Cued by their counterparts, the SEALs rained gunfire from the roof. Uniformed policemen crumpled next to dead narcos. Surviving cops scrambled back into their armored trucks.

Another grenade hit the ground. Jeremiah watched it roll between the wheels of the nearest truck and flinched—

Ka-BOOM! The ten-ton vehicle bucked, flames flaring as its gasoline tank exploded. Pained by the screams, Jeremiah briefly closed his eyes. The truck's front door flew open, and one lucky soul tumbled out.

A loudspeaker blared from the second truck. Scarcely audible over gunfire, a voice instructed the remaining officers to cover "the senator's exit."

Jeremiah scoffed at the title. Pity for the cops protecting that bastard made his stomach twist. He peeked around the corner—only to have bullets pepper the cinderblock and kick up dirt at his boots.

In that instant, a vision flashed across his mind's eye.

He keyed his mic. "Get word to the CIA to hold their fire! Hostages are coming out of the building."

"Copy that."

He held his breath, waiting. Less than thirty seconds later, an eerie hush fell over the compound.

Into the silence came the sound of the factory's front door groaning open.

A quick peek around the building revealed two men—neither uniformed, both armed—emerging into the light of the burning truck. All parties held their fire.

Then the *capo* himself appeared, clutching Sammy across his chest.

Jeremiah's blood ran cold. Not only was the bastard using Sammy as a shield, but his notorious blade was pressed to the little girl's throat. Worse, tottering behind him and tied to his elbows by a short rope were Emma and Katherine, protecting his flanks.

Disgust rising, Jeremiah shouldered his rifle and stared down its sights, waiting for a clear shot. Two more men followed, hampering his view.

"Bronco?" he growled. "Tell me you've got a shot."

"Can't take it, brother." Bronco's voice was gutted. "It'll go right through him into the kid."

"Shoot the tires on the truck, at least."

"Those kinds of tires don't go flat, brother."

Master Chief broke in. "Heads up. CIA's got a sniper with an

RPG. I can see him from here. If that truck drives away, they're blowing it sky high."

The blood drained from Jeremiah's head, leaving him dizzy. Three steps. That's all it would take for El Cuchillo to be inside the armored truck with his hostages. And as soon as it hit the clear street, the CIA would launch the RPG—collateral damage be damned.

Sammy and Emma would die in a flash. And Jeremiah's promise to protect them would die with them.

A bead of sweat slid down his temple. He would rather risk gunfire than see them blown to pieces.

Kuzinsky's order freed him. "Open fire, men. Don't let them drive off."

Jeremiah put his crosshairs on a man between him and the *capo*. Before he could squeeze the trigger, a shot cracked from within the yard, and the man toppled. As his companions swiveled to fire, a flash of blond hair ducked behind the rusting Fanta sign.

Ping, ping, ping, *pyong!*

Juliet. He'd thought he was hallucinating earlier when a lithe figure with long blonde hair dashed through the gate earlier.

Thanks to her, he had a clear shot at the capo's back. Exhaling slowly, Jeremiah squeezed the trigger. Two bullets streaked through the chaos and slammed into El Cuchillo's torso.

The *capo* pitched forward, spilling Sammy onto the backs of his men and dragging Emma and Katherine to the ground with him.

Gunfire erupted from all directions. Without warning, the remaining armored truck backed over two bodies, then surged forward through the open gate. Its rear doors swung wildly.

Three seconds later, the unmistakable sizzle of an RPG rent the air.

Whoosh—

Somewhere down the street, the truck detonated, blooming into a ball of fire so brilliant it lit the entire neighborhood.

A cheer went up from the CIA contingent. The SEALs stayed silent.

Jeremiah bolted from cover, hurdling bodies as he raced into the yard. He hit his knees beside Emma, leaving Sammy to Juliet, who hauled her off the corpses she was lying across.

A glance at El Cuchillo showed the man either dead or dying. Katherine, who's leg was pinned beneath him, was sobbing hysterically. Jeremiah shoved the corpse aside, keeping his rifle ready. Tristan dashed up, crouching next to Juliet to provide cover.

"I told you to stay put," he raged.

She shot him a glare, yanking her arm free. "*I'm* the reason you won this war."

Still scanning for threats, Jeremiah snagged the *capo*'s blade and sliced through the rope binding Emma and Katherine.

"Back into the building," he ordered. "Helo's on the way."

Helping a dazed Emma to her feet, Jeremiah studied her profile while Tristan aided Katherine and Juliet clutched Sammy tightly.

"I got you, Professor. Can you walk?" He wanted to sweep her into his arms, but she might not want that.

She nodded faintly.

"Ma'am, you're safe now." Tristan gave Katherine a slight shake as she continued to wail. "Let's get you back to your family."

Juliet, the only one unfazed, teased her niece as she guided her inside. "See, Sammy? You could never hide from me."

Skirting the bodies, Jeremiah ushered them into the dark factory. A backward glance showed the CIA sweeping into the yard to collect prisoners and bodies.

It was over. But until the hostages were airborne, Jeremiah wouldn't breathe easy. Fortunately, the steady throb of the approaching extraction helo sounded in the distance.

The smell inside the factory brought on a wave of déjà vu.

"We're almost out of here." Emma's silence gnawed at him. Had something happened to her while he was away?

Tristan gripped his shirt. "Bullfrog, Cougar needs your help stabilizing the kid. You'll never believe it—he shot and killed César Salvador. No one knows where the pistol came from."

Guilt knotted Jeremiah's stomach. Carter was a brave kid. But if he died…

"I'll check him out."

Tristan clapped his arm. "I'll take the ladies to the roof."

Reluctant to let Emma go, Jeremiah dropped a kiss on her ice-cold cheek. "I'll join you in a minute."

Her lack of response rattled him.

She's just in shock, he assured himself as he rushed up the stairs ahead of Tristan and ducked into the room that had been their prison. The only people he could see in the glow of Cougar's helmet light were Carter, his mother, and Joe.

The boy's pale, slack face made him look dead already. Cougar crouched beside him, keeping pressure on Carter's gut wound. His mother, sobbing quietly, held her son's head in her lap. Dropping to his knees opposite Cougar, Jeremiah nudged that man's hands aside to check the wound. Blood oozed sluggishly beneath the compress.

He wasn't dead yet. But even with an IV in his arm, Carter wouldn't survive thirty minutes without surgery.

Thank God for that helicopter. He could feel its vibrations now, shaking the factory walls.

Cougar stood and motioned to Carole. "Ma'am, it's time to go."

"No!" She shook her head firmly. "I'm not leaving him. I've already lost a husband. I won't lose my son."

Carter's eyelashes fluttered at her voice.

Sometimes it sucked to feel other people's pain. Jeremiah's heart folded in on itself. "Let her stay. Go fetch a stretcher."

Cougar nodded and vanished.

Moments later, Teddy and Hack rushed in, hefting Joe between them, morphine dulling his pain. The bore him to the stairs, leaving just Carter, his mother, and Jeremiah.

"Please don't let him die," Carole whispered through her tears.

Jeremiah closed his eyes and sent a plea to the Universe. *This woman has lost too much already. Let him live. Please.*

The *whup-whup-whup* of the helo finally thundered overhead. Plaster dust rained down on his shoulders as the bird landed. Jeremiah cast a wary glance upward. So far so good.

A minute later, two Navy med techs swarmed in with a gurney. "Sir, we got this."

Jeremiah helped them hook Carter up to a bag of blood, then

watched them slide him gently onto the stretcher. As they carried the boy toward the stairs, followed closely by Carole, Jeremiah took one last look around the room that had been their prison.

The rescue hadn't unfolded the way he'd planned—but most of them had survived. Bert and Joan's fate remained uncertain. And Carter's life hung in the balance.

I won't forget the lessons learned here.

Straightening, Jeremiah followed the others to the roof.

Even with wind whipping the *azotea*, the stink of burning gasoline from the armored truck was still apparent as Jeremiah took in the rooftop scene. The injured were being loaded first. Emma stood with the other freed hostages behind the entrance to the stairs, away from the helicopter's rotor wash.

Joining them, he caught Juliet trying to normalize the situation.

"Oh, shoot!" She raised her voice to be heard over the helo. "I forgot to buy souvenirs before we left." She ruffled her niece's hair. "Don't you always get a magnet for the refrigerator?"

Sammy managed a smile, but Emma, who stood with one arm around her daughter, her hair dancing wildly in the wind, stared into space, her jaw clenched.

Sidling up to her, Jeremiah lightly caught her chin and turned her face toward his. "You okay?"

Her distracted gaze focused briefly on his face before sliding away.

Alarm prickled his scalp. Had something happened to her while he was gone? Had she been… violated? Where was the confident woman who'd kissed him goodbye—and the kiss she'd promised to give him every time he returned to her?

Master Chief rounded the corner and leaned close to speak into his ear. "The attaché from the American Embassy wants you to stay with the hostages through the debriefing process."

Relieved not to have to leave Emma just yet, Jeremiah nodded. "Great."

"The helo's going to fly you all to Fort Sam Houston. You'll go straight to Brooke Army Medical Center, where the injured will be treated and the rest of you evaluated for twenty-four hours, then debriefed. Media's going to want a statement. Avoid getting your picture taken—no personal interviews."

"Goes without saying." Frankly, the Army's largest and busiest medical center sounded like a five-star vacation destination, especially if he got to stay there with Emma.

"I expect they'll shuttle you back to New Orleans after that to collect your things. You holding up okay?"

Jeremiah met Kuzinsky's dark gaze, a wave of familial affection rolling through him. Though only a decade older, all the firefights Kuzinsky had survived made him the granddaddy of all SEALs. Jeremiah sent him a grateful smile. "I'm good, Master Chief. Thanks for everything."

Kuzinsky slapped him on the back. "See you at Team Building on Monday, then. All right. Time to take your friends home."

Jeremiah turned to the others, raising his voice. "You heard the man. Let's go home."

~

"Juliet!" Tristan shouted Juliet's name a second time, but she still ignored him.

Abandoning his watch post, he sprinted across the roof through rotor wash and caught her arm just as she put a knee into the hold.

"What?" She rounded on him angrily, proving she'd heard him calling all along.

He pulled her away from the door, just far enough to speak privately. "I just wanted to say—good shooting out there. Unlike most guys, I admit it when I'm wrong. And I was obviously wrong about you. You caught the *capo*'s men totally off guard—us, too, by the way."

Her mulish expression faltered beneath his praise. For once, she was speechless.

"So… thanks." The rotors were spinning faster. Not much time left. Taking advantage of her astonishment, he caught her jaw in his hand and angled her face up for a firm, solid kiss.

"See you soon, honey." Giving her a gentle push toward the

door, he sent her into the helo and backed away, head low. The cargo door slammed shut between them.

As the V-22 Osprey's tail lifted, the skids rose off the ground. Up it climbed, pummeling Tristan with gale-force winds before streaking into the dark sky.

Watching it go, a strange sense of loss stung his eyes. *Just the smoke*, he told himself. But that didn't explain the ache in his chest.

Hell. He missed her already.

Juliet Rhodes wasn't like any woman he'd ever known. And that was a crying shame—because she was probably the only woman on earth capable of resisting him. But he'd be damned if he was going to let her slip away just like that. For a SEAL, quitting wasn't an option. If he had to humble himself to make her his girlfriend, so be it. Shoot, he might even marry her one day—if she'd have him.

But then he remembered her ultimatum: *Go celibate for six months. Prove to yourself and to me that you don't have to be in a relationship to be happy. Then I might even date you."*

He could do that. Of course he could. He was a U.S. Navy SEAL, for Pete's sake. He could do anything.

And what was six months of loneliness—if he could eventually call her his?

CHAPTER 20

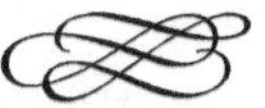

Jeremiah rapped tentatively on the hospital door, three rooms down from the one he'd been assigned. The colorful murals on the corridor walls made the stark factory building feel like a distant nightmare. Over the background hum of the seven-story hospital—the tramping of feet, the squeaky wheel of a gurney, a doctor being summoned over the intercom—he strained to hear Emma's reply.

Nothing.

Frowning, he glanced at his watch. Surely by 1 p.m., Emma, Juliet, and Sammy—who'd been allowed to stay together—were awake. Granted, they hadn't landed at Brooke Army Medical Center at Fort Sam Houston until three in the morning, where they'd been examined before finally getting rooms.

By the time Jeremiah had been looked over by a doctor and scrubbed the grime from his aching body, he'd barely been able to keep his eyes open. But even through the exhaustion, he'd craved Emma and Sammy's closeness. In the short time they'd been together, he'd grown used to their presence. Only knowing they were safe had finally allowed him to sleep.

Now, eight hours later, he couldn't stand another minute apart. He lifted his hand and knocked louder.

"Come in."

Relief and anticipation surged through him as he pushed the door open and stepped inside. Emma stood by the window, dressed in a peach sweater and cream-colored slacks—donated clothing, like the Army fatigues he wore. Looking at her, no one would've guessed what she'd just survived.

She glanced over her shoulder at him, offering a faint smile. Their gazes met briefly, but then she turned back to the view outside, and all the concerns that had gnawed at Jeremiah overnight rushed back with renewed force.

Crossing the room, he studied her carefully. She stood before the sunlit window with one arm across her waist, elbows tucked in, fingers curled toward her palms. The dazed, haunted expression she'd worn since he'd led her away from El Cuchillo's body still lingered in her eyes. Only a whisper of color had returned to her pale cheeks.

"Where's Sammy?" He glanced around the room, noting the three beds—one of them overflowing with stuffed animals, presumably donated by the same charity that had provided their clothing.

"Down there with Juliet," Emma murmured, nodding toward the window.

Jeremiah stepped beside her and peered down at the tree-lined lawn. Through the branches bursting with bright green leaves, he spotted Juliet walking hand in hand with Sammy, who appeared to be smiling, showing no signs of what she'd endured.

If only the same were true for Emma.

"I had trouble sleeping without you near me," he admitted softly.

Her soft blue eyes flicked toward him, then slid back to the view outside. No response.

"It's okay to be shaken up by what happened," he tried again. "You should never have had to experience violence like that."

A sheen of moisture gathered in her eyes, but she said nothing.

A darker thought twisted his gut. "Do you blame me for not coming back sooner?"

That got her attention. "What?" She turned, her gaze sharper. "You risked your life for us, Jeremiah." She placed a hand over her heart. "If not for you and your teammates, God knows where Sammy and I would be right now."

Relief loosened the knot of dread forming in his chest. Gently, he reached for her shoulders and turned her toward him. "You'll be okay, Emma. I know how you feel. It takes time to shake off the darkness, especially the first time—not that you'll ever have to go through that again. Once you're home, once life's normal again, this will feel like a bad dream."

Unless it didn't. Unless the trauma never let her go.

She shook her head faintly. "No. Nothing will be the same."

Her whispered words cut through him like a blade. She wasn't just talking about the ordeal. She was talking about *them*.

"Explain that to me."

His voice came out gruff, and she flinched, pulling free. Turning her back, she pressed trembling fingers to her forehead. "I can't be with you, Jeremiah."

The resolution in her voice landed like a hammer blow.

"I keep picturing Sammy in the *capo*'s arms, completely vulnerable. If someone had taken a shot at him—God, that bullet could've hit her. Even Juliet could have fired by mistake. And just like that, she would've been gone. I would've lost…" Her voice broke, and she dropped her face into her hands, shoulders quaking.

"Hey." He gathered her against his chest, relieved when she leaned into him, dropping her forehead to his shoulder. It was something. Maybe all she needed was this—time, comfort.

"Sammy's fine," he reminded her, voice low. His gaze drifted out the window. "Even Carter pulled through."

With a sharp sniff, she lifted her head, watching her daughter lean against the trunk of a tree, laughing at something Juliet said.

But instead of relaxing, she stiffened. "That's not the point." She pulled away from him, no longer touching.

Jeremiah's arms dropped to his sides. "Then tell me—what *is* the point?"

She swallowed visibly. "The point is I'm not strong enough to live this way. It feels like I just got over losing my parents. Or maybe I haven't. It was like my entire life was ripped away, and I had to start over. When I met Eddie, I thought I'd found something safe again. I thought I had everything I needed—until the day you stepped into my office."

He shifted uneasily, dread twisting in his stomach.

"You opened my heart to things I didn't even know were possible. Beauty. Depth. Connection. But to have that with you, I'd have to give up the safety I'd built. That's why I sent you away before. I was terrified of losing everything again."

Jeremiah blinked, the truth hitting him like a sucker punch. Fear still ruled her—fear, not love. Not faith. Not hope. Just fear.

"And then Eddie left me." Her chin wobbled, her voice breaking. "And I got knocked down again. It's taken me nearly three years to claw my way back from that."

She took a step closer and reached for his hand, gripping it tightly. "I'm not strong like you, Jeremiah." Her gaze searched his, pleading for understanding. "When you left us to get help, I *had* to believe you'd come back—but I didn't believe it, not really. Every time I doubted, it crushed me. You're here now, standing in front of me, but I can *still* feel that fear. Like if I blink, you'll disappear."

"That fear will fade," he promised.

She shook her head, despair rising in her voice. "That's easy for you to say. You're strong. You're a fighter. I don't have that kind of faith. And I can't live like this—waiting, wondering. One day you'll go fight another giant, and that'll be the end."

The worst part was—she was right. And he couldn't promise otherwise.

Tears filled her eyes again. "I don't want to go through that. I *can't*."

Just like that, the growth he'd seen in her—the courage, the spark—seemed to collapse under the weight of fear. She was retreating, back into the shell she'd lived in before him.

Dismay dragged his gaze to her donated shoes. His voice felt hollow when it finally emerged. "I see."

Why had he been given those visions of their future together if *this* was how it ended?

She squeezed his hand harder. "Please don't take this wrong. I want us to stay…friends. The best of friends. I want to email you every day, just to know you're okay."

His incredulous gaze lifted to hers. *Friends*? After everything they'd shared? Emails?

Frustration surged, sharp and hot. "I'm sorry, Emma," he ground out. "But I'm an all-or-nothing kind of guy. Being pen pals doesn't cut it for me."

She released his hand as burned.

With a sigh of regret, he crossed to the pen and clipboard hanging at the foot of a bed and scribbled his number on the chart. "But if you change your mind about the future, call me." His voice gentled. "I'll be here."

She had to change her mind. She *had* to. But he wouldn't force her. She had to find that strength herself.

Replacing the clipboard, he caught the torn expression on her face. Maybe she'd expected him to fight for her. Maybe part of her wanted him to. His frustration eased, replaced by sorrow. She was cheating both of them out of something beautiful because of fear.

One last time, he stepped close. He hugged her stiff, trembling body, pressing a soft kiss to her forehead, inhaling her scent to carry with him into the future. Then he thrust the slip of paper toward her.

"Tell Sammy I said goodbye."

Giving her shoulder one final squeeze, he turned away.

"Jeremiah, don't do this…"

His hand paused on the door latch. "Take care, Professor. And know that I love you. I always have."

It felt like wading through thick mud as he stepped into the hallway, each step heavier than the last.

What had he expected? That she'd transform into the woman she was meant to be in just one week? Her heart was still too raw.

Too fragile. She wasn't clinging to the thorns anymore, but the vulnerability she'd uncovered terrified her.

Still, those visions of their future together were *so* clear. It made no sense that she was pushing him away.

Unless... she wasn't ready yet.

But God help him, he hoped she would be soon.

With a growing sense of isolation, Emma scanned the crowded hospital lobby, searching desperately for Jeremiah. How could he have just walked away? Didn't he realize she'd expected him to reason with her, to fight for them? She'd counted on it—counted on him to want to stay in touch.

Where was he? His height usually made him easy to spot. "Come on, honey. Let's go find a seat." Tugging on Sammy's hand, she guided them to the long table where the other former hostages were gathered, wishing she could have left her daughter with Juliet. But the press had insisted on including the children.

"This is good." As they sat at the far end, Emma's gaze swept over the group. Everyone was present except for Carter, Joe—and Jeremiah.

Beyond the wall of reporters jostling for position, she noted the networks: CNN, NBC, Fox, and a slew of local Texas stations. The atrium-like lobby reverberated with their hushed energy beneath its soaring, glass-paneled ceiling.

Family members clustered off to one side. Juliet stood with them, steady and strong, her gaze promising Emma it would all be over soon.

Two framed photos rested before empty chairs—Bert and Joan, still missing. Another empty seat sat vacant. Jeremiah's.

"Excuse me." A CNN reporter's voice rang out to the Army public affairs officer who coordinated the event. "Where is the Navy SEAL who helped to rescue the hostages?"

Apparently, Emma wasn't the only one looking for him. The

press must have caught wind of Jeremiah's involvement. She leaned in, straining to hear the response.

The officer mouthed an "Ah," before raising a hand for silence. "May I have your attention, everyone."

Conversations died instantly. "The Navy SEAL mentioned in my earlier statement will not be attending this interview."

Disappointment rippled through the reporters. Emma's heart sank.

"I'm sure you understand that active-duty Special Forces members must protect their identities. You may refer to him as a special operator, first class, but the Navy requests you refrain from further identification. As patriots of this great country, we trust in your cooperation."

Emma's chest tightened, panic cresting. Oh, God. He hadn't just skipped the interview. He'd left. Just like at the university, when she'd pushed him away.

I'm an all-or-nothing kind of guy.

Why hadn't she seen this coming? He wasn't the type to stick around and plead for her love.

Heart unraveling, she closed her eyes, willing the interview to hurry along. The last thing she wanted was to relive their ordeal—or worse—the beautiful moments like when she'd realized her love for Jeremiah was more real than anything else.

Had she done the right thing? Emma swallowed against the dryness in her throat. Of course she had. How could she live with the constant fear of losing him to some mission gone sideways? Life didn't hand out happy endings. Jeremiah's optimism was naïve.

The interview began. The officer summarized the past week's events, then ceded the floor to an ABC reporter.

"Welcome home," the blonde woman said warmly. "Would any of you recount the moment your tour bus was overtaken?"

A heavy silence followed until the wife of Mike spoke up timidly. "At first, we thought they were soldiers. They checked our IDs, but when they started demanding our jewelry, we realized they were thugs. Then they ordered all the Americans off the bus."

"And the others?" The question was gentle, but they all knew the answer.

Mike's wife looked ill, prompting Mike to step in. "They were gunned down where they sat. Then the bus was set on fire."

A horrified murmur rippled through the press.

A Fox News reporter cut in, "Do you know why they only took U.S. citizens?"

Mike nodded grimly. "Because wire transfers from U.S. banks to Mexican ones don't require special permissions. Ransoms from other countries would've been harder to collect."

Emma glanced at Sammy. Pale, composed, but far too serious for a twelve-year-old. Therapy. Definitely.

"Ted Swisher, TXCN," boomed another reporter. "The Navy SEAL—how would you describe him, and when did you realize he was your ace in the hole?"

Pride surged in Emma's throat, but Cheryl answered first. "I noticed him before the ambush. He tried to convince the driver to take another route. It was like he already knew what would happen. And that first night, he told us he had military training. My boyfriend, Joe, and Jeremiah worked together to keep us calm."

"Can you tell us how Mr. Gardner was injured?"

Kathryn answered, voice shaking, recounting how Joe and Jeremiah fought two captors who'd snuck up in the middle of the night to assault them. "They could've stood by. But they didn't."

Emma found her voice. "Joe was every bit as brave as the SEAL." Jeremiah would want Joe to share the credit.

Dozens of microphones pointed her way.

"How did the SEAL escape?"

Emma cleared her throat. "He pretended to be a doctor—performed an operation on the leader's brother, who was injured. Then he convinced the leader he could help find the right antibiotic for his brother. Once he got outside, he broke away from his escorts and found his teammates."

"How did his team know where to find him?"

Emma shrugged, grateful she didn't have to reveal classified details.

"I want to talk about the actual rescue." CNBC's reporter cut in. "When did you realize a rescue was underway?"

Emma deferred to Carter's mother, who described the firefight, Carter's heroism, and how three of them—Emma, Kathryn, and Sammy—were dragged downstairs by the leader.

"What about you, Miss Samantha?"

Emma's spine stiffened as the reporter addressed her daughter.

"You must've been afraid when that man dragged you downstairs. Can you tell us about that?"

Sammy nodded solemnly. "My mom was screaming at them to let me go. I was so scared, but then I heard the SEALs coming, and I knew we'd be okay."

Emma blinked at her daughter, amazed by her faith.

"It's true he used us as shields," Sammy continued. "He squeezed me so tight I could hardly breathe."

"Were you scared then?"

"I guess. There were lots of guns. Dead guys on the ground. But I knew the SEALs wouldn't let them take us. Especially not my mom. 'Cause he loves her."

Chuckles and speculative looks followed, but Emma barely noticed. Her heart expanded at Sammy's words. *'Cause he loves her.*

"And then the man holding me was dead, and there were explosions. The last bad guys tried to drive of in a truck, but they didn't get far."

"It sounds like you're lucky to have survived all that."

Lucky.

Emma had never believed in luck. Yet here they sat—alive when, they shouldn't have survived. But they had.

"Oh my God," she whispered.

Jeremiah had been right. *Believing makes a difference.* Sammy's faith. Jeremiah's faith. Logically, they should be dead already, but they weren't.

"Ladies and gentlemen," the Army officer interrupted. "That concludes the press conference. Thank you."

Emma waved frantically at Juliet, who hurried over, concerned. "What is it?"

"I made a terrible mistake."

"What kind of mistake?"

"I let him go. Again. I need to find him and tell him I can do this. I can believe in a positive outcome."

Juliet's gray eyes glinted. "Damn right you can."

"He left his number. I'll call—"

"No. You'll tell him in person." Juliet spotted the public affairs officer. "Stay here."

Turning to Sammy, Emma found her bright-eyed, expectant. "How do you feel about Jeremiah being part of our lives?" she asked her.

Sammy thought a moment. "Do we have to move?"

"I don't know. Maybe. Would you mind?"

Sammy shrugged. "I guess not."

Juliet returned, victorious. "They put him on a bus to New Orleans to collect his stuff from the cruise ship."

Emma's heart jumped. "We have to catch up to him."

"Oh, we will." Juliet grinned. "We've got a ride on the officer's private plane. Leaving in an hour."

Emma gaped. "How?"

"Blackmail. I threatened to expose the CIA's involvement."

Emma looked back at the public affairs man. "He's CIA?"

"Educated guess. Anyway, don't just sit there. Go pack."

"I'm bringing all my stuffed animals," Sammy declared.

"You can have two," Juliet retorted. "It's a small plane."

Small plane. Emma pushed away the flicker of anxiety. *Don't manifest a crash.*

"Let's do it." She stood, grabbing Sammy's hand, channeling Jeremiah's confidence.

But what if it was too late?

Think positive, she reminded herself. *It'll all work out.*

~

The pink plaid suitcase sitting amid the collection stored in baggage claim riveted Jeremiah's gaze. No doubt about it—it belonged to

Sammy, the only little girl on that ill-fated excursion to Tulum. Which meant Emma's suitcase had to be here, too.

Doubt assailed him. What if his confidence that she would change her mind was misplaced? What if the future he'd envisioned was nothing but wishful thinking?

He should collect his luggage and go. But the urge to see the *Escapade* one last time held him rooted in place.

"Hey," he called to the lone attendant still lingering nearby. "Mind if I look at the ship first?"

The guy shrugged, clearly past caring, and gestured toward the departure tower. The place was deserted. Just the two of them, the hour pushing past one a.m.

Turning toward the glass wall overlooking the docks, Jeremiah mounted the tower stairs, his footsteps echoing up the empty stairwell. He remembered the last time he'd climbed this way, sunlight beaming down on the pristine, white ship, the air fragrant with the sweetness of spring.

Now, moonlight bathed the moored vessel, silver glinting off metal railings and deserted balconies. No bustling passengers, no eager crew—just a few dim lights glowing like the last embers of a dying fire.

The ship had returned with one crew member and twenty-seven passengers fewer than when it had left—twenty-nine if you counted Juliet and Tristan. Secured at its berth, the *Escapade* floated in somber silence, like a vessel adrift in grief, her decks haunted by the ghosts of the murdered.

Guilt gnawed at him, sharp and familiar. He hadn't saved them all. But overlaying that pain came memories that cut in the opposite direction. Emma, standing at the prow, her glorious rippling like a fiery ribbon as she tied it back. Emma gazing up at the heavens, naked beneath him, her bare skin bathed in starlight.

Always Emma.

The ache of longing curled tight in his chest, and he breathed deeply, grounding himself. There would be plenty of time for remembering on the long drive home. Having slept most of the nine-hour bus ride, he'd make it to Virginia Beach by dawn.

A child's voice drifted up the stairwell, stopping him in his tracks.

It can't be. Don't be stupid. That can't possibly be Sammy.

But before his mind could reject the idea entirely, he was bounding down the stairs, three steps at a time, his heart hammering with desperate hope.

The attendant's bored voice reached his ears. "He went that way."

Jeremiah burst into the terminal and skidded to a halt. His gaze locked on Emma, windswept and anxious, standing just beyond the turnstile.

She caught sight of him. "Jeremiah!"

"Jeremiah!" Sammy echoed, tearing away from Juliet and sprinting toward him, arms flung wide.

Warmth flooded him, fierce and paternal, as he scooped up the preteen and spun her in a circle, laughter filling his lungs. But even as he squeezed Sammy in welcome, his gaze never left her mother.

Emma approached more cautiously, a tentative smile on her lips, vulnerability in her eyes.

"Hey," she said softly.

Setting Sammy back on her feet, Jeremiah reached for her mother, pulling her into a three-way embrace. Hope gave him the confidence to say, "I knew you'd come."

Her eyebrows rose. "You did?"

"You think I would've left otherwise?" He held her gaze with certainty. "You're the love of my life, Professor. We belong together."

Tears sparkled in her eyes. "I know."

Two words. Simple. Eternal.

Relief nearly buckled his knees. "How the heck did you get here so fast?"

Emma glanced at Juliet, who hung back wearing a satisfied smirk. "Juliet persuaded the public affairs officer to give us a ride on his private plane."

That explained the wind-tossed look. And the exhaustion that clung to her like a second skin. "Let's grab your luggage and find a hotel. You look like you could fall over in a stiff breeze."

Emma leaned her head against his shoulder, exhaling a sigh that seemed to carry the weight of the whole last week. "I love you, Jeremiah," she whispered. "I'll never send you away again. I promise."

He pressed a kiss to her forehead, locking the moment in his heart. "I'll never give you a reason to."

An hour later, Emma nestled closer to Jeremiah's warm, naked body and hummed with contentment. "This is heaven," she whispered.

"Totally."

They'd found a modest hotel just outside the port. Juliet had managed to convince Sammy to share a room with her, assuring the child that her mom and Jeremiah had important matters to discuss about their future.

Not that we did much talking, Emma reflected with a secret smile. Instead, their bodies had spoken for them, declaring a passion and devotion that affirmed her decision. Everything really was going to be okay.

Even if Jeremiah perished someday on one of his blood-curdling ops, she would always have this memory. This peace.

"Well," she murmured drowsily, "Tennyson was right."

Jeremiah shot her a knowing look. "So you *finally* agree."

His satisfaction was so endearing she couldn't feel guilty for how long it had taken her to come around. Sighing again, she drifted toward sleep—until his low voice stirred her awake.

"You *will* marry me, won't you, Professor?"

Her eyes flew open to meet his. "Wait. Are you seeing the future, or actually proposing?"

He chuckled at himself. "Both. Maybe I should wait until I have a ring—assuming you'll say yes."

Happiness trickled into every corner of her being. "You don't need to wait."

He rose upon on one elbow to study her with gentle intensity. "You sure?"

The lamp's soft glow illuminated his hazel eyes—eyes that had haunted her dreams from the day they'd met. *This* was her future.

"I'm sure. From the day you first walked into my office asking questions, I've been yours," she admitted.

His grin deepened. "Then you do believe in soul mates."

"I certainly do. And I will," she added.

"Will what?"

She smiled dreamily, eyes drifting closed. "You already know."

His quiet chuckle was the last thing she heard before he reached back and turned out the light.

EPILOGUE

Sammy sidled up to the table bearing the wedding cake. Out on the dance floor, her mom and Jeremiah were gazing deep into each other's eyes, surrounded by fellow guests. Nobody would notice if she nabbed two more slices.

The hotel's reception room was packed. There had to be at least a hundred people—her mom's friends from the college, Sammy's friends from school, and SEALs from what Jeremiah called his Task Unit. The lights were dimmed, the music pulsed her chest, and the spice cake with cream cheese frosting was practically calling her name. The second slice was for her best friend, Gracie, who'd promised to visit after they moved to Virginia Beach, where Mom would teach at Virginia Wesleyan.

"I think you've had enough cake, honey."

Aunt Juliet's voice made Sammy snatch her hand back. She whirled to find her aunt stepping out of the shadows. *Dang it.*

Light from the chandeliers made her aunt's silver dress shimmer. Made from the same material as Sammy's, it made Aunt Juliet look like a fairy princess, while Sammy's own dress just hung from her bony shoulders. "It's for Gracie," she insisted.

"Sure it is." Aunt Juliet scanned the room.

"Are you looking for him?" Sammy pointed to the man about to tap her aunt on the shoulder.

Juliet jumped and spun.

"Boo." He flashed a grin—one that made him so handsome even Sammy felt a little weak in the knees.

Aunt Juliet took a steadying breath. "Tristan."

Sammy had learned his name back on the cruise ship—and of course she remembered him from the night of the rescue. He'd been the one to kiss Aunt Juliet just before she climbed into the helicopter. He looked a whole lot better in a tux than with black paint smeared across his face.

"Are you really trying to hide from me?" His teasing tone suggested it wouldn't work.

"Of course not." Aunt Juliet scoffed at the idea, but Sammy knew better. She'd dodged him the night before at the rehearsal and again at the dinner that followed. "So, how's it going?"

Juliet lifted her chin.

"Well, thanks for asking, honey." He shook his head sadly. "I've been pretty lonely, actually."

"Oh, why is that?" Juliet aimed for a bored tone.

"Been solo for the past three months." He sent her a slow, determined smile. "Only three to go, and then I get to date you."

Forgetting all about the cake, Sammy edged around the table for a better look at her aunt's face.

Hands on her hips, Juliet scoffed. "Says who?"

"Says you, honey." He slid an arm around her waist, drawing her against him.

Sammy expected Aunt Juliet to shove him away—after all, her hands were spread flat on his chest, and her spine was straight as a board. Instead she said in a faint voice, "I told you not to call me that."

He chuckled, leaning in to murmur something in her ear that made her close her eyes and sway against him.

"Well, that's not happening again," she muttered unconvincingly. Her chest rose and fell, as though she couldn't catch her breath.

"I think it is. You wouldn't go back on your word, would you?"

"I said I *might* date you after six months. I never said for certain that I would."

"Well, how about you dance with me now and decide?"

To Sammy's surprise, her aunt let him whisk her toward the dance floor. She obviously liked him more than she was letting on.

Watching them sway on the dance floor with their golden hair shining under the chandeliers, they looked like a prince and princess—except Aunt Juliet had more of an annoyed than regal expression. Sammy sighed.

One day, I'm going to fall in love like that. Turning back to the dessert table, she checked out of the corner of her eye to see if her aunt was watching.

Nope. Juliet couldn't seem to look away from Tristan's face.

With a smug smile, Sammy swiped two of the thickest slices she could find and hurried back to Gracie.

END

HOT TARGET

THE ECHO PLATOON SERIES, BOOK 4

The silhouette of a man standing in her darkened living room startled a gasp from her. The door thumped shut behind her. With the blinds closed and her lights out, the shadowy figure brought to mind her parents' killer.

Juliet's hand reached automatically into the depths of her purse where she stowed her 9mm pistol when she wasn't working. But then the intruder swiveled her blinds, flooding the room with light and revealing his identity.

"Tristan!" Astonishment rooted her in place. "How the hell did you get in here?"

He shook his head, tsking in disapproval as he walked toward her. His dark blue eyes gleamed predatorily. Every hair on her body rose in wariness as he closed the distance between them.

"You don't get to ask the questions, honey."

She ordered herself to pull out her gun, but she'd frozen. Jeremiah's earlier comment made sudden sense. *That's not the word I would use.* He'd known Tristan was beyond angry. He was, in fact, so upset he had left the restaurant to pursue her. Jeremiah and Emma hadn't managed to stop him. If anything, they had helped him find his way in.

Damn it, she wasn't going to get away with disappearing and apologizing later. Her resolve to stay single was suddenly under siege. If she didn't hold the line, she would surely suffer for it down the road. God help her because she wasn't sure she had the strength to resist what Tristan had to offer.

~

"Ah-ah." Spotting Juliet's hand sliding into her purse, Tristan wagged a warning finger at her. "No you don't. Give me the bag."

The outrage that had goaded him to ride his motorcycle like a demon through a suburban neighborhood still flowed through him like lava. The relentless and inexorable heat of anger staved off the insecure voice in his head insisting Juliet didn't want him. Like his birth mother, she'd rather walk away than get to know him.

"Give it to me." He thrust out his hand.

Her full upper lip curled into a sneer. Tristan had to give her credit for looking unafraid. Yet the flutter at the base of her slender neck revealed that he'd succeeded in freaking her out. Good. It was about time he got her attention.

"Or what?" she taunted.

He snatched the purse so fast she only had time to blink. Digging into it, he found her Ruger and tossed the handbag down. He made a show of checking the magazine and shaking his head when he found it full of bullets.

"If there's going to be a crime of passion here," he grated in his best Dirty Harry impersonation, "it's not going to involve bullets." Slapping the magazine closed, he laid the empty pistol on the narrow table in the entryway and gave her a "what now?" look.

Juliet lunged for the purse, most likely going for her cellphone. He grabbed her, catching her up in his arms and eliciting a growl as he carried her, fighting him vigorously, toward the couch. She landed a few good blows, but her physicality didn't surprise him. He'd found out down in Mexico she handled herself like a cage fighter. That was something he liked about her, actually. However, their wrestling wasn't so much a fight as it was a prelude to lovemaking.

Her heeled pumps struck his shins before they mercifully fell off. He tossed her onto the sofa, but she'd sunk her hands into his hair, so he went down with her. As they descended, she kicked his upper thigh—three inches from the nuts she was targeting.

He had to admit her training was thorough, but his was more extensive in scope. Plus, he was twice her size.

Exerting pressure on her wrists, Tristan freed his hair from Juliet's grasp. Straightening, he picked her up again and flipped her belly-side down onto the cushions, promptly sitting on her bottom to keep her from going anywhere.

"Get off me, you son of a bitch."

"No name calling," he warned. Catching Juliet's flailing arms, he pinned them behind her back. "You don't want to go there. I'm not the one reneging on a promise or running away from an honest conversation. If we start slinging names, I'm bound to call you a manipulative bitch or a low-life coward. See what I mean? Doesn't get us anywhere."

ABOUT THE AUTHOR

As the daughter of a foreign service officer, Marliss Melton grew up living all over the world. She was a military wife and raised five children. To this day, she relies on her many contacts in the Spec Ops and Intelligence communities to pen realistic and heartfelt stories about America's bravest defenders. She has written a medieval romance series and, under the pen name Rebecca Hartt, writes Christian military romance. An award-winning author with over 30 titles to her name, Marliss still finds time to teach high school Spanish. She lives in Williamsburg, Virginia, near her alma mater, The College of William and Mary.

www.marlissmelton.com

facebook.com/MarlissMeltonBooks

goodreads.com/346309.Marliss_Melton

www.ingramcontent.com/pod-product-compliance
Lightning Source LLC
La Vergne TN
LVHW091121080826
845145LV00008B/2002

* 9 7 8 1 6 1 4 1 7 8 4 8 4 *